Dancing hooves struck the ground inches from her head....

Laura awoke frozen in terror, waiting for the rider to bring his mount under control.

"Judas priest, woman!" came the roar of a familiar voice. "Don't you know this is private property?"

She sat up, and her brown eyes met the rider's gray ones. He stopped his tirade, the suntanned features under the dusty black Stetson registering disbelief. It was Cal Sinclair all right—grown a little wearier and somehow even more attractive.

When he spoke, his words were as hard and unyielding as his eyes. "You've been away too long. If you've come to see your sister, you're a little late."

Laura felt the sting of unexpected tears as she absorbed the cruelty of his remark. Angrily she blinked them away. "I had to put this place and everyone here behind me," Laura said quietly. "It was necessary."

"Necessary?" Cal boomed. "I guess you don't even care that Eve's gone."

"How could I not care? She was my sister!"

"And she was my wife," Cal reminded her, each word a hammer blow against the stake she felt sundering her heart.

Dear Reader,

Got the February blues? Need a lift? You've done the right thing—you've picked up a Silhouette **Special Edition**. Among the guaranteed-to-cheer-you-up offerings this month is a particularly inspiring love story by Bay Matthews, *Summer's Promise*. The compelling portrait of a family torn apart by tragedy, then made whole again by the miraculous healing power of love, it's a very special kind of romance, a radical departure from "boy meets girl."

Whether they're traditional or innovative, written by your Silhouette favorites or by brand-new authors, we hope you'll find all six Silhouette **Special Edition** novels each month to be heartwarming, soul-satisfying reading.

Author Bay Matthews says: "I believe we all read romances to recapture the breathless, sometimes bittersweet feelings of falling in love. As well as fulfilling that promise to the reader, Silhouette **Special Edition** features exciting plots grounded in the psychological and emotional makeup of the characters. **Special Edition** allows me to stretch the boundaries of romance, to create realistic people and explore their minds, their souls and the entire spectrum of emotions ruling them. As a writer *and* reader, to me, that's special."

Let us know what's special to *you*—all the authors and editors of Silhouette **Special Edition** aim to please.

Warmest wishes,

Leslie Kazanjian

Senior Editor
Silhouette Books
300 East 42nd Street
New York, N.Y. 10017

JOLEEN DANIELS
The Reckoning

Silhouette Special Edition

Published by Silhouette Books New York

America's Publisher of Contemporary Romance

SILHOUETTE BOOKS
300 East 42nd St., New York, N.Y. 10017

ISBN: 0-373-09507-4

First Silhouette Books printing February 1989

All the characters in this book are fictitious. Any
resemblance to actual persons, living or dead, is
purely coincidental.

®: Trademark used under license and
registered in the United States Patent and
Trademark Office and in other countries.

Printed in the U.S.A.

JOLEEN DANIELS

lives in Miami, Florida, where she tries to juggle a full-time job, a part-time writing career, an unmanageable husband and two demanding children. Her hobbies include housework and complaining to her friends.

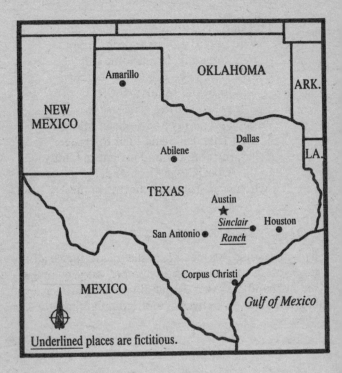

Amarillo

OKLAHOMA

ARK.

NEW
MEXICO

Dallas

Abilene

LA.

TEXAS

Austin
★

Sinclair
Ranch

Houston

San Antonio ●

Corpus Christi

MEXICO

Gulf of Mexico

N

Underlined places are fictitious.

Chapter One

Laura felt a shock of mingled apprehension and desire leap through her as she heard the click of the bolt, but no thought of protest occurred to her. The pelting of heavy raindrops on the roof echoed the pounding of her heart, and the sound of the howling wind was overcome by the exultant roar of the blood racing through her veins. No prior claims or family loyalty could outweigh her certainty that what was about to happen was right and good. If she had only this one night, then she would use it to love Cal as no woman had ever loved him before. She would leave her brand on his heart forever.

Cal's lips claimed hers for the first time. His mustache tickled her sensitive skin, as the scent of his aftershave and the slightly musky odor of his aroused maleness enfolded her. The work-roughened tips of his fingers stroked her jawline from ear to chin as his mouth moved against hers with gentle pressure. He sucked and nibbled and licked at her lips, slowly savoring them as if he had all the time in the world while in Laura's mind the seconds ticked away. She was desperate to make him hers completely, to possess him fully before this magical night ended and she had to face tomorrow alone....

"How would you like to be the new district manager for Texas?"

Laura Wright looked up, having been rudely recalled to reality by her boss's voice. She was surprised and a little dazed. One minute she'd been sitting in her office doing her paperwork, and the next her mind had unexpectedly plunged her seven long years into the past. The memories had been recalled more and more often lately, and she seemed unable to prevent it, unable to keep them buried any longer.

With effort, she organized her errant thoughts. "I'm sorry, Steve," she said with a soft, subtle hint of a drawl. "You startled me. I didn't hear you come in. In fact, I didn't even know you were in town. What was that question you asked me?"

"How would you like to be the new district manager for Texas?"

Laura's brown eyes widened in disbelief, and she experienced a surge of near panic. Texas! But Cal lived in Texas. She could never go back there. Biting her lip, she fought for control. She was being ridiculous; it had been over between her and Cal for seven years. He was ancient history—nothing more than an unpleasant memory. Slowly the feeling of disorientation faded away, and she was able to return her attention to the man in front of her.

Steve Randall was grinning at her, his boyish face making him appear younger than his thirty-two years. "I'm not taking no for an answer, Laura," he assured her, his blue eyes meeting hers directly. "You've done an excellent job managing the New York City International Inn for the past three years. Now that the company is expanding into Texas, it's time for you to move up."

The last of Laura's apprehension disappeared as she gazed into her boss's deceptively guileless eyes and wondered what he was up to. She'd first met him while working her way through college as a part-time desk clerk at this very hotel. He'd been the assistant manager and quickly recognized that Laura would be an intelligent and talented ally—a protégée who could help him fulfill his own ambitions. And it hadn't taken Laura long to realize that despite Steve's aura of charm, warmth and approachability, he possessed all the lethal potential of an aroused pit bull. She didn't quite trust Steve Randall, but she respected him. More than that, she identified with his goals and his ambitions. She wanted to achieve what he had achieved.

Steve sat precariously on the corner of her desk and casually ran a hand over his short reddish-blond hair, waiting for her to speak.

Knowing that any roundabout approach would be useless, Laura asked the question that was on her mind. "So tell me. What's in it for you?"

Steve smiled in amusement. "Always trying to second-guess me, aren't you? Well, this time I have no hidden motivations. You're from Texas. You're familiar with the people and the area. And I know how dedicated you are. This job isn't just a job to you—it's the most important part of your life. We're a lot alike when it comes down to it. That's why I keep hoping that someday—"

Laura shook her head in annoyance, her dark shoulder-length hair shimmering under the lights. "I know where this is leading, Steve. We've been down this road before. I'm getting a little tired of fielding your passes. I thought that you understood how I feel. I won't have anyone saying that I got ahead by sleeping with the boss."

Steve raised an eyebrow. "Don't be so naive, Laura. They're saying it now. If you're already condemned, you might as well commit the crime. What's the difference?"

Laura looked up at him, her jaw set, her voice firm. "The difference is that I know it's not true. I know that I'm being promoted only because of my ability. The other way I'd never be quite sure."

Steve leaned closer to her. "That's your one weak point Laura. Integrity. Aren't you ever going to give in? It won't be just a one-night stand. I'm madly infatuated with you, you know."

Laura smiled despite herself. "I can't imagine you 'madly' anything. And you haven't answered my original question. What's in it for you if I go to Texas? I can't really help your career from that far away. Your base is here in New York."

Steve's eyes glinted with mischief, revealing that he'd saved the best news for last. "Oh, I'd be down in Texas checking on you regularly. In fact, I'd still be your boss. The company is splitting the Southern region in two. You're looking at the new regional manager for the area from Florida to Texas."

Laura beamed her approval. "I should have guessed. And just how did you manage that coup? I can't believe it!"

Steve pushed himself upright and walked around to her side of the desk. "Believe it. Believe that what I want I eventually get. And I want you."

Laura groaned. "Don't you ever give up?" Giving him a reproachful look she stood up and moved away from him, her tall, slim figure complementing his stockier build, her dark good looks contrasting with his lighter coloring. "Give me time to think about your offer, Steve. It's after ten. I'm tired and I'm going home."

As she retrieved her purse from the bottom drawer and straightened, he put his hands on her shoulders and forced her to face him. Caught off guard, she looked at him directly.

"I understand why you might not want to be my mistress, Laura, but why would you even think twice about the promotion? I really need you to be there for me in Texas as district manager. You know that."

She pulled away and, picking up a portfolio full of paperwork, started for the door. Steve followed close behind her. "I know that, and I'm grateful for the chance—don't think I'm not. In all probability, I'll accept the promotion. There are just other considerations, other parts of my life..." She let the sentence trail off without further elaboration.

Steve frowned in puzzlement. "What other parts of your life? Marriage? Children? You need to succeed every bit as much as I do. Don't tell me you'd give up your career to sit at home with a bunch of squalling kids? You'd be lousy at it."

Laura's chin lifted defiantly, as it always did when her ability was challenged. She saw a familiar calculating look in Steve's eye and knew the exact second he decided that he had nothing to gain by pressing the Texas issue any further. Predictably he smiled.

"All right, Laura. You have a vacation coming up. Why don't you take some time off to assess your priorities? I'll be in Texas the rest of this week and part of next week. You can locate me through my secretary. If you feel like coming down, I'll show you the sites of the new hotels. Woodley's a competent assistant manager. I'm sure that he'll be more than glad to take over for you temporarily."

Laura laughed. "He'd be glad to take over for me permanently if I let him," she said as they walked into the lobby together.

Every International Inn was decorated to reflect the culture and environment of a foreign country. The theme of Laura's hotel was France. It was evident in all aspects of the hotel, from the French cuisine served in the restaurant to the gendarme uniform worn by the doorman. Copies of famous paintings by French impressionists graced every room. A mural depicting downtown Paris, with the Eiffel Tower and the Arc de Triomphe in positions of importance, covered one entire wall of the lobby. Laura examined it critically as they passed by. Its flaws never failed to grate on her because she knew that she could have done better. But, of course, hotel managers didn't have the time to paint murals.

As they emerged from the revolving doors and stepped out into the muggy summer night, Steve turned to speak to her again, but Laura silenced him with a warning look. "I'll call you and let you know what I decide."

She turned away before she could change her mind. As she walked the few short blocks to the apartment that she shared with her friend, Susan, she reviewed her options while keeping an eye out for potential muggers. Steve was quite attractive when he wasn't insulting her intelligence by trying to con her into bed. He was never too pushy or too forceful about it, but what bothered her was his motivation. She suspected that he only wanted to take her to bed in order to cement their business relationship. He had come out with all those corny lines because there were no real feelings for him to talk about. He was "madly infatuated" with her and wanted her to be his "mistress." Laura smiled. She couldn't imagine Cal ever saying things like that. Slowly her smile faded.

Cal was yesterday's dream. Her potential promotion was the only issue she should be thinking about now. But weren't her feelings for Cal an unavoidable part of that issue? She'd be resurrecting the past if she returned to Texas. Was she ready to face the possible consequences of that?

And what about her painting? In New York she took art classes, belonged to an artists' guild, and participated in shows. Now and then she even sold a painting. Of course she could do all that in Texas, but there was really nowhere like New York for art.

Hurrying across a busy intersection, she remembered that having to relocate to Texas was only part of the problem. If she became a district manager, her involvement with art would come to an end regardless of where she lived. She simply wouldn't have time for painting or any other hobby. She'd be required to put in long, grueling hours—six, sometimes seven, days a week. She'd have little time for any kind of personal life, let alone a romantic relationship. Laura shook her head angrily, annoyed with herself. She'd been in love once, and it had been the most painful experience of her life. Why was she anxious for a repeat performance? The only person she could count on was herself. She had become successful and independent through hard work and by taking advantage of her opportunities. That was reality. Making a living as an artist was a childish dream, and true love was a pretty but ultimately disappointing illusion. Resolutely, she made up her mind to call Steve in the morning and accept the promotion. After all, Texas was big enough to hold both her future and her past without the two ever having to meet.

As Laura approached the stoop of her apartment building, she noticed the outline of a man leaning against the railing beside the door. A thin line of smoke from his cigarette drifted upward on the barely moving air current to ring the yellow outside light with an artificial halo. The same light revealed his lean face and heavy, muscular body. A chill of premonition made Laura shiver in the warm night air. Even before he spoke, she knew that he had come for her.

"Laura Wright."

It was a statement, not a question. Laura realized that although she'd never seen this man before, he had definitely recognized her. Had someone shown him her photograph?

The man slowly descended the steps, reaching into the breast pocket of his suit jacket. Laura's eyes never left the stranger's face as he approached. He stopped about a foot away from her and handed her a long, plain white envelope. Then with a nod and a half smile he passed her and walked down the street.

Laura didn't turn to look after him. She quickly tore open the envelope. A plane ticket for a flight leaving New York for Houston early the following morning fell into her waiting hand. Slowly she unfolded the single sheet of paper that had accompanied the ticket. A mixture of dread and longing filled her as her eyes quickly found the signature at the bottom: Henry Sinclair.

Laura's thoughts turned to the kind, vital man who had raised her after the death of her parents. She frowned in concern. The signature was shaky and ill formed and didn't match the writing that made up the body of the letter. The feeling of premonition grew stronger. She rapidly scanned the first few lines on the paper.

Dear Laura,
The man who gave you this letter is a private detective. I know that you didn't want to be contacted, but it was something I had to do. We just found out recently that your sister, Eve, passed on last September.

Laura gasped and squeezed her eyes shut, oblivious to the furtive stares of two hurrying passersby. Tears began to stream down her cheeks as she ran up the front steps and unlocked the outside door, still clutching the crumpled letter in her hand. It was impossible! Not Eve...beautiful, spoiled, heartless, unmanageable Eve.

Laura refused to accept the death as real. Eve had haunted her nightmares for too long. But as she slipped into her deserted apartment and locked the door behind her, Laura could only remember the younger sister who had run to her for comfort when life had disappointed her with everything from a skinned knee to a dented fender. But if Eve were dead, that meant that Cal...

She pushed that thought away and swiped at her tears, her sniffling sounding thunderous in the quiet room. Flopping down on the beige sofa, she kicked off her shoes and lay back. Her eyes stared at the ceiling unseeingly. It had happened ten months ago, and she hadn't even known. But it was her own fault—she'd wanted to break completely with the past. For six years no one from Texas had her address, no one had known for sure where she was. Now the past had sought her out, and she realized that she'd been a fool to believe that she could run away forever. A part of her had always been in Texas with the people she'd thought she'd left behind.

Frowning, she reread the first three sentences in the pale moonlight that shone through the living-room window. What was going on? Apparently the Sinclairs had just found out about Eve themselves. She switched on the end-table lamp and, smoothing out the letter, continued to read.

I'm sorry to have to bring you bad news like this, but there's good news, too. Eve and Cal had a beautiful little girl. Her name is Melissa. She's almost six years old now, and the spitting image of her mother.

The bolt of gut-wrenching jealousy that shot through Laura was as unexpected as it was painful. She blinked in surprise and sat up, her breathing rapid and uneven. This was the reason she'd decided to cut all ties with Texas, why she'd never wanted the Sinclairs to find her. She would have expected this pain seven years ago, but the magnitude of her present reaction came as a complete shock. She'd thought the wound would surely have healed by now. She'd made a new life for herself. Why, she hardly even thought about the way things had been...before. Laura flushed as she remembered her earlier daydream about Cal. Who was she trying to kid? It was all as real to her as if it had happened only yesterday. Unwillingly her eyes strayed back to the letter.

You have to come and see her, Laura. It's important. It may be the most important thing you've ever done. There's an airline ticket enclosed. I'm asking you as a personal favor to use it. If any of us you used to think of as family still mean anything to you, please do as I ask.

The only thing that followed was the uncharacteristically frail signature. Laura let the letter drop onto the coffee table in front of her. She owed so much to Henry. Now he was asking for her, and she couldn't refuse to go. She smiled slightly. Of course, he would have counted on that. At any rate, if she was going to take that job in Texas, she'd have to confront this situation sooner or later.

Then she thought about Cal again. Even thinking about him was a kind of exquisite self-torture. What would seeing him be like? she wondered, and then shuddered involuntarily. Pain—more pain than she could handle. But maybe... maybe there was a chance...

She laughed out loud. It had a bitter, empty sound even to her own ears. It was all a fairy tale conjured up by a young girl and nurtured by a grown woman too foolish to know any better.

She stood and began pacing, upset and agitated as she hadn't been for years. She dealt with crises at work in a manner that had earned her a well-deserved reputation as a cool, reliable professional, and here she was trembling like a frightened kitten because of some man that she hadn't seen in years. Why, he was probably fat, bald and even more arrogant and evil tempered than ever. He'd probably seem like a laughable, chauvinistic hick to her now. But a nagging little voice whispered that she would always love Cal no matter what he looked like, no matter how badly he behaved. Setting her jaw, Laura decided to go to Texas and resolve the issue—it was time to separate fantasy from reality.

She picked up the phone and dialed Steve's number, waiting impatiently through the recording on his answering machine to get to the beep. "Steve, I'm leaving this message to let you know that I'm taking a two-week vacation starting tomorrow morning. You're right, I need some time off to think things out. I'll be at the following address and phone number..."

She recited the address and phone number of Sinclair Ranch from memory and quickly hung up before she could change her mind. Then she called her assistant manager at home to notify him. His barely concealed astonishment caused her to smile. In the years she'd worked with him, she hadn't exactly made spontaneity a habit. She set the receiver back in its cradle. Maybe it was high time she did something unexpected.

She packed slowly, her mind jumping from the past to the future and back again. She was sure of only one thing: whatever happened in Texas would hurt deeply. But she was determined to face the pain and ride it out. After all these years, it was time to stop hiding.

Chapter Two

Laura turned the key in the ignition of her rented car and was rewarded by a dull, grinding noise. Pulling the lever to release the hood, she stepped out onto the dirt shoulder of the road. Instantly her expensive white shoes were coated with a fine layer of windblown dust.

She peered at the cloudless morning sky, shielding her eyes against the glare of the bake-hot Texas sun. It was the same sky, the same dust, the same heat she'd left behind. But then nothing really changed this country, least of all the passing of a few years. It was she who had changed. The naive young girl of twenty-one who had left this place to finish college in New York was now a successful and self-assured woman.

Laura smiled grimly at her thoughts as she raised the hood of the car to confront the steaming radiator. She might be successful and self-assured, but she was certainly no auto mechanic. To make matters worse, she had stalled out on the access road. No one passed this way unless they were traveling to or from Sinclair Ranch. There were no other houses, no phones, no gas stations between her and the ranch house, which was a distance of about ten miles.

Resolutely Laura opened the car trunk and unzipped the red leather sack that served as her overnight bag. She slipped her purse and her case of art supplies inside. The inclusion of the latter had been an afterthought that she was already beginning to regret as she lowered the heavy bag to the ground and slammed the trunk shut. At least she didn't have to worry about carrying her suitcase; the airline had somehow managed to misplace it.

"I should have taken that as a warning and caught a plane right back to New York," she muttered with futile hindsight.

Bending down beside the driver's seat, she left the car keys under the floor mat. She intended to call the rental company and give them a piece of her mind—if she lived to reach a telephone.

Casting one last look back at her disabled car, she slung the strap of the bag over her shoulder and began walking. She was suddenly grateful that she'd worn a cool, short-sleeved blouse, comfortable slacks and low-heeled shoes. Her floppy hat protected her face and head, but before five minutes had passed the blazing sun had turned her white blouse dark with perspiration.

Through the haze of heat and dust, Laura began to recognize one landmark after another as she made slow progress along the road. She'd ridden over every inch of this land as a girl, and it was as familiar to her as her own face. A warm, nostalgic sensation crept over her, only to be replaced by an uncomfortable feeling of apprehension as she realized that each step brought her closer to a confrontation with her past.

In the shadow of the great arching signpost of the ranch she halted, letting her burden slip to the ground. With a soft groan, she flexed her shoulders and swept the hat from her head. Sweat had reduced her stylish hairstyle to a damp ruin. She pushed the long dark strands away from her cheeks and peered upward, drinking in the letters on the sign with thirsty eyes: Sinclair Ranch.

A feeling of almost unbearable homesickness swept through Laura as she stared at the letters that were burned so deeply into the weathered wood. She suddenly realized that they were branded on her heart just as irrevocably. No matter how far she traveled or how long she stayed away, this place would always be a part of her.

She glanced back the way she had come, sorely tempted to flee before anyone knew that she'd arrived. Then she thought of Henry and all that he'd done for her, and she knew that she would have to face her past or live in its shadow forever.

Laura picked up her bag, grimly determined to reach her goal. But after another hour and a half of walking in a simmering inferno, she was more than ready for a break. Lured by childhood memories, she veered off the road and quickened her pace, stumbling over the rough terrain. By noon, she had reached the temporary shelter of the glade, a cool oasis of water and shade in the midst of a vast expanse of dust and dryness.

Parboiled by the blazing heat, she sank to the ground beneath the welcome shelter of the trees and slowly eased her shoes off her aching feet. Then she dragged her weary body to the edge of the pool and, lowering her head, sipped the crystal-clear water from her cupped hands. Her thirst slaked, she lay on her back and closed her eyes.

She knew there were at least another three miles to the ranch house. The sun was now directly overhead and the thought of continuing seemed unbearable.

Rolling to her side, she stared into the depths of the pool. It looked so cool, so inviting. She remembered the feel of that smooth blue water against her skin—skin that was now sticky with drying sweat.

Exerting every ounce of willpower, she turned her head away. She wasn't a child anymore. She couldn't go skinny-dipping in the middle of the day. What if someone came along and saw her? Then she laughed to herself. She'd walked seven miles without getting that lucky.

Her gaze returned to glide over the water again. She really ought to keep walking. She'd be at the house soon enough, and she could take a shower there. "But that's three long, hot miles away," she whispered, not realizing that she spoke aloud.

Before many minutes had passed, the lure of the tempting pool proved too great for Laura to resist. Throwing off her sweaty clothes, she walked to the side of the pond where the bank fell away sharply into deep water and dived into the all-enveloping coolness. Breaking the surface, she filled her straining lungs with warm, sweet-smelling air and yelled in sheer delight.

She swam for what seemed like an eternity, luxuriating in the sensuous caress of the rippling water on her smooth, firm flesh. Finally, out of breath, her muscles trembling, she pulled herself onto the bank.

She lay flat on her back in the soft green grass and found herself looking up at a tree that had shaded her on another summer day twenty years before. She drifted off to sleep listening to its leaves rustling. It sounded like the murmur of an old friend's voice welcoming her home.

As Laura sank into the deeper stages of sleep, she began to dream. In her dream, she was once more a little girl of eight, as free as the wind that ruffled her long, dark hair. Wearing only her skin, she plunged into the pond and swam out to where ten-year-old Cal Sinclair was treading water. He was the one who had taught her how to swim, how to ride and how to climb a tree. He was the big brother she'd never had, the hero of all her childish fantasies.

As she drew near he smiled, his white teeth glistening, water plastering dark hair to his forehead in random swirls. To Laura his careless warmth was as unself-conscious and nurturing as the sun's.

"Cal, you promised you'd come tell me a story!"

Laura's heart sank as she glanced toward the bank where her six-year-old sister, Eve, sat in her pretty pink dress. Her golden hair shone in the dappled sunlight, and her vivid blue eyes threatened to spill tears of disappointment at any moment.

"Don't cry, Eve!" the boy called out. "I'm coming!"

As Cal waved and started for shore, Laura wanted to beg him to stay with her. But she kept her silence, feeling betrayed and rejected. Tears streamed down her tanned cheeks and mingled with the water of the pond. But the other two never noticed that she was crying.

The sound of pounding hoofbeats brought the dream to an abrupt end, and jerked Laura awake. Her eyes snapped open, and she found herself in the towering shadow of a rearing horse. She lay frozen in terror, waiting for the rider to bring his mount under control.

"Judas priest, woman," came the roar of a familiar voice. "Don't you know that this is private property?"

Grabbing her blouse, Laura draped it over her bare breasts. She sat up and her brown eyes met the rider's gray ones. He stopped his tirade and the suntanned features under the dusty black Stetson registered frank disbelief. It was the same ruggedly handsome face that Laura remembered, the same strong jaw and the slightly crooked nose that had been broken in a school fight when he was twelve. The lines around his mouth were deeper, and there was a permanent crease between the heavy black brows as if the intervening years had held more pain than happiness. The gray eyes that had at first expressed astonishment now turned cold and flinty with suspicion. The generous mouth under the bushy black mustache drew up at one corner in a cynical smirk. It was Cal Sinclair all right—a little older, a little wearier and somehow even more attractive. It was the face of the boy she had dreamed about, the face of the man she had once loved.

Laura felt a pressure in her chest as though a steel vise were being slowly tightened around her wildly beating heart. She had lived this moment in her mind a thousand times, but now she couldn't remember even one of the glib and clever remarks she'd rehearsed so often. She could only sit drinking in the sight of Cal like some tongue-tied teenaged groupie who is suddenly confronted with the rock star of her dreams.

She had wanted to overwhelm him with her big-city sophistication. Now here she was with her hair hanging in wet strings and her makeup washed away except for the inevitable smudge of mascara beneath each eye. Instead of her expensive, tailored clothes, she was wearing only her skin, and her usual easy confidence had fled to parts unknown.

If Cal was experiencing any similar discomfort, it certainly wasn't apparent to Laura. When he finally spoke, his words were as hard and unyielding as the look in his eyes. "If you've come to see your sister, you're a little late."

Laura felt the sting of unexpected tears as she absorbed the calculated cruelty of his remark. Angrily she blinked them away. When she had imagined this moment, she had pictured herself as composed and aloof, polite yet basically indifferent to the situation and to the man before her. It wasn't fair that he still had the power to shatter her with a few hostile words.

"I had to put this place and everyone here behind me," Laura said, finding her voice at last, holding her tattered dignity like a shield. "It was necessary."

"Necessary?" Cal boomed, causing his horse to shy nervously. "That old man in the house up there took you in when you had no one and nothing. He made you a part of our family. Every day he expected you to come back. Every night he sat and worried about why you stayed away. But I guess an old man's feelings aren't real important to someone like you. I guess you don't even care that Eve's gone."

Laura glared at him with a mixture of anger and guilt, her tone rising to match his. "How could I not care? She was my sister!"

"And she was my wife," Cal reminded her, each word a hammer blow against the stake she felt sundering her heart.

"I know that," she snapped. "Eve called me right after the ceremony to tell me that you two had eloped."

Cal studied the toe of one worn boot in eloquent disinterest. "Too bad you couldn't have been there, but it was a spur-of-the-moment decision."

"I'll bet," Laura retorted quietly, though her nerves were screaming. "Even if I had been invited, I'm sure I could have found a better use for my time."

"So don't you have better things to do now?" he shot back. "Why'd you bother to come back here at all?"

"I'm here because Henry sent a private detective after me. He invited me here. And I've come to see my sister's daughter. *Your* daughter."

"Melissa?" Cal said in disbelief. "You're here to see Melissa? When did you find out about her? She's almost six years old now, and this is the first time you've so much as expressed a passing interest."

"Well, I'm interested now," Laura said determinedly, with fire in her eyes. "And I'm not leaving until I've talked to Henry."

Cal grunted noncommittally, obviously not liking her statement, but not contradicting it, either. "That your car out on the access road?" he asked, his voice a shade less belligerent.

When Laura nodded, he tilted his hat back on his head and leaned forward, resting one arm on the pommel of his saddle. "Well, I'll be damned if I'm going to sit here any longer arguing with a naked woman. Get dressed and climb up or you can walk the rest of the way."

Laura blushed to the roots of her hair, suddenly made painfully aware of her undressed state. Well, she'd be damned if she'd walk when she could ride, and she'd be damned if she'd amuse him by asking him to look the other way while she dressed. With a burst of bravado she hadn't known she possessed, she stood up and, turning her back to him, quickly began to pull on her clothes.

Clad in her white lace bra and matching bikini panties she turned to find his warm glance caressing her body. "Caleb Sinclair!" she exclaimed in exasperation. "Just what do you think you're staring at? You and I have been skinny-dipping in this pool ever since we both learned to walk."

Cal lifted one expressive eyebrow, obviously enjoying her discomfort immensely. "That's God's truth, Laurie," he drawled, using her name for the first time since their conversation began. "But you're sure no child anymore and neither am I."

Stuffing her panty hose into her bag, Laura straightened to meet his gaze. She saw the wanting look simmering in his eyes, and an electric current of pure desire shot through her body. In seven years she hadn't wanted another man the way she wanted Cal right now. If he had climbed down from his horse, lowered her to the ground and made love to her right then and there, she would have welcomed him body and soul.

Trembling, she forced herself to look away, confused and angered by the intensity of her response to this man. Reaching for the rest of her clothes, she resumed dressing.

"No, I'm no child anymore, Cal. You saw to that, didn't you? On the night I went back to college for the last time."

Cal's face hardened again. "You weren't exactly fighting me off, and you sure as hell didn't have any complaints afterward—leastways none that ever got back to me. You left for New York in such a damned quick hurry that I never was quite sure."

Laura hung her head. Anger, hurt and regret were warring for the center stage of her emotions. Slipping into her shoes, she walked over and silently handed Cal the leather bag. He slung the strap over his saddle horn, avoiding her gaze as studiously as she was now avoiding his.

Absently she stroked the horse's glossy neck, buying time to slow the runaway pounding of her heart and to choose her words carefully. When she spoke she was cool, calm Laura Wright—logic personified.

"Why waste time talking about bad memories, Cal? Whatever happened between us was over for good seven years ago."

Taking a deep breath, she searched his face for some flicker of caring. She waited in vain for him to disagree with her statement, but he only kicked his boot free of the stirrup nearest her and offered his arm to help her up.

Placing her foot in the empty stirrup, she grasped his upper arm as he leaned down to grip her elbow. Her heart skipped a beat as her fingers closed over the hard, tautly flexed ridge of his biceps. She felt the incredible heat of his skin through the thin cotton of his shirtsleeve as the firm, but gentle pressure of his hand closed around her soft flesh.

After what seemed like an eternity, she was on the horse behind him. The tender skin of her arm still tingled from his touch. If his hand had affected her so deeply, what would closer contact do to her fragile composure? Trembling, she reached out and tentatively placed her hands on the thick belt that circled his waist. If he guided his mount at a sedate pace, that tenuous grasp might be enough.

The horse, unaccustomed to the weight of two riders, chose that moment to prance sideways, almost unseating Laura. She threw her arms around Cal's waist and pressed herself up against him like a second skin, her hands gripping his shirt where it covered his hard, flat abdomen. She heard his sharp intake of breath and felt the muscles under her fingers tense in response to her touch.

Furious with herself, but unable to deny her need, she leaned her cheek against his broad shoulder. She inhaled the spicy odor of after-shave that mingled with the sweet tang of sweat on clean skin. She felt the heat of his body radiating through his shirt, and the tips of her breasts hardened in reaction.

With a muttered curse that sounded like a groan, Cal touched his blunted spurs to the horse's sides. They galloped across the rough ground, every jarring stride sending a new jolt of desire through Laura's body.

Cal, Cal, Cal. The name was a drumming rhythm in her fevered brain. She wanted to leave the real world behind and ride with him like this forever. Every molecule in her body, every minuscule pulse beat of her emotions sang in response to this man. Dizzy with the rapture, she wondered how she had managed to exist through all the cold and lonely years without hearing the sound of his voice, without seeing his face, without feeling the warmth of his flesh against her own.

She was shaking when he finally pulled his horse to a halt behind the big two-story white ranch house. Clasping her arm, he hastily lowered her to the ground and dropped her bag in the dust at her feet. Gray eyes locked with brown, and Laura saw an anger and an arousal that equaled her own.

Cal looked down at Laura, surprised and repelled by the attraction he felt for her. Over the years he'd convinced himself that he hated her. Then today he'd unexpectedly come face-to-face with the truth: he didn't hate Laura. In fact, he still wanted her. He wanted her more than he'd wanted any woman since the day she'd left. The fact that she could still have that kind of effect on him after all that had passed between them was infuriating.

Their gazes held with fierce intensity before Cal's voice broke the silence. "Damn you, Laurie! I wish to God you'd never set foot on this ranch. I only hope I have the pleasure of saying goodbye to you real soon.''

Laura went cold under the hot summer sun, chilled by the unmasked loathing in his gaze. Tears blurred her eyes as she watched Cal ride away, tall and straight in the saddle. He was like the cowboys of the wild West, yet he was also a totally modern man who held a degree in engineering and ran one of the most innovative companies in the United States. She had never understood how he moved so effortlessly from one role to the other, anymore than she'd been able to fathom the dark emotions and subtle motivations she'd seen in his eyes today.

She hadn't thought she'd be welcomed with open arms, but she hadn't expected such blatant hostility, either. Once upon a time, many years ago, she'd been sure that he loved her. Now he seemed so bitter, so angry. There was no sign of the gentle, warm, compassionate man she'd dreamed of all these years. Was it possible that that man didn't even exist anymore? That the surge of feeling she'd experienced when their bodies had touched a moment ago had been nothing but pure physical attraction? Maybe that's what it had been all along, and she'd just deceived herself into thinking that it was more. Maybe she had needed to believe that she was in love in order to justify giving herself to him in the first place. But if she wasn't in love with Cal, why did she suddenly feel as if all the pain in the world had gathered inside her chest?

"You're not the only one who wishes I'd never set foot on this ranch, Cal Sinclair," she whispered softly.

Tearing her gaze away from his retreating form, she shouldered her possessions and resolutely mounted the steps to the wide back porch. A short, stout Mexican woman with streaks of gray in her jet-black hair opened the heavy screen door. Her brown weathered face, which had once been beautiful, was now etched with deep lines of age and laughter. Her flashing dark eyes widened in surprise when she saw Laura.

Wiping her hands on her huge white apron, the housekeeper ran outside. "Ah, Laurita!" she exclaimed, tears wetting her leathery cheeks. "You are home after so many long years."

She held Laura at arm's length and inspected her before drawing her close. "But I was beginning to think that you had decided not to come. Where have you been? Your hair, it is all damp!"

"I rented a car, and it had engine trouble..." Laura began, but the housekeeper continued to ask question after question without once pausing to listen for an answer.

Laura let herself be led into the sunlit kitchen that smelled of cinnamon, allspice and freshly baked bread. In the blink of an eye, she was overcome by a feeling of warmth and belonging, a feeling of homecoming. She buried her face in Juanita's soft shoulder.

"Oh, Nita, I've missed you so! I'm sorry that I didn't write, but... Cal..."

"I know, Laurita. I know everything. It does not matter. You are home now."

The older woman held Laura and gently stroked her hair while the story of the disabled car and the stormy meeting with Cal spilled out.

"Do not worry about Mr. Cal," Juanita told her soothingly. "He is very glad to see you. He just does not know it yet."

Laughing through her tears, Laura sat down at the kitchen table. She wiped her eyes dry and nibbled on a cold chicken sandwich while she told Juanita about the

past seven years of her life. She spoke with pride about
her career in hotel management, but her voice quickened
with enthusiasm when she talked about her art classes
and the paintings that she'd sold.

"You always had a gift for art...and for love," Juanita
commented softly.

Laura smiled ruefully. "Neither of which is practical.
I've made a place for myself in the world, Juanita. I don't
have to take handouts anymore." She quickly overrode
the housekeeper's objections. "I'm sure that's not how
Henry saw it, but it was really charity when he took Eve
and me in. Well, now I don't have to ask anyone for
anything."

"That is good. I am glad of that. But are you also
happy?"

The question hovered in the air between them as if it
had a life of its own. Laura finally shrugged and stood to
take her dishes to the sink. "I've given up on happy. I just
want to be content . . . satisfied with myself and my life."

Juanita opened her mouth as if to retort, but evi-
dently thought better of it. "Come," she said. "Let me
take you to see Mr. Henry. He has been waiting for you."

Laura picked up her bag and slowly did a complete
turn in the middle of the kitchen floor. "It's just like I
remember it from when I was a child, Nita. I remember
so much warmth in this house, so much love."

The expression on the housekeeper's face darkened.
"The beautiful house where you and poor Eve and Mr.
Cal used to run and laugh as children is empty now.
There is no joy here."

Laura frowned. "But what about the little girl...
Melissa?"

The housekeeper sighed heavily. "She is a sweet child,
but quiet and shy—like a little white mouse. She keeps

always to herself and talks to her dolls as if they were playmates. Ah, Laurita! She saw so much when she was little. Eve and Mr. Cal had horrible quarrels. It was shameful. And Eve, she made the little one afraid of Mr. Cal. Now he only looks through the child as if she is not there, or snaps at her like an angry dog. There is no love in this house anymore. When Eve left with that man and went to Europe, I thought things would be better.''

Laura had been about to follow Juanita out of the kitchen. She stopped as abruptly as if she'd run head-first into an invisible brick wall. ''What are you talking about?''

''Two years ago, Eve left Mr. Cal and ran off to Europe with another man—making sure to take plenty of money with her, of course. We did not hear any news of her until last month. A friend of hers who was vacationing in France saw Eve's boyfriend on the street and asked him about her. He said that he had not seen her for a long time himself, but that he had read in the newspaper that she had died of a drug overdose last September.''

Laura felt shock and outraged anger. How could Eve do that to Cal and their little girl? How could she do it to herself? No wonder Cal seemed so bitter and hard. So much had happened, so much she'd known nothing about.

''When Eve's friend told us what she had learned, Mr. Henry immediately sent a detective over to France to investigate. Every word of the story was true. Eve's landlady identified the body for the police, but all she knew was Eve's name and that she was an American. All Eve's papers and all her money had disappeared, so she was laid to rest in a potter's field. There was no way to trace exactly where—no way to have a proper funeral. I am sorry.''

"How Eve would have hated that," Laura whispered with a small, sad smile. "No attention, no frills or fuss. She was a pain in the backside, Nita, but she was so…full of life. I just can't get used to the idea that she's gone."

Considerably subdued, Laura trailed the older woman into the huge living room with its gleaming hardwood floor and heavy, overstuffed furniture. The brown leather upholstery was worn in places by years of comfortable lounging, and her eyes found the spot on the arm of the couch where a ten-year-old Cal had carved his initials. Wood was stacked by the fireplace ready to add warmth to cool evenings, and two portraits hung above the mantel.

Halting, Laura examined the paintings carefully. The first was a portrait of Henry Sinclair that she had painted when she was eighteen and the old patriarch was in his late fifties. He was seated in the massive chair of his business office, looking every inch the iron-willed, steel-fisted dictator. The strong features of the Sinclair family faced at the world squarely, ready to take on all comers.

The portrait of Cal hung next to his father's and showed some of the same characteristics. It was the callow, unlined face of a man of twenty-two, and the glint of good humor in the eyes almost belied the firm set of his jaw. Laura had painted him clad in chaps and Western shirt, with one foot resting on a fence rail. That was Cal's rightful place just as the throne in the executive suite had been his father's natural setting. She had painted Cal for his college graduation, a year before she'd left the ranch. The portrait of Eve that Laura had completed during her final evening in this house was conspicuously absent.

Juanita interrupted her reverie. "When you see Mr. Henry, *niña*, you must remember that he has been very sick. Come now, he is waiting."

Laura automatically started up the wide, oak-banistered staircase that led to the bedrooms on the second floor. The housekeeper stopped her, a note of sadness in her voice. "He is downstairs now. We have turned the study into a bedroom for him. He is confined to bed for much of the time, and when he does get up he sits in a wheelchair. The stairs are impossible for him."

Standing very still, Laura let the full meaning of Juanita's simple words penetrate her consciousness. She couldn't imagine the vital, compulsively active man she remembered transformed into a helpless invalid. "I'd read in a business magazine that Cal had taken over the company, but it never occurred to me..." She shuddered involuntarily.

Putting an arm around the taller woman's shoulders, the housekeeper led Laura to the door of the study. "It was hard for all of us to accept at first, *especially* for Mr. Henry to accept. It happened gradually. The doctors say that it is some evil thing called emphysema that strangles his lungs. He began to do less and less, and now there are some days—like today—when he can do nothing at all."

The painfully thin, white-haired old man dozing in the railed hospital bed bore so little resemblance to the Henry Sinclair Laura remembered that, for a moment, she felt she was intruding on a stranger. Then the gray eyes snapped open and focused on her, and she felt the unbreakable will that still resided in the man and the undimmed power of his formidable mind.

Setting her possessions down, she rushed to kiss his ashen cheek. He looked up at her and held her hand tightly. "Where have you been, girl?" he asked in a low whisper that was a mockery of his old, booming greetings.

A sense of overwhelming remorse caused Laura to stammer as she tried in vain to answer.

Henry reduced her to silence with a few softly spoken words of total acceptance. "It's no matter, child. You're here now."

Laura knelt by the bed and pressed her cheek against his hand, unable to speak for a long moment. Finally she drew a long, shuddering breath and moved back so that she could see his face.

"Why did you ask me to come home now, Henry?" she asked. Her voice held puzzlement and not a small amount of challenge. "Your letter told me about Eve's accident. You mentioned something about Melissa, but there wasn't anything specific." She barely noticed that Juanita had set a chair close by and was guiding her into it.

"I sent for you because I want you to help Melissa. She's your sister's daughter—your own flesh and blood. You've got to make Cal accept her and give her the love she's entitled to or, by God, you've got to take her out of this house!" The old man sank back against the pillow, panting breathlessly, leaving Laura sitting before him in speechless surprise.

"Me?" she asked incredulously. "You want *me* to convince Cal to love his daughter? How can I do that? That's not just something you can talk a person into."

"You've been closer to Cal than anyone, Laura. You two grew up together. He won't listen to anything I have to say about Melissa. Maybe he'll hear you out. He can learn to love that little girl, I know he can. But he has bad memories of the child's mother, and Melissa's got Eve's look about her." He shook his head tiredly and took a deep, wheezing breath before he continued. "If you can't make him see the truth, Laura, then you have to take the child. Take her before he ruins her."

"But what makes you think that he'd just let me walk off with his daughter?" Laura asked, finding all of this very hard to comprehend. "I'm only the child's aunt, after all."

"That may give you more of a right to her than you know," Henry told Laura without bothering to elaborate. "Anyway, Cal won't raise a fuss. He'd hardly notice that the little one was gone."

"What about you, Henry?" Laura wanted to know. "You must love her or you wouldn't be worrying so. Do you want to lose her?"

The man sighed deeply. "I don't have much time left, girl. I've already turned this ranch and the Sinclair Company over to Cal. Truth to tell, I didn't expect to last this long."

Laura felt her throat tighten. "Don't take on like that," she begged.

Henry waved one large, blue-veined hand as if to dismiss her objection. "I've lived my life, child. I have a lot of good memories and damned few regrets. I'm ready for whatever comes. But I refuse to leave my only grandchild unprotected and unloved."

Laura frantically sought a way out of her dilemma. "What about your daughter, Ellie?" she asked finally. "She was only twelve when I left, but—"

She was interrupted by a dry chuckle from the man on the bed. "Ellie? You mean 'Delphine,' don't you? She's using her full name now—thinks it's more sophisticated. Ellie was a sweet child. Delphine is a woman who doesn't care about anything except clothes, jewelry and high living. Maybe in a few years when she gets a handle on who she really is she'll settle down and become a force to reckon with. God only knows. She's getting married in this house next week to some man from up North who doesn't give a damn about her. He's the one who got her started on all this fancy business. The money and property that Ellie got from her mama and our family connections, those things are what he really wants."

"How do you know that for sure?" Laura asked, trying to reason away some of his worries.

"I had him checked out." He returned the look Laura gave him with no hint of repentance. "I had a right. She's my only daughter, you know. The only thing I could find to fault him on is that he lied about his family. He came out of the worst slum in New York, not from highbred stock like he claims. Now I don't hold that against him. Hell, I admire him for getting out. But he's hiding it, and if he'll lie about that—"

"That's not such a terrible lie," Laura said gently. "You Sinclairs could scare a better man than that into stretching the truth."

The old man patted her cheek affectionately. "You always did see the good in everyone, Laura. Well, you just meet him. Then you can judge for yourself."

Henry waited so long before continuing that Laura grew concerned. But when he began to speak again, his voice was stronger and more forceful than before. "Your daddy was my foreman for a long time, Laura. You and Eve had the run of this house like you were my own children. When you were only teenagers your parents died in that car accident, and I took you in. I never thought of repayment other than the pleasure and happiness you brought to my home. Maybe I didn't give you as much as I should have. I let you make your own ways. Eve married Cal, and you left to make a name for yourself in New

York. You've become a fine, strong woman, Laura. That's more than I can say for my own daughter. So maybe I chose the right way with you after all. Now I'm asking for your help with Melissa. Don't let me down, girl.''

Henry's head dropped to one side, and he gasped for breath. Immediately Juanita rushed to the bed and slipped a nasal cannula into position on his face. He lay still, breathing in the oxygen, his eyes closed.

Laura was stunned by Henry's illness. One minute he'd been talking to her, the next he could hardly breathe.

"He will sleep now," Juanita explained matter-of-factly as she gently propelled Laura to the door. "Today has been one of the bad days."

Following Juanita up the curving stairway to the second floor, Laura felt herself bearing an unwanted invisible burden much heavier than her red leather bag. It was a responsibility that she had no notion of how to deal with and no hope of escaping from. She couldn't even decide what to do with her own life, and now she had another problem to cope with: a child she'd never seen. All she had to do was use her incredible influence with Cal. Laura smiled grimly, remembering the look in his eyes when he'd left her an hour ago. He'd be glad to tell her just what to do with her advice. So then what? If she took Melissa away with her, where would she ever find the time to raise the child?

She was still lost in thought when the housekeeper made a right turn and ushered her into the third bedroom down the hall. A plethora of pink assaulted her eyes. The brass bed was decked out with a pale pink satin quilt and a matching ruffled canopy. Even the wallpaper, both dressers and the bedside table were pink. The carpet was a particularly glaring shade of the same color.

"My lord!" Laura exclaimed, all but blinded by the vivid hues. "This is Eve's old room, isn't it? But it's been...uh...redecorated since I was here last."

"Si," Juanita told her, hastening to open the window. "Eve did it herself after she married Mr. Cal. He never would set foot in this room. At first because he said he couldn't stomach the color. Later on he said it was because he couldn't stand the person who slept here." She looked at Laura apologetically. "I am sorry, Laurita. I am only speaking his words."

Laura met the housekeeper's gaze frankly. "No need to be sorry, Juanita. We both knew what Eve was from the time she was a child, and we both loved her anyway. But Cal...Cal was bewitched by her. He never saw her as she really was. To him she was some kind of impossibly perfect fairy princess. God knows, with her blond hair and those big blue eyes, she surely looked the part. When Cal finally realized the truth, it must have been awful for him."

"It was awful for all of us who lived here. And I do not think that Mr. Cal will ever be the same again. His smiles used to light up my days. Now I cannot even remember the last time I saw him smile. He is so hard and so bitter that my heart aches for him."

Mine, too, Laura thought. In more ways than one. Aloud she only said, "I don't think that I can stay in this room, Nita."

"But it is the only empty room. Mr. Cal, he has the room to the right of this one, and Delphine, she is on your left. Her fiancé is here for the wedding, the Sunday after next. He has your old room at the top of the stairs."

"But surely one of the other—?"

"All the other rooms have been closed up since Eve left. No one has bothered with them since. They have no furniture, no rugs, *nada*. Your sister, she was redecorating again, and she had them stripped bare. Mr. Cal, he never let her touch his room or anything downstairs, thank the Lord. Certainly there are things throughout this old house that could be made better. But Eve made changes with no respect for the spirit of the house or for the feelings of the men who live here. Delphine, she wanted to buy furniture, to finish the decorating, but the men would not trust her to do the job. Now she is leaving to go to a home of her own. Me, I have no talent for things of this nature. Mr. Henry is sick, and Mr. Cal just does not care."

Laura set her bag on the bed with ill-concealed reluctance, finally talked into submission. "I'm not going to enjoy this."

Juanita clucked in sympathy. "I have packed away the things that Eve left behind. The bureaus and the closet are empty, the linens are fresh and clean. You must do your best to accept the situation, Laurita. After all, you will be right next door to Mr. Cal. If you want to talk to him, that will prove very convenient."

Laura's eyes narrowed suspiciously as the housekeeper quickly slipped away to start dinner preparations. Had that whole long story about decorating been merely a ruse to see that she stayed in the room next to Cal's? Surely Nita wasn't suggesting that she...? Laura felt her cheeks flame. No, she must be mistaken. The old housekeeper had been like a mother to her. She would never condone such behavior. Or would she? Laura felt like her whole world had been turned upside down. Wasn't anything the same anymore?

Still, she couldn't help but remember the reaction of Cal's body to her closeness this afternoon. It was strangely at odds with the total rejection she'd seen in his eyes. If she were ever bold enough to slip into his room uninvited, would he throw her right back out or would he make love to her? Even thinking about that possibility caused her pulse to race crazily. And maybe afterward he wouldn't look at her as if she were a lower form of life. Maybe they'd be able to talk about the things that had gone wrong between them—and about Melissa.

Feeling a little more optimistic, Laura used the pink telephone to call the rental car agency and arrange for a pickup and replacement. Then she set about unpacking her overnight case. Unfortunately all it contained in the way of clothing was some extra underwear and a night-gown that she'd originally forgotten to pack in her suitcase. Silently she berated the airline again for losing her bag. She'd just have to make an emergency shopping trip to Houston if it didn't turn up soon.

Suddenly there was a knock on the hall door, and a very tall young woman wearing a deep green designer dress came into the room. The strong jaw and nose that made Cal so ruggedly handsome had been duplicated in Delphine with less pleasing results. She could be called striking, but never pretty. Laura noticed with astonishment that the chunky, awkward child she'd known had turned into a woman as thin and graceful as any high-fashion model. A muted reddish hue had been added to the original dark brown of her hair, turning it a rich shade of auburn. Clusters of smooth curls softened the hard angles of her face and neck, while artful makeup emphasized her Sinclair gray eyes. The total effect was one of attractive elegance.

When Delphine saw Laura, she paused as if some-what taken aback by the other woman's bedraggled ap-pearance. Then, after her initial hesitation, she walked forward with studied poise, extending one well-manicured hand.

"Hello, Laura. I'm so glad to see you again."

The soft, well-modulated voice that bore no trace of a Texas accent was yet another surprise. Laura had no idea how to relate to the stranger who stood before her. In her memory, Ellie had remained a twelve-year-old ugly duckling. The nineteen-year-old swan who confronted her was a shock to say the least.

Elizabeth Sinclair had died giving birth to Delphine and, despite everyone's best intentions, the motherless baby had grown into a difficult, moody child. Laura had felt vaguely sorry for her, but she'd been too wrapped up in her own adolescence to worry much about the problems of a girl just starting grammar school. Now she smiled warmly, genuinely glad to see that things had worked out so well for the other woman.

"It's good to see you again, too, Ellie. I mean, Delphine."

A knock at the door signaled the arrival of a second visitor. The expression of pride and love that came over Delphine's face made her seem almost beautiful.

"I asked my fiancé to stop by so that you could meet him. He's from New York, too." Crossing to the hall door, Delphine threw it open. "Laura, this is my fiancé, Steve Randall. Darling, this is Laura Wright, Cal's sister-in-law."

Steve stepped into the room, and Laura's jaw dropped in amazement.

A corner of Steve's mouth curved in an apologetic smile as he reached forward to grasp Laura's limp hand. "This certainly is a coincidence. I didn't get your message from my secretary until about an hour ago."

Delphine looked from one face to the other, her eyes assessing them speculatively. "You two know each other?"

Laura glared at Steve, withdrawing her hand as if she'd touched a hot stove. "I *thought* I knew him. He's been my boss for six years."

"The last person in the world I expected to see here was you," Steve commented ironically.

"I'm sure of that," Laura said sharply. "After all, I didn't get a wedding invitation, did I?" *And yesterday, when you were trying to seduce me, you neglected to mention the fact that you were engaged and getting married in a few days! Of all the rotten, double-dealing...*

Steve's smile widened as if he could read every thought. "I'm sorry, Laura. We're just having a small wedding, and all the guests are from Delphine's side. I only invited my best man. You've heard me speak of my cousin, Fred."

"Fred," Laura echoed. "How appropriate." It would be safe to invite his cousin, Fred, the successful attorney from Chicago. He was probably as self-conscious about the family past as Steve was. No one would find out anything from him.

"Of course, we're delighted that things happened to work out this way," Steve continued smoothly. "I expect that as the new district manager you'll take the time to tour the new hotels with me before joining us for the wedding."

Laura was about to tell him just what he could do with his expectations and her promotion when she caught sight of Delphine. She had almost forgotten that there was someone else in the room. The woman's face was flushed with anger, and she was looking at Laura with undisguised jealousy. Laura searched frantically for something she could say to explain the misunderstanding and ease the tension of the situation, but Delphine spoke first.

"What *are* you going to wear to dinner?" she mused out loud in an ice-cold voice. Slowly she looked Laura up and down, making her distaste for the older woman's sweat-stained clothes blatantly obvious.

"I have no idea," Laura responded more sharply than she'd intended. "Since the airline lost my suitcase, I'm rather short on clothes. But when I used to live here, no one dressed for dinner."

"Why, it's been a tradition since Eve married Cal. It's expected. But don't worry, Laura," Delphine told her, a peculiar gleam in her gray eyes. "I have just the dress for you. Come on, Steve."

Before Laura could protest or offer thanks, Delphine had swept from the room.

Steve paused in the doorway. "That deal we discussed in New York? I'd appreciate it if you'd keep it in strictest confidence until I have a chance to explain more fully."

"I'll bet you would," Laura snapped, still angry at his behavior.

"Steve?" Delphine called.

"We'll talk later," he told Laura as he hastily stepped into the hallway.

As soon as the door shut Laura threw herself facedown on the soft bed, her mind still reeling from the impact of the day's events. Setting aside her bruised ego, she tried to look at the situation objectively.

Steve had offered to enter into a long-term affair with her only yesterday. That meant he couldn't really be in love with Delphine. So his marriage was probably motivated by the gain of property and family connections as Henry suspected. But what could she do about that?

Even if she were to warn Delphine about Steve, the girl was so obviously in love with him that she might refuse to listen. If she did decide to risk talking to Delphine, would it make Steve angry enough to fire her?

There was an even more important consideration: Steve had taught her everything she knew about the hotel business. She owed him a lot. It all boiled down to one very simple question. Was the loyalty she owed Steve stronger than the older tie that bound her to the Sinclair family?

Laura tossed on the bed, her mind a whirl of confusing images: Steve with his hidden past and questionable future; the elegant but still insecure Delphine; Juanita, as feisty and loving as ever; Henry, an invalid confined to bed, but still holding sway over her life; and finally, Cal. She had returned to the ranch hoping to prove that he meant nothing to her. Instead she'd only succeeded in ripping open an old wound that had never truly healed.

She replayed the day's encounters over and over again in her mind until visions of the ranch's occupants began to whirl around inside her head like the mismatched pieces of an annoying jigsaw puzzle. She fell asleep knowing that she couldn't turn them into a coherent whole because there was still one piece missing—Melissa.

Laura woke in the gray semidarkness of evening with the overwhelming feeling that she was not alone. Lying very still, she let her eyes grow accustomed to the dim light. She could barely make out the figure of a slender, blond child fingering the material of a dress that was draped over the chair by the door.

She studied her visitor for a few moments, finding her features symmetrical, flawless and strangely familiar.

Then she moved slowly to sit up. The little girl started and fled toward the door.

"Melissa!" Laura called out desperately. "Melissa, don't go. Please!"

The child paused with one hand on the doorknob, eyeing the woman suspiciously.

"Melissa, I'm your Aunt Laura," she began softly. "I came all the way from New York to see you. I brought you a present, too. May I turn on the light and show it to you?"

The child hesitated and then nodded vigorously. With a smile, Laura switched on the bedside lamp and rummaged through her art kit. Her hand emerged a minute later with a sketch pad and a charcoal pencil.

"What's that?" Melissa wanted to know.

"Come closer. I'm going to show you how to draw pretty pictures."

The child made no move to approach her, so Laura began making marks on the sketch pad. When she looked up again, Melissa was trying to peer over her shoulder.

"What are you making a picture of?"

"You."

A slow smile spread over the child's features as she gazed down at the replica of her face on the pad. "Can you really teach me to draw like that?" Melissa asked eagerly, her eyes sparkling in the lamplight.

"I can try," Laura said, absorbed in her attempt to translate the child's fragile beauty into charcoal lines on paper. Porcelain skin, a rosebud mouth and button nose. Two large sapphire-blue eyes framed by long lashes a shade darker than her fine, pale blond hair. The child looked like an angel who had come briefly to rest on Earth. Eve had possessed that same ethereal loveliness when she was young, and it had only deepened as she grew to womanhood. But Laura sensed a goodness and sensitivity in this child that would have been foreign to Eve.

Thrilled by her discovery of a kindred spirit, she molded the child's fingers around the pencil and positioned it over a sheet of blank paper.

When Juanita came into the room a half hour later, Laura and Melissa were still huddled in concentration over the sketch pad. "I see that you have met my sweet little Melissa," the housekeeper observed.

Laura glanced at her. "Yes. And I'm very glad I have."

The child ran to Juanita excitedly. "Look! Look what I drew! It's Daddy's horse, Dancer."

"It looks just like him!" Juanita exclaimed. "Did you do this all by yourself?"

Laura saw the child waver uncertainly. "Well," she said finally, "Laura showed me where to put the lines."

The housekeeper laughed in delight. "It is truly beautiful, little one. But now we have to get dressed for dinner."

"When can we draw some more, Laura?" the child asked as Juanita led her from the room.

"Tomorrow," Laura told her. "If you sit still for me a while and let me make another picture of you, I'll give you a second lesson. Is it a deal?"

The little girl nodded eagerly as the bedroom door closed softly behind her.

Laura went into the bathroom for the hot shower she'd been promising herself all day. Then she slipped into her clean underwear and sat down at the dresser to apply her makeup. Surveying the results of her efforts in the mirror, she grimaced at her reflection. She had the flawless olive skin of her father's Spanish grandmother and high cheekbones that revealed a hint of American Indian blood. Her sister, Eve, on the other hand, had inherited the Nordic beauty of their mother's Swedish ancestors. All her life, Laura had existed almost unnoticed in the shadow of that perfect beauty, feeling herself ugly in comparison. Since leaving the ranch, she had learned to accept and even to appreciate her unique looks, but she still couldn't think of herself as a beautiful woman.

Standing, she held up the dress that Melissa had been so interested in. Inevitably it was pink. With a sigh of resignation, she slipped it over her head and gazed at her reflection in the full-length mirror on the back of the closet door. The dress was short and sleeveless with slits on both sides up to midthigh. The mandarin collar circled her throat like a band of steel, and the satin bodice molded her breasts so tightly that she was afraid to take a deep breath.

"You look like a receptionist for a Shanghai opium den," Laura told the stranger in the looking glass. "You definitely do not look like the manager of one of the finest hotels in New York City."

She had almost decided to change back into her soiled slacks and blouse when Juanita knocked on the door, and called to her that dinner was about to be served. Slipping into new panty hose and her only pair of shoes, Laura ran a brush through her hair. With a final sidelong glance at the mirror, she walked out into the hallway feeling as if she were going to a masquerade party.

Descending the staircase, she saw Steve and Delphine seated side by side on the living-room sofa, sipping drinks. Cal was standing in front of the fireplace gazing at the unlit logs. Laura was not surprised to see him outfitted in jeans and an old green shirt. She made a silent resolution to dress similarly from now on, no matter what Delphine said.

Laura became absorbed in the handsome profile of the man before her. His thoughts were obviously a million miles away. Was he remembering what had passed between them this morning? she wondered. Was he sorry that he'd been so harsh?

She remembered the steel of his muscles under her fumbling hands and the unguarded arousal she'd seen in his eyes as he'd watched her dressing in the glade. Desire spread through her body like wildfire. He'd had a chance to recover from the shock of her sudden appearance. He'd had time to think through his anger. What would his face reveal when he turned and looked at her now? She trembled in nervous anticipation as, with every step she descended, she walked closer and closer to the answer.

Cal's sister saw her first and greeted her with a smirk. "I see you found the dress, Laura."

The two men looked up at the newcomer. Laura first read surprise, then amusement and finally, lusty speculation in Steve's blue eyes.

Taking a deep breath, she forced herself to look at Cal and her heart seemed to stand still. His face was a frozen mask of stunned disbelief, as if he were seeing a creature conjured up by dark forces to torment his soul. As she watched in horror, his right hand began to shake. His glass shattered under the pressure of his fingers sending sharp fragments and cold Kentucky bourbon cascading onto the hardwood floor.

"Are you all right?" Laura cried, rushing toward him, forgetting her own wounded feelings in her concern for his safety.

His only response was a withering look that warned her to keep her distance. She had never seen so much violence in his eyes. She got the frightening impression that he was barely restraining himself from striking her. Then the moment passed. Without a word he turned and stalked into the dining room.

Laura followed, hurt and perplexed. She hardly remembered to thank Steve when he pulled out her chair for her. She couldn't understand what had gone wrong.

Cal had taken Henry's old place at the head of the table, and when Juanita brought Melissa in, she seated the child one chair away. The housekeeper was about to return to the kitchen when she saw Laura and stared openly.

"Heaven help you, Laurita," she said in a frantic whisper. "Where did you find that dress? It belonged to Eve!"

Laura choked on the ice water she was sipping. She looked accusingly at Delphine's bland, too innocent face. The fact that the girl had thought nothing of upsetting her brother in order to get back at her for some imagined slight was infuriating. "Well, Delphine. Apparently you went to a lot of trouble to make me look foolish, but what about Cal? Don't you have any consideration for his feelings?"

"My goodness, Laura," the younger woman exclaimed ingenuously. "I just didn't think. You're about the same size that Eve was, so naturally I just went through some of her things. Anyway, I hardly expected that reaction from Cal. He never notices what anyone wears."

"Come off it!" Laura snapped. She was aware that Cal's eyes were on her, but she didn't dare look at him. Why hadn't she realized? The dress was so obviously something that Eve would have worn. All she'd wanted was to be closer to Cal. Now they'd been pushed even farther apart.

She met Delphine's burning gaze without flinching. "If you've got something to say, spit it out, and we'll settle it here and now before any real harm is done."

Delphine rose to the challenge. "I saw the looks that you and Steve were exchanging earlier. I know that there's something going on between you two that has nothing to do with business."

"Don't be ridiculous!" Steve blurted out desperately.

Both women ignored him.

Laura actually smiled in satisfaction, disregarding the insistent nudge of her boss's toe against her calf under the table. "Good, Delphine. Now we can stop playing stupid games. If anyone at this table has a specific question, I'd appreciate it if they'd come right out and ask it."

Unfortunately Melissa saw no reason why Laura's invitation shouldn't apply to her. "Daddy, do you want to see the picture that I drew of Dancer?"

"Not now," Cal told her gruffly.

The little girl's mouth quivered. Swallowing hard, she reached for her water glass. Her hand slipped and the entire contents of the glass flooded the table, soaking the cloth and Melissa's drawing.

For the first time that night, Cal looked at his daughter. "Get away from this table," he said in a low growl. "Go eat in the kitchen with Juanita."

Laura burst out in anger. "There was no call for that, Cal."

"This is no place for a child right now."

"All right, but you don't have to talk to her as if she were a stray dog!"

He looked at her coldly. "She's my daughter, this is my house, and you are only a guest here. I'll thank you to mind your own business."

Laura stood up and threw her napkin down on her plate. "I'll be careful to do just that from now on. I'm sure you don't mind if I eat in the kitchen, too. The food is just as good, and the company has to be much more pleasant."

She turned to Cal's sister. "Just for the record, there's nothing 'going on' between Steve and me. But I want to thank you for the fine welcome anyway, Delphine. You know, I really liked you a lot better when you were just plain Ellie."

She had the satisfaction of seeing the girl flush and lower her eyes.

"Come on now," Steve said, attempting to smooth things over. "There's absolutely no reason for anyone to be upset. I don't believe this all started over a piece of clothing. I'm sure Delphine was just trying to do you a favor, Laura. The dress is a little...exotic, but it's very attractive on you."

Laura grimaced. "I knew that I could count on you to appreciate it, Steve," she said sarcastically.

Then she caught Delphine's hard stare and knew that the girl disapproved of Steve's remark and of her response, but she was too angry to care about Delphine's feelings. As for the disgust she saw on Cal's face, she wasn't about to waste any more regrets. If he couldn't see that the dress was Delphine's fault and that he was wrong to talk to his daughter the way he had, then he was more unreasonable than she'd thought!

Seething, she burst into the kitchen and found Melissa sitting on Juanita's lap, sobbing uncontrollably.

"Oh, baby," she said, bending over to stroke the child's silky hair. "Don't take on so. Your daddy was just angry with me. That's why he hollered at you. Honest!"

Melissa sniffed and looked up at her in confusion. "But why was he angry at you?"

Laura hesitated. How could she explain to a child what she didn't really understand herself? "I guess he just didn't like it that I wore your mama's dress."

Melissa thought for a moment. "It's an ugly dress anyway," she declared solemnly.

Laura laughed and gave her a hug. "You have the soul of a true artist."

"But my pretty picture," Melissa said sadly. "The water made it all wet."

"We'll make a new one. It'll be better than the old one, you'll see. Now come on and let's eat dinner. I walked a long way to get here today, and I am soooo hungry!"

At ten o'clock, Laura dragged herself up the stairs to her bedroom weighted down by three helpings of Juanita's pot roast and a big wedge of apple pie. She hadn't realized how much she'd missed the Mexican woman's delicious home cooking. She'd better be careful or the clothes she had to buy would end up being a size bigger than usual.

In the company of the housekeeper and the child, she'd been able to forget that Cal was just one room away. Not that distance mattered. The man obviously hated her. He even resented his own daughter!

For the first time since she'd arrived, she seriously considered taking Melissa to live with her. She'd need help if she took the little girl in, but Nita would never leave Henry. Maybe she could hire her own house-keeper...

Laura brought those thoughts up short. She couldn't take Melissa away from Cal. Melissa needed her father, and Cal needed the child—even if he didn't recognize that fact. Someone had to help him heal and show him how to love again. He wouldn't let her close enough to do it, but surely he could be convinced to accept his own child. She knew there was laughter and gentleness buried beneath Cal's angry facade. If only he'd let it out!

As Laura undressed, she tried to make sense of the evening's events. She felt ashamed of the responses Cal and Delphine had elicited from her. During the last seven years, she'd come to think of herself as a rational, even-tempered person. Even Steve admired her self-control and cool thinking. She hadn't even been back on the ranch for twenty-four hours, and already she was locked in a contest with Delphine to determine who was the most illogical and immature female in Texas. It was as if the emotions she had repressed for so long had all surfaced at once.

Whatever the provocation, she decided things would be different from now on. She promised herself to keep a tight rein on her feelings and let her mind dictate her actions from here on in.

Drowsily she pulled off the infamous dress and left it lying on the chair. After removing her makeup and brushing her teeth, she slipped into her long, pale blue nightgown, and throwing the wall switch, plunged the room into darkness. Burrowing under the covers of the big double bed, she was asleep almost instantly.

Moments later, she struggled back to consciousness, suddenly aware that she was no longer alone. Someone was sitting on her bed shaking her awake with cool, smooth hands. She heard Steve's voice in the darkness.

"Come on, Laura, wake up. I don't know how anyone can go to sleep that fast. It's unnatural."

"Watch it!" Laura pushed the hands away and groped around trying to turn on the bedside lamp, forgetting in her confusion that she'd thrown the wall switch off before going to bed. "Are you crazy? What are you doing here?"

Steve chuckled. "It's not what you think. Of course, I might not turn you down if you insisted."

Laura's silence seemed to echo in the darkness of the room.

Steve cleared his throat. "Well, actually, I just wanted to talk to you without an audience before you and Delphine had a chance to get together again. I knocked, but there was no answer."

"So you just came in anyway and, when you realized I was asleep, you proceeded to wake me up! Of all the—"

Just then the door connecting her room with Delphine's opened without warning. The younger woman walked in and flipped the wall switch, flooding Laura's room with light. "I knew that I heard Steve's voice!" she cried.

Steve stood up to face his fiancée as Laura sighed in resignation. With his half-buttoned shirt and mussed hair, he looked like an overgrown child who'd been caught with his hand in the cookie jar.

Delphine stared at the scene before her and experienced a fiercely possessive rush of jealousy. She had never noticed any lack in the way Steve responded to her until she'd seen him with Laura. The respect and affection with which he'd looked at the other woman, the genuine warmth in his voice when he spoke to her, made Delphine painfully aware of a deficit in their own relationship that hadn't been apparent to her before. And the naked desire in his eyes when he'd first seen Laura coming down the stairs in that tarty pink dress had made Delphine seethe. Not once had he looked at her that way!

Now as he stood and confronted her, the thinly veiled contempt in his eyes erased the last vestige of her self-control. She began to scream accusations at Laura in her true Texas accent, liberally laced with obscenities and speculations concerning the other woman's ancestry.

Laura listened numbly, unable to comprehend why this was happening to her. It seemed like a particularly distasteful nightmare. She'd never forgive Steve for this. Never.

"What in the hell is going on in here?"

Laura tore her eyes away from Delphine to see Cal standing in the open doorway that connected his room to her own. In the confusion she hadn't even heard him come in.

He was shirtless, barefoot and rumpled as if he'd just climbed out of bed and pulled on his jeans. Her eyes were drawn to the hard, rippling muscles that made up his wide chest and the soft, springy hair sprinkled across it.

Cal turned to meet Laura's eyes, and his mouth was a grim line. Earlier that evening, he had noticed the same feeling between Steve and Laura that his sister had sensed. The fact that he gave a damn one way or the other only served to increase his anger. By the time the unholy din coming from Laura's room had attracted his attention, he'd already been tossing and turning for an hour without being able to sleep. The sight of Laura in her nightgown with Randall not a foot away did nothing to improve his mood.

Laura jumped guiltily when Cal turned and caught her openly assessing him, but for all the attention he paid her she might as well have been invisible. No such luck, she thought miserably.

"I found them in bed together!" Delphine wailed. "They—"

"I needed to talk to Laura about business," Steve insisted, "so—"

"Just how stupid do you think I am?" Delphine raged. "I know what I saw! You were—"

"No, we weren't—" Laura began.

"Quiet!" Cal bellowed. The sudden silence was a blessed relief. "I don't care if you people swing on chandeliers in New York City," Cal continued, his face impassive, "but in this house we respect other people's possessions. Laurie, that man happens to belong to my sister—whether he knows it or not. Do we understand each other?"

Laura opened her mouth to protest, but Cal was already herding Delphine and her fiancé into the hallway. "Other people are trying to sleep," he admonished. "So if you want to fight, do it quietly, or go check into one of his hotels."

The door closed behind the wrangling couple, and all at once Cal and Laura were alone in her room. His eyes burned with white-hot anger and glared at her accusingly.

Laura's sense of unreality vanished. Hurriedly she tried to explain. "Cal, listen—"

"There are three doors that lead into this room," he snapped, ignoring her attempt to speak. "They all have locks. If you're going to make a habit of receiving night visitors, you ought to bear that fact in mind. Or did you plan on getting caught?"

Laura stood and, quivering with righteous indignation, walked toward him, heedless of the inadequate covering of her nightgown. "We were only talking!"

Cal rolled his eyes toward the ceiling. "Just like you were only talking to me this morning? Hell, you would have let me take you right then and there! Wouldn't you?''

Laura stood mute, unwilling to damn herself by admitting that she had so little power to resist him.

"Now, a few hours later, Delphine finds you snug in bed with Randall. And while all hell was breaking loose with them, you were sitting there calmly looking at me like you were the cat and I was the cream. You're playing us one against the other. Who's the object of the game, Laurie? Him or me?''

"I—''

Cal's cold fury overrode her protest. "And you had the brass to lecture Delphine about playing games! She's an amateur compared to you. I almost believed you were sincere. All that tender concern about my feelings—that was a real nice touch.''

Laura stepped closer, determined to convince him of her honesty and saw his gaze dip reluctantly, drawn by the provocative sway of her breasts. Words froze in her throat as his eyes burned their way down her. She was suddenly aware that every line of her body was visible through the semitransparent material. She felt her nipples jut their pink tips toward him in wanton invitation. The pounding of her heart drowned out the sound of her own breathing as his gaze fastened on the dark triangle of curls below her navel.

Let it happen, Cal, she begged silently, her anger swept away by sweet yearning. Come to me and let me show you the only truth I know.

The lines around Cal's mouth deepened, and she saw the heavy muscles of his throat jerk as he swallowed convulsively. For an impossibly long moment, she watched him fight a war within himself and knew by the shuttered look that came over his eyes that she had been the one to lose.

When he finally spoke, his voice sounded strained. "You don't owe me any explanations, Laurie, not after all these years. Maybe I was wrong about tonight, I don't know. But I do know one thing for sure, the sooner you leave here, the better it'll be for all of us."

He stared at her coolly, letting the words—and his rejection—sink in. Then he went back into his room, closing the door between them with shattering finality.

When she heard the sound of the bolt being driven home on his side of the door she clenched her lips together to keep from screaming. It was the worst insult that he had ever offered her. Did he really think that she'd come crawling into his bed after the things he'd said?

An inner voice mocked her. You were thinking of it this morning. It's a good thing he locked that door. He's saved you from spending the last of your pride in a futile attempt to revive a love that died years ago. Thank him, the voice urged gratingly. Next time you see him, thank him.

Laura spent the rest of the night simmering in a stew of frustrated passion and outraged innocence. With her resolution to retain her equanimity shattered, she tossed and turned for hours. Her thoughts alternated between anger at Cal's high-handed behavior, and devising persuasive explanations that would make the actual events of the evening clear to him. One thing was certain, if Cal thought that loud talk and hard looks could intimidate her into leaving, he had a surprise coming. She fell asleep just as the first rays of sunlight filtered through the billowy curtains, determined to stay and face whatever challenges the new day would bring.

Chapter Three

This is great!" Laura told Juanita. "Thank you."

A call to the airline had ascertained that they'd still been unable to locate her luggage. She'd been worrying about what to wear for the day when the housekeeper had turned up with some of her old shirts, jeans and boots that she'd left behind years before.

"Where did you dig these up?" she asked as she slipped into the freshly laundered clothes, delighted to find that they still fit perfectly.

"They were in the attic. I got them down yesterday afternoon and washed them for you. I also found an old easel of yours and some blank canvases. Would you like one of the men to get them for you?"

Laura quickly nodded. "I sure would."

After drinking a cup of coffee in the kitchen, Laura decided to stop by Henry's room. She found the older man sitting up in bed reading the business section of the morning paper. Relieved by the obvious improvement in his condition, she leaned down to kiss his cheek.

"What was all that ruckus upstairs last night?" Henry demanded without preamble.

"Well, I . . ." Laura stammered, surprised and embarrassed by the unexpected question. "That is, Steve and Delphine had an argument."

Keen gray eyes bored into hers.

"In my room," Laura added, feeling like a ten-year-old trying, futilely, to cover up a misdeed. "Cal came in and . . . settled things down."

"Cal did that, did he?" Henry muttered skeptically. "Seems to me he's spent a lot more of his life stirring things up than he has settling them down. Glad to know the boy's making a change for the better."

Laura didn't try to hide her smile, which Henry returned. "Don't go taking everything he says to heart, girl. Cal's been through a lot these past years. Sometimes the anger and the pain just seem to get the better of him."

Laura nodded solemnly, but inwardly she groaned. First Juanita, and now Henry. Cal apparently had a champion in every room.

Henry now seemed satisfied that he'd gotten his point across. "You run along outside now, Laura. No sense wasting a beautiful morning like this cooped up in the house. Don't worry about me. I'll be up and around by tomorrow."

Five minutes later, Laura found herself obediently wandering out into the shade of the front veranda. Somehow her old clothes no longer felt strange. It was as if she were sliding back into the past and the all-engulfing problems of her adopted family, despite her best efforts to retain her hard-won independence. She felt like a helpless spectator watching herself becoming increasingly involved in a situation that both angered and frightened her.

"Yeeeee-ha!"

The yell drew Laura's attention toward the corral about twenty yards away. A young cowboy bounced in the saddle of a bucking Appaloosa, both hands firmly gripping the rope reins. Snorting fiercely, the stallion continued its jolting gyrations, its spotted coat gleaming under the blazing sun. Seconds later, the rider went sailing over the horse's head to land on his side in the dust.

Other men leaped into the corral to shoo the skittish bronc away from the injured rider as Steve and Delphine leaned over the surrounding fence for a better view of the spectacle. But Laura only had eyes for Cal as he slipped between the rails and knelt in the dust beside the fallen cowboy.

She walked down the steps, drawn to the scene against her better judgment. Delphine glared daggers at her as she approached.

"Are you still here?" the younger woman asked in icy tones. "I thought that after last night you'd have the decency to leave. But then maybe that word holds no meaning for you."

Laura looked at her evenly and kept her voice civil. "Nothing happened between Steve and me last night. Nothing has ever happened between us. If you want to invent a problem where none exists, be my guest."

Climbing up to stand on the lower rail of the fence, she purposefully turned her attention to the scene below. Several of the old hands greeted her and quietly welcomed her back to the ranch as they waited for a diagnosis on the injured rider.

Cal was conferring with an older man in a checkered shirt. The man shook his head sadly. "It's broke. His leg's broke bad, maybe in more 'n one place."

"Damn!" Cal exclaimed. He bent over the young cowboy again. "Okay, Jimmy. Frank and Len are going to drive you into town to the hospital. You behave yourself, and you'll be back home in time for the big barbecue."

The injured man managed a weak grin. "Nothing could keep me away from that, come hell or high water."

"You betcha." Cal patted Jimmy's shoulder as the other men helped the boy up and carried him carefully toward a white pickup truck.

"We got any other rider who can break that horse?" Cal asked, turning back to the man in the checkered shirt.

Laura, still smarting from Cal's rejection of the night before, had the words out of her mouth before she even realized she'd intended to speak. "I know a man who used to be good enough—once upon a time."

Cal peered at her from under the wide brim of his hat. "I've won my share of buckles, lady. I've got nothing more left to prove—to anyone."

Laura felt her mouth curve in a derisive smile. "Well, I guess the Sinclair money can buy you another young cowboy to do the hard work for you. No need to get *your* hands dirty."

"Does the chance of seeing me fall on my backside mean that much to you?" Laura's face turned red as Cal pointed a gloved finger at her. "I wouldn't go taking any bets on it happening, if I were you!" Cal walked toward the Appaloosa with determination.

Three cowboys held the horse steady as Cal mounted, then nodded his readiness. The other men quickly moved out of the way as the stallion exploded into a blur of motion.

A bolt of fear shot through Laura, and she cursed herself for a fool. She vividly remembered the rodeo held the year Cal turned eighteen and the broken shoulder he'd brought home as a souvenir. All the anger she'd felt evaporated in the intensity of her concern for his safety.

"He's rather good, isn't he?"

Laura looked down to see Steve beside her. She wasn't ready to forgive him yet. Just looking at him seemed to make her more annoyed than ever. He didn't belong with Delphine or on this ranch. She was about to tell him so when she suddenly realized what was happening: She was becoming one of the family again, closing ranks against outsiders. The direction her thoughts were taking frightened her more than she cared to admit. Nervously she turned her attention back to Cal.

"He's not just good, he's the best," Laura exclaimed with feeling.

Steve looked at her oddly as if wondering at the intensity of her declaration. Then he shrugged. "If you're into the phony macho type, I guess he is."

Laura found it hard to say the words, but she knew them to be the simple truth. "There's nothing phony about Cal Sinclair, never has been, never will be. I'm the one who's the phony. He just seems to bring out my worst—"

Her words broke off with a gasp as the horse slammed its side into the fence, and Cal's leg received a glancing blow. Watching his face go white with pain, she knew she couldn't stay any longer. She jumped down from the rail and ran into the house and up the staircase.

"I've got to talk to you, Laura!"

Reaching the second floor, she paused briefly to gaze down at Steve, who had followed her. The sound of her voice arrested his progress at the foot of the stairs.

"You really don't have to justify your actions to me. I'm your employee, not your friend. If I thought that Delphine would listen to what I had to tell her about you, I'd make the effort. Unfortunately, she's stupid enough to love you."

She turned and fled down the hall, ignoring him as he called her name. Then she heard Delphine's voice and knew for sure that he wouldn't follow. All she was concerned with now was the fact that Cal had been hurt...maybe seriously, and definitely because of her. All she wanted to do was hide behind the locked door of her room until she could regain some vestige of composure.

Absorbed in her tumultuous thoughts, she blindly stumbled through the wrong door and found herself in Cal's room. She froze on the threshold, unbidden memories flooding her consciousness with vivid images of the past.

The beige-and-brown room had changed little in seven years. The athletic plaques and trophies were still in the glass case by the far wall, and the mounted set of Texas longhorns still hung above the headboard of the heavy mahogany bedstead.

She had spent many happy hours in this room with Cal just talking or watching TV, even trading baseball cards. With a smile, she found herself wondering if he still had his old collection.

Sitting down on the bed, Laura ran her hand over the faded, but still beautiful, patchwork quilt that Cal's mother had made the winter before she'd died. And, slowly, she drifted back to the last time she'd been in this room...

* * *

...Laura had been home for the Christmas break, and was scheduled to return to college in New York the next day. Her bags were packed and she'd arranged for Frank to drive her to the airport at six the following morning. She'd said goodbye to everyone, and finally she'd come up to Cal's room to show him the finished portrait of Eve that she'd painted as a Christmas present.

"I showed it to Eve before she left for her friend's bridal shower," she told Cal with a smile. "She liked it, so I guess it's going to be hanging downstairs whether or not anyone else approves."

As Cal held the canvas up to the light to admire it, Laura felt her heart contract in envy. She had always loved him, ever since she could remember. Not that they hadn't had their share of fights. They were both stubborn and strong willed, and they had butted heads more times than not. Despite their arguments, Cal had been an idolized older brother whose exploits had excited her girlish imagination. But for the past few years he had been arousing other feelings in her—feelings that were painful and difficult to deal with.

She had never been able to bring herself to tell him how she felt because she was afraid of losing the part of Cal that did belong to her. Even when he'd called her in New York and casually mentioned that he and Eve had started dating, she'd kept her own counsel. Now, as she watched him staring at the portrait of her sister, she felt an overwhelming desire to run her fingers through his curly black hair, to caress his strong, handsome face, to make those gray eyes look at *her* that way.

"She's so beautiful," he said with a shake of his head. "When she turns those blue eyes on me and smiles, I feel like a firecracker on the Fourth of July."

Laura was numb with despair. "Yes, she is beautiful."

Cal frowned, and set the portrait on a chair. "The only thing is, we just don't have that much to talk about—not like you and me."

Their eyes met, and Laura's heart began to flutter wildly.

"When I'm near her, it's like I'm under some kind of spell. I can only think about how much I want her. But when I'm away from her, I start to have doubts."

Laura had to keep herself from telling him the truth—how Eve had laughed about the teasing game of pretended innocence she was playing with Cal. Laura knew the true extent of her sister's sexual experience, and the idea that Eve would lie in order to manipulate Cal's feelings disgusted her. Hurriedly she searched for something to say that would protect Cal without maligning her sister.

"Give yourself time to be sure of your feelings, Cal. You're twenty-three and Eve's only nineteen. It's natural to have doubts. Don't rush into a commitment that you may regret later."

"I'm not afraid of commitment... to the right woman." His gray eyes seemed to be looking down into her soul. "I missed you, Laurie. When you were away at school, I thought about you all the time. So many things happened that I wanted to share with you, but I couldn't because you weren't here. I wish you weren't going back to New York tomorrow."

Laura turned away before he could see her reaction. She knew that he was offering her a brother's affection, and that made her own feelings seem inappropriate. Ashamed and confused, she walked toward the door, intent on escape, babbling the first words that came into her mind. "I've got to go back to school. I've got to get back to my job, too. Did I tell you that I was working part-time at a hotel now and—"

"Only about a hundred times."

Then Cal's hands were on her shoulders, and her whole body began to tremble.

"I want to talk about us, Laurie. You and me."

He forced her to turn around and face him. She knew he had to be aware of the effect his nearness was having on her, but she was so startled by what he'd said that she forgot to be self-conscious.

"You want to what?"

He took her face in his hands and Laura closed her eyes, afraid that he would read too much in them. But she could still feel his fingers on her skin, his warm breath against her cheek. His voice was a sultry whisper.

"I want to know what it's like to touch you the way a man touches a woman, to get closer and closer to you until there's nothing left to separate us."

Laura felt cold and then burning hot as the shock of what he was saying rushed through her. She couldn't believe that her fantasy was coming true at last, that Cal wanted her the way that she wanted him. Her eyes flew open, and her lips curved in an incredulous smile as she saw the burning light in his gaze and realized that he was shaking, too.

Then her smile slowly faded. It wasn't just she and Cal in this room; there was an invisible presence.

"What about Eve?" she asked slowly, reluctantly.

Cal's eyes didn't try to hide anything. "I'd be a liar if I told you I know my own mind where she's concerned. But I do know that I want you, when you're with me and when we're apart. It doesn't allow me a moment's peace, Laurie. I had to tell you or go crazy!"

He pulled away and looked at the floor. Laura had never seen him so miserable.

"I know that's a lousy answer, and I know it's not fair to you. It's just the best I can do right now. Tell me to go to hell, and I won't blame you."

Laura felt a surge of temper. It *was* unfair! She wanted to yell at him and tell him to talk to her again when he'd grown up enough to be able to make a choice. Only she knew he'd choose Eve in the end. Eve's beauty always got her everything she wanted, and Eve wanted Cal.

But now Cal was offering her a chance at a relationship. Even if it didn't work out, he would still be hers for a few hours. And maybe, just maybe, he really was in love with her. If she could only make him realize it! Clinging to that slim hope, she forced herself to swallow her pride. Only one nagging doubt remained.

"What's wrong?" Cal asked, sensing her inner conflict. "Tell me what you're thinking, Laurie. Call me names if you want to. Just talk to me!"

Laura hesitated, her thoughts racing. She might lose the one chance she'd ever have to be with him, but the possible consequences were too grave. She had to tell him.

Awkwardly she struggled to find the right words. "I ... I want you, Cal. But I've never been with a man before, and I'm not ... prepared."

Cal took a deep breath, his face reflecting the clash of divergent emotions. Desire warred with protectiveness, and he looked at her as if he were in awe of the gift she was offering.

"I can take care of things, Laurie. I promise you don't have to worry about that. But are you sure that this is right for you? Is this really what you want?"

She felt Cal's concern wrap itself around her like a familiar embrace, and she was grateful for his caring. But he had to understand that being with him was something she wanted with all her heart. If Cal came away from this thinking that he'd harmed her in any way, he'd carry the guilt with him for the rest of his life. She had to reassure him.

"I've dreamed of this happening for a long time now, Cal. I guess I've just been waiting for you to ask."

She watched him hesitate for what seemed like an endless moment, as if he were weighing her words in a vain attempt to justify taking what he wanted, what he needed.

Laura spoke quickly, urgently, unable to bear the pain she saw in his face. "This isn't only your decision to make, Cal. You asked and I said yes. It's that simple."

He smiled as though beguiled by her sudden assertiveness. "Is that so?"

"It is, and you'd better accept what I'm trying to give you or I'm going to be very insulted."

"Well, I can't let that happen, can I?"

His smile faded and he gently stroked her cheek, his eyes as soft as a gray dove's wing, his voice a silken caress. "I can keep fighting my own wanting for a while longer, Laurie, but I can't fight yours, too. I'll try my best to make it good for you. Just remember, if you change your mind in the middle of things, tell me and I'll stop."

With his eyes watching hers for any sign of objection, he reached behind her and quietly locked the door.

Laura felt a shock of mingled apprehension and desire leap through her as she heard the click of the bolt, but no thought of protest occurred to her. The pelting of heavy raindrops on the roof echoed the pounding of her heart, and the sound of the howling wind was overcome by the exultant roar of the blood racing through her veins. No prior claims or family loyalty could outweigh her certainty that what was about to happen was right and good. If she had only this one night, then she would use it to love Cal as no woman had ever loved him before. She would leave her brand on his heart forever.

Cal's lips claimed hers for the first time. His mustache tickled her sensitive skin, as the scent of his aftershave and the slightly musky odor of his aroused maleness enfolded her. The work-roughened tips of his fingers stroked her jawline from ear to chin as his mouth moved against hers with gentle pressure. He sucked and nibbled and licked her lips, slowly savoring them as if he had all the time in the world, while in Laura's mind the seconds ticked away. She was desperate to make him hers completely, to possess him fully before this magical night ended and she had to face tomorrow alone.

Throwing her arms around his neck and pulling his mouth more firmly against hers, she tried to communicate her need to him, but he only continued to treasure her swollen lips with maddening thoroughness.

"Easy, Laurie," he murmured. "Easy. Don't rush things. Just relax. Close your eyes, relax and let it happen."

His fingers moved up to massage the tight muscles in her shoulders as his tongue found a sensitive spot just below her ear.

Gradually the soft, unhurried sound of his voice flowed through her. She stopped thinking about what he was doing and began to feel it instead. Like Alice stepping through the looking glass, she crossed a threshold into an unfamiliar universe of dizzying sensation. Cal's hands and mouth made her experience things she had only read about before.

The sensuality that had lain dormant within her through clumsy high-school kisses and the self-imposed celibacy of college suddenly knew no bounds. As Cal's lips trailed down her throat she shivered and pulled her clothing aside, straining toward him until he captured one sleepy, rose-pink nipple, waking it with his tongue. The sweet tug of his mouth drew out the essence of her soul to merge with his.

Touching, seeking, finding, locked in each other's arms, they fell back onto the bed, impatiently shedding the barrier of their clothes until there was only skin against skin, warmth against warmth.

She had waited and watched and wanted for so many years that passion took over with a stunning completeness. Boldly she reached out to claim what her heart had always known belonged to her.

She was familiar with every scar, every curve, every line of Cal's body, but now she rediscovered them as his lover. Smiling up into his face, she pushed a stray lock from his forehead and memorized the texture of his hair. With aching tenderness she pressed her lips to the jagged white scar on his shoulder, just as she had yearned to do for years. Trembling with desire, she ran her fingers over his smooth back and explored the taut, firm muscles of the chest she had admired a thousand times from a distance, but had never dared touch before. Yet the more she knew of him, the more she wanted to know.

Hesitantly she reached down to touch the miraculous change—the hardness where only softness had been before. Smiling, he curved his hand around hers, teaching her, guiding her with the same patience she had trusted since the first faint awareness of memory.

Then his easy smile disappeared, and her breath quickened as she saw the fire building in his eyes. "Do you know what you're doing to me, Laurie?" he asked, his voice raw with want.

"Yes," Laura whispered fiercely. "I'm showing you how much I love you."

With a groan, he forgot all restraint and buried his tongue in the warm haven of her mouth, leaving no corner untasted. His muscles vibrated with the force of his tightly reined passion while he lifted her hand away and rolled her over until she lay flat on the bed. His fingers eased between her thighs and found the bud that had been aching for his touch.

She opened her body to him as she had long ago opened her heart, as naturally as a flower opens to the life-giving rays of sun. She had been born for this man, for this moment—born to feel the rapture that only his touch could inspire.

Before Cal, she had been kissed, but never excited, touched, but never aroused. Her stubborn body had waited for Cal to awaken it. Now it ached for the fulfillment only he could give.

His kisses covered her face, her neck, her breasts, and moved lower until his tongue was teasing the sensitive nerve endings that his fingers had caressed only moments before.

Laura twined her hands into his dark curls, pressing him closer, adrift in delicious sensation. She didn't think to object, to push him away. Her body had become an extension of his. His wishes, his desires had become hers. There was no holding back, no embarrassment, no pretense. She freely offered him everything she possessed and, in the miracle of love was given back full measure and more.

Her breath began to come in short gasps. Her hands gripped the quilt, her body reached instinctively for the release that Cal was bringing closer.

"Please," she begged, not even knowing what it was she asked for. "Please."

Suddenly there was no Cal, there was no Laura; there was only a breathtaking golden world of pure feeling. The most intense pleasure that she had ever known coursed through her, going on and on until she was sure that it would never stop, that she would never have to return to the cold loneliness of the everyday world again.

Wrapped in the soft, hazy cocoon of fulfillment, she saw Cal hovering above her and held out her empty arms for him to fill. She drew him against her and felt an unbearable pressure trying to invade the untried tenderness of her body, and then a swift burning pain as her flesh yielded inevitably to his.

She moved into the pain, welcoming it—welcoming an end to the years of longing, the years of separateness. She would have endured far worse, would have walked through hellfire itself, for the privilege of becoming Cal Sinclair's woman.

She looked up and the warm, loving light in Cal's eyes took her breath away. He leaned forward to reverently kiss her forehead, her cheeks, her eyelids, her lips while he buried his hands in her long dark hair. His eyes pleaded for forgiveness.

"I'm sorry I had to hurt you, Laurie."

Her heart seemed to overflow with love as she reached up to touch his cheek. "I don't remember any hurting," she whispered, surprised to find that she told the truth.

As Cal began to move inside her—first cautiously, and then more forcefully, the last of her pain faded, a warm glow steadily building in its place.

Trembling, she gazed into his eyes and saw her passion reflected there as he touched her to the limits of her womanhood. Each stroke was like the turn of an invisible key winding an internal mainspring ever tighter.

Then Cal slipped one hand between their bodies and the spring snapped in an excruciatingly pleasurable release of tension. He smothered his name against her lips as he drove into her even harder. His every movement created shock waves of ecstasy for Laura.

In the final strokes of their passion, Laura wrapped her arms and legs around him possessively, never wanting it to end, never wanting his body to leave hers. This morning she wouldn't have believed it possible to love him more. Now she felt that parting from him would mean more agony than she could bear in a lifetime.

Shuddering, he clung to her, running his hands over her flushed skin, whispering her name until his breathing gradually quieted. Tears filled Laura's eyes as he pulled his body from her warmth with a sweet, lingering kiss and a long sigh.

Propping himself on one elbow, he gazed down at her as if he were seeing her for the very first time. His eyes searched her face in surprise and disbelief as though he were questioning what alchemy could change a girl into a woman, a friend into a lover, in the space of a few heartbeats. He found the answer in her eyes, and his lips touched hers in tentative wonder.

"You're a genuine treasure, Laura Wright," he said softly, wiping away her tears with one not quite steady hand. "I'll remember this night until I draw my last breath."

Later, as they lay quietly in each other's arms, she whispered, "Cal, we have to talk."

But he was already snoring gently, the hard plane of his face cradled against the soft curve of her breast.

Laura lay awake for a long time, cherishing the weight of his body, knowing that this might be the last time she'd be able to hold him in her arms. When she'd imagined making love to Cal, she'd thought of enfolding him, of caressing him, of giving him love and pleasure. But he had given, too—so much more than she'd expected, so much more than she'd thought possible. Yet not once had he said he loved her. She was still leaving in the morning. Nothing had really changed.

Maybe Cal needed more time to sort out his feelings. Things had happened so fast, and he wasn't one to say "I love you," unless he was sure.

At least she knew that no matter what happened, he'd still be her friend. They'd still see each other. If she were ever to lose him completely she wouldn't be able to bear it. Shivering, she buried her face in his hair and snuggled closer to him, finally falling into an exhausted, uneasy sleep.

She woke with a start to singing birds and the ambiguous promise of a dawning day. The clock on the wall above the desk read twenty minutes to six. Cal's front was pressed up against her back, and his left arm was draped over her waist. She remembered their lovemaking of the night before and sighed. She didn't feel a trace of regret. Eventually Eve might have Cal's name, his body and his children, but Laura would have the memory of last night to carry with her until the day she died.

Pushing aside a feeling of paralyzing sadness, she carefully slipped out from beneath Cal's arm and stood naked gazing down at the man she loved. He shifted restlessly in his sleep as though aware of her desertion.

Laura's eyes traced his features once before she reluctantly turned away. She quickly showered in Cal's bathroom and threw on her clothes from the previous night. Thankfully she was already packed. All she had to do was collect her coat and suitcase from her room.

Pausing with her hand on the doorknob, she fought an overwhelming desire to burst into tears. She wanted so much to say goodbye, but she was afraid the sound of his voice would shatter her heart into so many pieces that she would never be able to put it back together again. She'd call him later in the week when she wasn't feeling quite so vulnerable.

She jumped when the bedsprings creaked behind her.

"What's going on?" Cal murmured sleepily.

Laura held her chin high, trying to hide the pain. "I...I was just leaving."

"What are you talking about?" Cal asked, sitting up and rubbing his eyes.

"About going back to college," she told him, her voice shaking. "I have to leave in a few minutes."

"Whoa, girl," he exclaimed. He jumped up naked, leaving a trail of bedclothes across the floor and grabbed her by the shoulders. "You're not going anywhere. I love you."

The three little words hit Laura like a tidal wave, leaving her knees weak. "But...but what about my sister?" she asked incredulously. She felt something inside her die a little as a flicker of uncertainty crossed his face.

"It's not that I feel anything less for her, I just feel more for you. I can't explain it, Laurie. I'm not sure I even understand it all myself. It's not something I can pick apart and analyze under a microscope." He looked at her with all the love she'd longed for finally present in his gaze. "Close your eyes."

"What?"

"Just close your eyes, will you?"

Her head was a whirl of jumbled thoughts, but Laura did as she was told. She heard the sound of a drawer being opened, and then something hard and cool was slipped on to the ring finger of her left hand.

"See?" Cal said, his voice vibrant with happiness. "It's a perfect fit."

Laura opened her eyes and a swirl of diamonds and emeralds gleamed at her. She gasped in delight. "Your mother's ring!"

"It's been sitting in that drawer for a long time," Cal said softly. "Somehow it never did seem quite right for Eve." Gently, almost reverently, he took her face in both his hands. "Marry me, Laurie. Marry me right away, and then we'll never have to be apart again."

Laura threw her arms around Cal and hugged him passionately. "Do I have to tell you what my answer is? Oh, Cal, I love you so much! I'm so happy! We can have a June wedding right here at the ranch after my graduation."

Cal held her away from him, his suddenly serious gray eyes staring down into her laughing brown ones. "I want to get married now, Laurie. I don't want to wait till June. What do you need to finish college for anyway? You won't ever have to work."

Her smile fading, Laura stepped away from him, a cold, sinking feeling filling the pit of her stomach. She spoke softly, choosing her words carefully, knowing that what she said now would determine the course her life would take from this moment forward.

"Cal, there's a part of me that wants nothing more than to be just your wife, to love you and have you love me. But there's another part that needs to grow, that needs to achieve, that needs to prove something to the world. Or maybe I need to prove something to myself. I've been living off Henry's generosity for years. I need to know that I can stand on my own two feet and make it. I need to know that I can go after what I want and get it. Me, all by myself. The first step is for me to go back to New York for four months and finish college. If I don't, I'll always feel like a quitter. Can you understand that?''

Cal was looking at her as if he couldn't quite believe his ears. "No, I'm sorry, I don't understand. Why do you think you need a degree or a job to be a complete person? I can't remember a time when I needed to prove anything to anybody. I know who I am, and I'm satisfied with that. If the rest of the world doesn't like it, they can go to hell. I only went to college to have fun and to learn more about something that interested me. I only went into the company because Daddy wanted me to, and it pleased me to make him happy. I'd just as soon spend all my time on the ranch and forget the business. Success and money isn't worth a hill of beans if that's all you have, Laurie. This ranch and my family is what I want, what I care about."

Laura frowned, frustrated by her failure to get through to him. "We're different people, Cal. Our needs are different. I don't know why, but I've always had a feeling of incompleteness, a nagging voice inside that keeps whispering 'You're not good enough, you're not strong enough to go the distance.' I've got to go out and run the race, Cal. I've got to know that I can make it to the finish line. You can't do it for me, your money can't do it for me. It's something I have to do for myself, or I'll hear that voice forever."

Cal stared at her hard, making a visible effort to hold his temper. "All right, Laurie. Get a job. Get two jobs. Become whatever you think you ought to be. All I ask is that you stay with me while you're doing it. Transfer to a college down here."

Laura's eyes widened in disbelief. "Are you serious? It's my last semester! If I transfer now, the new college would only accept so many credits. I'd have to go an extra year at least and—"

"And I'm not worth it."

Anger covered Cal's face like storm clouds sweeping across a sunny sky. He was Henry Sinclair's only son, a star athlete and the valedictorian of his college class. He wasn't a good loser because he'd had so little practice, and he wasn't used to hearing the word "no." Laura knew all about his stubborn pride, but she was too angry to try to cajole him into a compromise. "Well, if you want to be with me so badly, why don't you just come up and stay in New York for four months?"

"I couldn't breathe up there! Besides, I don't want to leave the ranch, and Daddy needs me in the business. And there's someone else who'd miss me if I left."

Laura felt as though he'd slapped her. "Well, why don't you say it?" she demanded. "Go ahead, say her name."

Cal's face was a study in defiance. "Eve."

Laura shook her head angrily even as tears welled in her eyes. "Don't try to threaten me, Cal Sinclair! Either you really love me or you don't. If you do, that feeling will still be there four months from now or four years from now."

"You want to talk feelings?" Without warning, Cal reached out and pulled her to him, bringing his lips down on hers. When he finally released her, she was breathless and wanting.

"Listen to me, Laurie. These are the facts of life. I'm only flesh and blood. I'm not going to walk around here miserable and frustrated for four months while you're wasting your time in New York. Eve's a beautiful woman. Any man would be proud to have her. When I'm near her, I want her so bad I can't think about anything else. She doesn't need a diploma with her name on it to hang on the wall so she'll know who she is. Me and the ranch, we're all she wants."

A bitter laugh bubbled through Laura's lips. She pulled away from Cal and began pacing the floor, all her old resentment of Eve boiling to the surface. "You don't know her, Cal, not even after all these years. She's like a cat. She takes, she doesn't give."

He was looking at her with disgust. "I think it's *you* I don't know, Laurie. Your sister is the sweetest girl in the world. She always has been."

Laura threw up her hands in exasperation. "She's flattered you and catered to your whims ever since she was a child, but only because it was in her own best interest to do so. Even back then, you'd bring her candy or pretty presents as a reward. She doesn't ever want that to stop, Cal. You've got enough money to buy her anything she desires. That's what she wants: the Sinclair money, the Sinclair name and a husband to worship her, a husband she can show off to the other cats she calls her friends."

Cal was shaking his head. "You're jealous, Laurie. All these years she's gotten your share of the attention, and it's made you hate her."

"You're wrong," she cried. "I don't hate her. I know her better than anyone. I know what she is, and I still can't hate her! If I thought she loved you—that she would be hurt by what happened between you and me—then maybe I wouldn't have let it happen in the first place. But it won't hurt her, Cal, because she doesn't feel that deeply. She's incapable of loving anyone except herself.''

"Supposing all this is true," Cal said, his voice cold with skepticism. "Why wait until now to tell me all this? You've known for months that I've been going out with her.''

Laura shivered in the warm room. "I didn't say anything because I knew what your reaction would be. People can't accept the truth about Eve. They think that what's beautiful must also be good. Well, that's not the way the world is. That's not the way Eve is.''

A strident blaring interrupted them as Frank sounded the car horn in the yard below. Laura jumped, startled by the sudden noise.

Cal's eyes were like two steel darts pinning her down, freezing her where she stood. "If you leave now, Laurie, I'm not going to come after you, begging with my tail between my legs. And I'm not going to wait around for you to change your mind—not even for four months. I wouldn't do it for you or for any woman born.''

Tears filled Laura's eyes, but her voice cracked like a whip. "You don't want a real woman who tells you about her needs, who's honest enough to say what she feels to your face . . . someone who'll argue with you when she feels she's right and criticize you when she thinks you can improve. No, you want a woman who'll tell you 'yes, sir' and 'no, sir' and wrap you around her little finger. Except she's really out for all she can get, and she won't think twice about breaking your heart along the way. But

I guess that's all the woman you can handle, Cal Sinclair, because you've got an ego the size of Texas!''

They stood toe-to-toe, glaring at each other like two battered gladiators who'd fought to a standstill. When Cal finally spoke, his voice filled every corner of the quiet room.

"You've had your say, and I've had mine. You know what my terms are. If you don't want to abide by them, there's the door."

Laura looked into his face and felt as though her heart were being ripped in half. He was leaving her no choice, no alternative that she could live with. She hated him for hurting her like this, for refusing to give an inch.

"Well, if that's how you feel," she heard herself saying, "then I guess I can't keep this." Reluctantly she took the emerald ring off her trembling finger and placed it on the bedside table.

Cal's face registered disbelief and anguish. But before Laura could reach out to him, that chink in his armor closed, and he became as unyielding as stone. "What are you waiting for, then?" he yelled. "Get out of here. Go!"

With a strangled cry of pain, Laura whirled and ran into her own room, leaving behind a lifelong dream that had inexplicably turned into a nightmare. Blindly she slipped into her coat, grabbed her suitcase and stumbled down the stairs. Half of her hoped that Cal would come after her, carry her back upstairs and never let her leave; the other half would have beaten him senseless if he'd tried.

She heard Juanita preparing breakfast in the kitchen and it tugged at her heartstrings, but she couldn't stop for even a moment. If she did, she might not leave at all. She fled through the front door and the chill January morning seemed to freeze her tears as she turned up the collar of her coat to hide her face from Frank.

"You know, I've been waiting out here for a good, long while, Missy," the old wrangler grumbled in annoyance as he took her suitcase.

Incapable of replying, Laura jumped into the car and wrapped her arms around herself, rocking back and forth, trying to quiet the agony in her heart.

Frank climbed into the driver's seat and frowned when he glimpsed her grim, pain-racked face. "You okay?" he inquired with concern. "You want to go back into the house?"

"I can't," she whispered, the tears she had held back all morning finally steaming down her cheeks. "I just can't."

The same abject misery was still with Laura when her plane landed in New York. In the week that followed, it became an old familiar friend. She haunted the dorm switchboard and checked the mailbox five times a day. She picked up the telephone and dialed Cal's number a hundred times, but always hung up before it began to ring. She relived their one night together over and over in her mind, her body yearning for the satisfaction only Cal could give.

Knowing that she'd done the right thing didn't stop the pain. She was so unhappy that she hardly ate, had trouble sleeping and couldn't concentrate on her schoolwork. During her lowest moments, she wondered how anything could be worth all this suffering.

She was sorely tempted to yield to Cal's demands. But she knew that if she gave in now, she'd always resent him for it, and she wouldn't like herself very much either.

The memory of the love she'd seen in Cal's eyes was the only thing that gave her hope. She knew there had to

be a way to work things out, a way for them to be together without one hurting the other. She'd given up too
easily, cut and run because they'd hit a rough stretch in
the road. Well, she'd had a chance to cool down and so
had Cal. He might be hurting as badly as she was. Maybe
she could make him listen to reason if only she could see
him and talk to him. Tomorrow was his birthday, and
that was all the excuse she needed.

Once her mind was made up, she couldn't wait to put
her plan into action. Within the hour, she'd secured a
ticket for a flight leaving at seven the following morning. In a matter of hours she'd be in Cal's arms again,
and then everything would be all right. They'd work
things out together. She went to bed and slept soundly for
the first time since she'd left the ranch.

At four in the morning, she was awakened by the ring-
ing of the phone. "Hello?" she mumbled sleepily.

"Hello, Laura."

The sound of Eve's sweet soprano voice made Laura
sit bolt upright, her heart pounding with sudden dread.

"Just wanted you to know that Cal and I eloped this
morning. You were a fool to try to take him away from
me. You should know by now that what's mine stays
mine until I get tired of it."

The dial tone echoed painfully in Laura's ear. Slowly
she replaced the receiver in its cradle, and then she fell
back onto the bed, sobbing uncontrollably, cursing herself, Cal and especially Eve.

In the weeks that followed she went through the mo-
tions of living until the horrible pain diminished and a
grim determination to survive took its place. She chan-
neled all her hopes and energies into her schoolwork and
job, knowing that now she had to succeed. If she didn't,
then she'd have given up Cal for nothing.

After graduation, Laura got a full-time position at the hotel. She moved out of the dorm and took an apartment with her college roommate, Susan. She left no forwarding address and didn't list her number in the telephone directory. Dutifully she sent the family a Christmas card each year with a brief note but no return address. She simply didn't need the pain of receiving gloating letters from Eve, of receiving any kind of communication that mentioned Cal.

For seven cold and lonely years, she'd managed to pretend that there was no such place as Sinclair Ranch, no such man as Cal Sinclair. She had existed, but hadn't really lived. Her emotions had been frozen until the day a letter, delivered by a private detective, had forced her out of hiding to resolve unfinished business she should have dealt with long ago. . . .

"What's the matter? Didn't you have the stomach to stay and see it through to the end?"

Laura looked up, jolted out of her reverie, and saw Cal's large frame filling the doorway.

"You'll be happy to know that I outlasted that ornery old hunk of horseflesh. I had him prancing around that corral like a show horse in a parade." He winced involuntarily as he limped into the room. "Of course, he did get a piece of me first."

"I'm sorry, Cal," Laura said contritely, her gaze fixed on the floor. "It was a stupid thing to do, goading you like that. You could have been seriously hurt. But I was mad at you for what you said last night."

"I meant every word of it, Laurie," he said sternly. "And cozying up to me now isn't going to change that."

She blinked in surprise. "I'm not cozying up to you!"

His gray eyes seemed to be laughing at her again. "Then what are you doing in my room? Sitting on my bed?"

Laura stood, realizing she had no plausible answer to that question. "Remembering the good old days," she muttered under her breath on her way to the door.

He grabbed her arm as she passed and swung her back toward him. "And weren't they just," he said huskily.

She felt dizzy at his nearness, and she didn't dare meet his eyes. "Is that bourbon on your breath?" she asked, stalling for time.

"My leg hurt," he said, pulling her into his arms. "I let some little witch make me act like more of a fool than I usually do." He put one leather-gloved hand under her chin and she raised her eyes to his. "You at least owe me some comfort, girl."

Laura moaned softly as his lips came down on hers, and she tasted the coffee and bourbon on his tongue. Forgetting her anger and pride, she threw her arms around him, touching the sweat-dampened hair at his nape with trembling fingers.

After all the tear-filled, sleepless nights, she was back in Cal's arms at last. Nothing else mattered, no other reality existed. Half drunk from sensations she'd thought she'd never feel again, she pressed closer until the hardness of his body nested in the hollow between her thighs. She wanted nothing more than to stay with this man for the rest of her life, no matter what price she'd have to pay, no matter what sacrifice she'd have to make.

All at once, Laura heard footsteps behind her. Startled, she tore her mouth away from Cal's and turned to see Melissa poised hesitantly in the open doorway, about to take flight.

"What do you want, Melissa?" Laura asked breathlessly, annoyed in spite of herself.

She felt Cal move away from her and watched with concern as he sat down on the bed favoring his injured leg.

"You said you'd help me draw another picture today," the child said, her voice barely above a whisper.

Laura felt a sharp sting of remorse. She quickly went to Melissa and drew her into the warm circle of her arms. "I haven't forgotten you, darling. Go play for just a little while, and I'll find you when I'm finished here. Okay?"

The child nodded and gave her a ghost of a smile. Then she vanished as suddenly as she had appeared.

"What is it you want from me, Laurie?" Cal asked her, his voice weary, sounding as if all the passion had been drained out of him. "You want money? I'll give you money. Whatever you want."

At first she thought that she'd heard wrong. Her head was still spinning, her body still aching for his touch. "What are you talking about?" she demanded.

"If you leave here now, you can have however much you want." He looked up at her coldly. "That's plain enough, isn't it?"

"I don't want your damned money!" she yelled at him in an outpouring of confused hurt and anger.

"Then go because we used to be friends," he said, staring down at the floor, his voice hard. "Do it because we used to mean something to each other. Do it for any reason you care to name. Just see that it gets done. Leave me be. Get out of this room and get out of my life."

Laura fled through the door, slamming it shut behind her. The hurt his words had caused was so bad that it nearly doubled her over with pain.

"Forgive me, Henry," she whispered to the empty hallway. "I just cannot cope with this any longer!"

Running to her room, she began to throw her few possessions into the red leather bag. Juanita interrupted her before she was finished.

"What do you think you are doing?" the housekeeper demanded.

"I'm getting out of here," Laura told her, eyes blazing. "I don't know how I could ever have imagined that I was in love with that mean, spiteful—do you know he offered to pay me to get out? If he hates me that much..."

"He does not hate you—he is afraid of you! He is so afraid that he is willing to say anything, to do anything, so that you will go away."

Laura laughed. "Cal was never afraid in his life, at least not of anything that walked, talked or breathed."

"Nevertheless," the housekeeper said emphatically, "you, he is afraid of. Please, stop and think about it. He knows how you feel about taking other people's money, does he not? He knew just how hurt you would be when he made you that offer."

Laura stopped packing as she realized that what Juanita said was true. She'd been so upset by what had happened that she hadn't been thinking straight. She'd missed what should have been obvious.

"Your sister, Eve, she hurt him, Laurita. When he found out that she was not the sweet girl she had pretended to be—when he discovered that she was a cold, vicious she-devil with a heart of ice—he didn't want her anymore. But Eve, she would not give him up so easily. She learned to drink, and when she drank, she looked for the blind worship Mr. Cal had given her in the arms of other men. She flaunted the others in his face, as if she were proud of them. God forgive her, I even heard her tell Mr. Cal that my princess, my Melissa, was not his child."

"So that's why..." Laura whispered, suddenly understanding. "And that's what Henry meant when he said I might have more right to Melissa than I knew. If Cal's not her father, then I'm her closest relative. Her *only* relative."

"I believe with all my heart that Mr. Cal is Melissa's father," Juanita told her. "Eve would have said anything to hurt him, to make him even notice her again. But her actions drove him away. For months before she left, he hardly ever came home. Even when he was here, they did not touch. They did not even speak to each other."

"It must have been a nightmare for both of them," Laura observed sadly.

"It was," the housekeeper agreed. "And that is just why Mr. Cal wants you to leave. He is afraid that you will make him feel again, hurt again."

Laura shook her head. "You don't understand, Juanita. It's not that simple."

"Perhaps not," the Mexican woman said doubtfully. "But it is what I believe. Even if I am wrong, what about Melissa and the promise you made to Mr. Henry?"

Squeezing her eyes shut, Laura felt the weight of the world resting on her shoulders. "I'm lost in a maze, Juanita, a maze that has no way out."

The housekeeper stroked her hair tenderly. "Your feet are already on the right path, my child. You need only follow your heart."

Chapter Four

The next morning Laura was still on the ranch. After yesterday's talk with Juanita, she'd tried to forget her emotional dilemma and had worked furiously making dozens of preliminary sketches of Melissa. Now, she was ready to put brush to canvas.

She had the child seated under a massive oak tree near the house and was just beginning to make her first stroke when she heard her name being called from the veranda. She was pleasantly surprised to see Henry roll out onto the porch in his wheelchair. Her heart began to beat faster as Cal followed and came to stand at his father's side.

"I'm glad you're feeling better today!" she called up to the older man, happy to see his improvement. She tried her best to ignore her distressingly predictable reaction to Cal.

Henry nudged his son in the ribs with his heavy gold-headed cane. "Don't just stand there, boy! Go down and look at the picture. Tell me what it's like."

"I really only just started," Laura protested, glancing at the solitary line she'd painted. But Cal, still limping slightly, was already down the stairs.

Laura turned away, afraid her eyes would reveal too much. All her other senses remained tuned to his approach. She heard him coming closer, and every nerve in her body seemed to strain toward him. Then his shadow fell across her shoulder, and a carelessly exhaled breath shivered along the side of her neck. Basking in the warmth his presence exuded, she inhaled the sharp citrus tang of his after-shave and the fresh scent of his recently laundered shirt. She closed her eyes, fighting the urge to lean back and lose herself in the feel of his body against hers.

"Is there some reason you're still here?"

Cal's hostile voice dragged Laura back to reality with cruel abruptness. Eyes flashing, she whirled around to confront him, almost knocking her canvas off the easel. "Do I bother you that much, Cal? Why is it so important to you that I leave?"

Cal glared at her, but was saved from replying when he was distracted by an approaching car. Laura turned to follow his gaze and saw a shiny red convertible roar up the road that led to the house, kicking up a cloud of Texas dust a mile wide.

The car pulled up beside Cal, and a sleek redhead with a beautiful face and a centerfold figure climbed out from behind the wheel. With her artful makeup and a pale green suit that accentuated every curve, she looked like she'd just stepped off the cover of a fashion magazine. Despite her elegant appearance, she managed to project a wholesome, unassuming air that only added to her attractiveness.

"A certain prominent businessman doesn't have his mind on his work," the redhead began in a gently teasing tone. "I stopped by the office this morning to get something out of my desk. While I was there, I noticed that you'd forgotten to take home those papers you wanted to look over."

Cal responded with a charming smile that set Laura's teeth on edge. "You didn't have to go to the trouble of bringing them all the way out here on a Sunday."

"I don't mind. I know you want to be prepared for the meeting tomorrow morning. And, honestly, it was an opportunity to remind you about our date tonight."

A puzzled look came over Cal's face, and then the light dawned. "Is that tonight? Damn, I forgot all about it!"

"That's all right," she assured him with apparent sincerity. "I can always go by myself."

"Honey, any man who would break a date with a sweet thing like you would have to be a born fool."

Cal turned to Laura with what she could have sworn was a self-satisfied smirk. "Laura Wright, I'd like you to meet my executive secretary, Honey Lambert. Honey, this is my sister-in-law."

The secretary smiled, revealing two dimples and gleaming, pearllike teeth. "Very pleased to meet you, Laura," she said, extending one perfectly manicured hand. Long red nails glistened in the sunlight. "It's hard to believe you're Eve's sister. You don't resemble her at all."

You do, Laura thought despairingly as she wiped the paint from her palm and then touched fingers briefly with the redhead. Unreasonable jealousy surged through her. Was Cal's ego really so shaky that he needed to display gorgeous women like hunting trophies in order to make himself feel like a man? Hadn't he learned anything from his disastrous marriage? Then she realized she was being unfair and berated herself soundly for judging Honey by her appearance. The secretary seemed like a genuinely nice person. At any rate, Cal's choice of companions was none of her concern. But knowing that didn't stop the gnawing pain of seeing Cal with another woman. It was bitter torment to watch him freely give to Honey all the attention and approval that he had denied her.

"Well," she heard Cal saying, "since you drove all the way out here, you might as well stay for lunch." He gazed down at Honey with a smile and offered her his arm.

Laura felt as if someone had plunged a sharp blade into her heart. "I think Melissa and I will pack a lunch and go riding," she said, keeping her voice steady. "I don't think this setting is right for the portrait."

"Can we go to the glade, Laura?" Melissa begged, claiming her full attention. "I can go swimming there!"

Laura looked thoughtful. "Well . . ." she began.

"I'll get my bathing suit!" Without waiting for objections, the child ran up the steps and into the house.

"Laura," Henry called from the porch. "You have worked a miracle with that child. I've never seen her so happy and full of life."

"It's a pity I don't have that effect on everyone," she murmured with a sidelong glance at Cal.

The tall man deliberately put an arm around Honey's shoulders. "It's all a matter of personalities, girl," he said pointedly to Laura. "Some women are just easier to get along with than others."

Laura felt another stab of jealousy. "I imagine it is real hard to have a disagreement with someone who makes sure everything is done your way," she said caustically.

Closing her easel with a snap, she stalked off to the stable.

The quiet glade did little to lighten Laura's mood, but she still managed to enjoy Melissa's company. They spent a pleasant hour together, huddled over a sketch pad. Laura watched as the child drew a picture of a tree. Then she made suggestions for improvements, guiding the small hand when necessary. After a while, Laura slipped away, opened her easel, and began to paint Melissa's portrait. The little girl sat nearby on the bank of the pond so absorbed in creating her own sketches that she hardly seemed to realize she was posing for Laura.

Although coming to the glade had only been a ruse to avoid Honey and Cal, Laura was surprised to discover that it was the perfect site for Melissa's portrait. The child had an elfin, other-worldly beauty that came alive in this verdant, fairy-tale setting.

Melissa eventually tired of her new hobby and put aside the pad and pencil. After changing into her bathing suit, she dived into the pond. Laura's mind was free to return to thoughts of Cal and Honey, and she brooded on the subject for the rest of the afternoon.

Honey's appearance had brought back Laura's old insecurity, the fear that her flawed looks would never be enough to compete with that kind of beauty. But was Cal attracted to Honey solely because of her looks? The secretary obviously respected Cal and looked up to him. She seemed to consider his needs more important than her own. With Eve all of that had been a pretense. Honey seemed sincere. But regardless of motivation, a woman who displayed those traits appeared to be the kind of woman Cal was attracted to.

Did he really need a woman who'd be willing to put herself in second place, who'd support him instead of competing with him, in order to be happy? Laura doubted if she could ever learn to be that kind of a woman. Could she live with herself if she did? Could she live without Cal if she didn't?

The more she thought about the situation, the more depressed she became. She sat gazing out over the water, seeking answers and finding none, until the sun set, and she realized how much time had passed. Glancing at her watch, she hurriedly called Melissa out of the pond. By the time they returned to the ranch, it was pitch-black, and the child was sneezing repeatedly.

"Ah, little bird, you are catching a cold!" Juanita exclaimed. "Get upstairs and get into your pajamas. I will bring you some soup and some nice hot chocolate."

The housekeeper turned to Laura as the child left the room obediently. "I kept your dinner warm for you. Everyone else has already eaten, except for Mr. Cal. He said that he was having dinner in town tonight."

Laura's stomach tightened. "I'm not hungry," she said flatly, fleeing the kitchen before Juanita could ask any questions.

She passed by Steve and Delphine as the couple sat talking in front of the fireplace. "How's the portrait coming?" the man asked with polite interest.

"Just fine," Laura answered without breaking her stride. "I think I'm going to paint in the glade every day now. It's an ideal setting."

"Yes. Delphine showed it to me. Perfect spot for a lunch date, isn't it?"

Laura didn't miss his implication. She knew that he wanted to meet her in the glade to talk, but the thought of providing yet another opportunity for a misunderstanding made her feel ill.

Ignoring Steve, she went up the stairs, fully aware of Delphine's poisonous glare scorching her back. Condemned without a trial again, she thought angrily.

After undressing, she showered, then lay in the dark trying to fall asleep. Annoying thoughts continued to nag at her. Maybe she *should* talk to Steve. His attempts to gain her attention were only making things worse. There didn't seem to be any action lately, any word she had said, that hadn't been misinterpreted by someone.

Switching on the lamp, she picked up the thick paperback novel she'd bought to read on the plane. She couldn't concentrate on the book, and her mind kept straying to the way Cal's lips had felt on hers yesterday, the way the hardness of his body had pressed against the softness of hers. Finally she looked at her travel alarm, noting in disgust that it was only eight o'clock.

Here she was on vacation, and all she could think of doing was sulking in her room in some kind of jealous snit. It was a waste of time brooding over something that she couldn't change. If Cal could go out for the evening, then so could she. Making a sudden decision, she threw down the book and began to pull on her jeans.

Feeling better than she had since her arrival, she bounded down the stairs and exited the house through the kitchen. Crossing the yard, she made her way toward the light shining from the open doorway of the bunkhouse. Inside Frank and three other gray-haired hired hands were sitting around an old folding card table playing poker.

"Hey, girl," Frank greeted her, "you wouldn't want to sit in on this here game, would you? I'm tired and these old goats won't let me quit."

Laura shook her head with a smile. "No, thanks. I just came out to get my car. I'm driving into town."

Frank looked at her with a glint in his eye. "Gonna give those young bucks somethin' to fight over, are ya? If I was just twenty years younger—"

A sarcastic snort from the man on his left interrupted the old wrangler. "How many years was that, Frank? Twenty? Hell, you'd still be older than Methuselah!"

Leaving the men to their amicable argument, she climbed into the dark blue rental car that the company had brought out as a replacement and snapped on the headlights. The beams did little to hold the inky darkness at bay once the car left the lighted ranch buildings behind. She crept along at a slow pace for several miles before she reached the spot where the access road ended. Turning onto the hard asphalt of the main road, she headed for the outskirts of Houston.

When she pulled up outside the nightclub in Pasadena, it was after nine o'clock. She found a space at the far end of the crowded parking lot and, climbing out of her car, walked toward the brightly lit honky-tonk. Pushing through the double doors, she entered a huge open area filled with neon beer signs, blaring country-and-western music and the sound of people having a good time. She pressed through the crowd and made her way to the bar.

"Hey, Laura! Laura Wright!"

Interrupted while ordering a beer, she peered through the smoke-filled air searching for the man who had called her name. She saw a young cowboy coming toward her wearing the standard uniform of boots, jeans, Western shirt and wide-brimmed hat. His boyish, smooth-skinned face fairly glowed with health and exuberance, his brown eyes shining in recognition.

"Oh, lord! David Perkins! I don't believe it."

They came together in the middle of the dance floor, and Laura threw her arms around her old high-school beau, giving him a resounding kiss. He hugged her enthusiastically, his gaze sweeping her face.

"You're still the best looking girl in Texas," he told her gallantly.

Laura laughed. "I'm still holding together fairly well, I guess. And look at you. I swear you look younger now than when I last saw you!"

David sighed in resignation. "I know, isn't it terrible? I ought to grow a beard or something. With this face, I'm lucky if they serve me a beer without checking my ID first."

"I remember you used to hate that face. But look on the bright side. Twenty years from now, you'll still be able to get all the young girls."

David made a derisive sound. "'Still'? Who says I'm doing that well now?"

He took her in his arms and they began to move to the rhythm of a slow tune as they talked.

"What are you doing for a living now?" Laura asked, her fingers brushing the close-cropped brown hair at the nape of her partner's neck. David had all the natural appeal of a warm, cuddly puppy, and she relaxed, glad that she had decided to go out tonight.

"I'm a lawyer, just like I always said I was going to be. I work with Legal Aid. Not much money there, but I enjoy my job."

Looking into the velvet-soft eyes that were exactly on a level with her own, Laura felt a rush of affection. "You always were a good person, David," she told him sincerely.

The object of her compliment bowed his head in mock humility. "Aw, shucks, ma'am. T'ain't nothin'."

Laura giggled and held him close, remembering the night of the senior prom when they'd danced until dawn. "You married yet?" she asked curiously.

"Nope. I guess that after you left . . ."

Their eyes met again, and Laura saw in his the flicker of an old ember about to burst into flame. "David, I . . ." she began to protest.

Then they danced blindly into a jarring collision with another couple. Laura broke away from David's embrace laughing breathlessly. "I'm sorry," she said, turning around. "I'm afraid we weren't watching where we were going."

Her heart gave a sickening thud as she found herself staring up into Cal's unreadable eyes. She noticed that he held Honey by one sequin-bedecked arm. The secretary's black leather pants were so tight they looked as though they'd been painted on.

"You remember David Perkins," Laura finally blurted, puncturing the uncomfortable silence.

Cal looked the other man over carefully. "He's the boy you had moping around our house like a lovesick calf for three years. How could I not remember that sweet baby face?"

David blushed and gave Cal a brief nod of recognition.

Laura's eyes narrowed, but before she could tell Cal what she thought of his remark, he had shouldered David aside and taken her in his arms. "Excuse me, Honey," he told his secretary. "But I have something to discuss with Laurie here." Then he indicated Honey with a jerk of his head. "Perkins, dance with the lady, will you?"

Ignoring David's open-mouthed stare and Honey's arched eyebrows, Cal maneuvered Laura across the dance floor. They were out of hearing range of the other couple before Laura found the words to adequately express her exasperation.

"Of all the rude, high-handed—"

He interrupted her before she could really light into him. "What are you doing following me?" he demanded angrily.

"Following you?" she sputtered, her voice rising a full octave.

"Turn your volume down," he commanded, casting a glance around the room. "People will think I'm dancing with a crazy woman."

"Following you?" she said again, louder than before. "You egotistical . . . I didn't even know you were here!"

"I'm sure of that," he shot back, just as loud.

"Who'd think you'd be out dancing? You with that leg of yours hurt so bad." She lowered her gaze pointedly to indicate the leg Cal was dancing on quite gracefully with no sign of pain.

"It feels better," Cal told her, enunciating each word. "Not that I have to justify my actions to you."

"I couldn't care less what you do. Now let me go!"

She tried to extricate herself from him, but he pulled her closer until her body was pressed firmly against his.

The stubborn set of his jaw infuriated her. "You let me go," she snapped, still struggling, "or I'll scream the roof down!"

"You keep rubbing up against me like that, and you're going to get something you didn't bargain for," he growled.

Laura felt her face burn as her eyes found his. All the sensory impressions she had ignored in her fit of anger suddenly began to come through loud and clear. The warmth of his chest seemed to seep through the material of their clothes, and her blush deepened as she felt the tips of her breasts respond to his nearness. She was close enough to him to verify that his last statement had been no idle threat.

She took a shaky breath, fighting to regain her equilibrium. "You like to pretend you're tough, Cal Sinclair," she said, her voice only a little above a whisper. "You seem to forget that I've known you all my life. You have more tenderness, more gentleness inside you than any man I know."

She restrained a triumphant smile as she watched a faint pink stain creep up under the bronzed skin above her collar. His gaze shifted away from hers abruptly.

Laura shook her head, refusing to accept his withdrawal. "Do you think I don't remember the night we spent together, the way you touched me, the things you said?"

Slowly, reluctantly, Cal's eyes returned to hers. "People change, Laurie."

"Not that much. Not you."

She reached up to touch his cheek, and the overwhelming rush of love sweeping over her made her feel as if she were in a high-rise elevator free-falling out of control. She wanted to talk to him for hours until every moment they'd spent apart had been accounted for and forgiven. She wanted to make love to him night after night, year after year. She wanted to feel his child move within her, and hold it in her arms. She wanted to grow old with him and wake to see his face every morning of her life.

His eyes seemed to absorb her and draw her down into their depths, his mouth moving closer and closer to hers.

"Hey, y'all, the dance is over."

Laura jumped and looked over Cal's shoulder to see David standing beside them, Honey hovering nearby.

"Why don't we all sit down together?" the secretary suggested. "David was telling me all about your high-school romance. I really miss those days, don't you?"

Feeling emotionally drained by her encounter with Cal, and ill at ease in Honey's presence, Laura sank into a chair that David had pulled out for her. Cal took a seat across from her as if nothing had happened and waved a pretty waitress over to their table.

"Get us four beers, will you, Julietta?" He winked and slipped a twenty dollar bill into the ample cleavage revealed by the girl's tight red tube top.

"Anything you say, Cal," the waitress told him with a dazzling smile. "We try to keep our customers completely satisfied."

Cal leaned back in his chair, apparently oblivious of the stare Laura was aiming in his direction. She was sure that what she had felt in his arms had been totally one-sided. His response had been purely physical, one that any attractive woman could have evoked. Her heart sank to her boots.

Suddenly the music stopped, and an expectant hush fell over the crowd. A man with a microphone walked out onto the bandstand. "Okay, folks. Now comes the part of the evening that y'all have been waiting for. We're holding tryouts for our mechanical bull-riding contest, ladies' division."

Whistles and cheers rose from the audience, drowning out the announcer's words. "Quiet down, now! Any lady who wants to participate can find a release form at the end of the bar."

David nudged Laura. "What are you waiting for? Or are you signed up already?"

Laura shrugged. "When I was twenty I thought that was real great stuff, but I'm not twenty anymore. Besides, I haven't done that for so long, I'd probably break my neck."

David was practically jumping out of his chair with excitement. "But you used to practice on that bucking machine at the ranch, the one that the cowboys rode to train for the rodeos. You were the best!"

Honey's name was called and she stood up, drawing on a pair of black leather gloves. "That was before *I* came to town," she said with a laugh and a wink.

The redhead strutted off to mount the bull while Laura stared after her with narrowed eyes.

"Aw, Laura," David pleaded. "You gotta ride! You can't let her get away with that. You're good enough to take her, hands down!"

Cal's eyes never strayed from Honey's curvaceous form, but his words were meant for Laura. "I know a woman who used to be good enough—once upon a time."

She pushed back her chair, and it scraped the floor savagely. Seething, she marched over to the bar determined to meet Cal's challenge and put Honey in her place.

Signing the release form that absolved the nightclub of any responsibility in case of injury, Laura turned to watch the beginning of Honey's ride. As a man on the sidelines manipulated the controls, the bull came to life, and the redhead was thrown high into the air, her full breasts bouncing under her black sequined shirt. Her knees firmly hugging the sides of the mechanical device, the secretary held on to the front grip with her left hand, flinging her other arm rhythmically over her head.

The bull bucked and swiveled, but Honey rode on, her white teeth gleaming under the lights, her hair a shiny red mane. She finished her ride to applause and whistles then jumped down to rejoin the men at the table.

Laura kept her place at the bar, watching as several other women tried out. Some were bucked off the device, falling onto the mattresses that had been spread out on the floor around the bull. Others rode poorly, a few rode well, but none were as good as Honey. Then, with a hammering heart, Laura heard her own name called.

She walked forward in a daze of fear and excitement, keenly aware that all eyes were focused on her. Coming to a stop in front of Cal, she silently held out her left hand.

He looked up at her, a smile playing around the edges of his mouth. He drew a single glove out of his pocket and held it while she slipped her fingers inside. Laura made a fist and then slowly relaxed her hand. The glove was too big, but it would wear better than bare skin.

"I won't take it kindly if you fall on your backside wearing my glove," Cal told her softly.

Laura lifted her chin. "I wouldn't take any bets on that happening if I were you."

Leaning over to David, she gave him a brief kiss. "For luck," she whispered, fully aware of Cal's disapproving glower.

She walked toward the tryout area, all her fear evaporating as she faced the familiar machine. Taking a running start, she vaulted lightly onto the bull from behind. Scooting forward, she positioned herself gingerly, her gloved left hand searching for just the right grip on the rigging. Shaking with anticipation, she dug her knees into the bull's leather sides and raised her right hand above her head. As she nodded her readiness, the mechanical monster sprang to life, jolting Laura down to her toes.

Arching her back, she beat a steady rhythm with her right arm, and kicked out with her feet in a rodeo style that would score important points with the judges. All the while, she maintained a precarious grip on the mechanical beast with her knees and thighs. When the eight-second ride came to an end, she dismounted to a standing ovation.

The emcee whistled into the microphone and clapped his hands. "Best yet, little lady. We'll see you back here for the contest next week."

With her legs and backside aching dully, but her spirits soaring, Laura concentrated on carefully putting one foot in front of the other. She had almost made it all the way back to her table when a big, burly man with two days growth of beard reached up with beefy hands and pulled her roughly down onto his lap. "Come on, sugar, let's see you ride me as good as you rode that there mechanical contraption."

David was at her side instantly. "Let her go, mister," he ordered the stranger.

"No, David! Don't—" Laura began.

The man laughed loudly and, in the process of getting to his feet, dumped Laura unceremoniously onto the floor. Her mouth fell open as she looked up at her heavy-handed admirer. He was a drunken tower of muscle, standing head and shoulders above poor David.

As she watched helplessly, the stranger drew back one gigantic fist and hit David squarely in the face. The lawyer went sailing through the air and landed on a nearby table. It splintered into several pieces under the impact, and he fell to the floor only half-conscious. The big man crossed over and, grabbing the groggy David by his collar, drew his huge fist back to hit him again.

"Excuse me, mister."

The giant's fist paused in midair as he searched the room to see who had dared to interrupt him.

Taking a long swig of beer, Cal stood slowly. He walked toward the giant, shaking his head, his Texas drawl in full evidence. "Any hombre who could put his fist through a face that looks like that just ain't no damned good."

The hulking Gargantua dropped David like a crumpled beer can and spat out a brown stream of tobacco juice that splattered the floor near Cal's boot. "I'm good at takin' apart smart-mouthed jackasses like you. No one ain't never knocked me down in a fair fight."

"Well then, I guess I'd be a fool to try to fight you fair."

Picking up a chair, Cal shoved the upper edge of the back support into the stranger's abdomen with a terrible force. As the man doubled over with a gasp of pain, Sinclair raised the chair and broke it across his opponent's head. The burly man collapsed in a heap, and Cal stepped over him and offered his hand to Laura.

Ignoring his hand, Laura got to her feet by herself. "You didn't even give him a chance! That was the most disgusting display I've ever seen, and it was totally unnecessary. If you hadn't interfered, I could have handled things on my own without any violence."

The gray eyes boring into hers were cold, the voice low enough that only she could hear. "At the risk of contradicting you, it was your friend over there who interfered." He jerked his head in David's general direction. "The violence had already started when I stepped in. I was just trying to stop it. The last man who crossed Paul

Bunyan here ended up with a broken back. He's in a wheelchair permanently. I was here the night it happened, and it wasn't a pretty sight. I'm not any storybook hero, Laurie. I have more sense than to let that monster get his hands on me. Now you'd better see to Perkins. You may have to peel him off the floor."

With a final glare, Cal took Honey's arm and disappeared out the door.

Her cheeks flaming from the sting of Cal's words, Laura rushed through the cheering crowd to David's side. Carefully she helped the bleeding man to his feet.

"Damn!" he grunted through bruised and swollen lips. "I didn't even get one punch in."

Laura had guided him out the door of the club and into the parking lot before she stopped to take a good look at his face. "Oh, David!" she gasped. "That moron broke your nose! Do you want me to drive you to an emergency room?"

David shook his head, feeling his newly rearranged features gingerly. "Who knows?" he said hopefully. "This may be what I've waited for all my life. Do I look macho now?"

"You're a mess!" Laura exclaimed with feeling.

"Thanks a lot," David responded, dabbing at the blood on his face with a formerly pristine handkerchief. He pointed to a green Mustang parked two spaces down from where they stood. "Here's my car."

"Is there anything I can get for you, David? Anything I can do?"

He faced her hesitantly. "I don't suppose that I could talk you into coming back to my apartment tonight? I'm a lot more fun than I was in high school."

A third voice interrupted them before Laura could answer David's question. "You have something that belongs to me."

Whirling around, Laura saw Cal standing behind her. "What are you talking about?" she demanded, his nearness causing her pulse to race.

"My glove, woman. I don't see anything else around here that I have any claim to."

With a sinking heart, Laura drew the item of clothing off her hand and passed it back to its owner.

Giving David a long, hard look, Cal turned and walked back to where Honey sat waiting for him in his beige Mercedes.

Laura's gaze followed the vehicle until its taillights winked out of sight. Only then did she become aware that David was speaking to her.

"I just don't believe Cal's still playing big brother," he commented wryly. "That look he threw me had hands-off written all over it."

Laura shrugged. "You're just imagining things."

"Then what about my proposition?" he pressed eagerly. "Maybe it could lead to something permanent . . . if that's what you're looking for."

Laura smiled at him sadly. "You know, that's the nicest offer I've had in a long time. You don't know how much I wish that I could take you up on it, Dave. It's just that my feelings are kind of mixed up right now, and until I get myself straightened out—"

"My God, it's Cal, isn't it?" he exclaimed, replaying the evening's events from a new perspective.

Laura nodded reluctantly.

"I just don't believe it! You and Cal? After all these years . . . You picked one damned hard row to hoe, lady. You know that?"

She laughed mirthlessly. "Better than anyone."

"Well, just remember, if you ever change your mind, Laura, my number's in the book."

Leaning forward, she gave him a gentle kiss on the cheek. "Every girl needs a knight in shining armor sometimes, David. Thanks for being mine tonight."

During her solitary drive back to the ranch, she called herself every kind of fool imaginable. David had offered her an alternative to her loneliness, and she'd pushed him away without so much as a second thought. And for what? Why was she in such a hurry to rush back to her cold and empty bed and her cold and empty life? With a sigh, she left the car in the driveway, noting without surprise that Cal's Mercedes was not there.

Upstairs in bed, she reviewed the words she'd flung at Cal after his assault on the man in the nightclub and groaned aloud. She'd been unfair, but she'd been so shocked. She had never seen Cal use such cold, calculated ruthlessness against anyone before. Had he changed that much in seven years? She shuddered and turned over in bed. No, she was sure that the kind, gentle Cal she remembered still existed, that his anger and sarcasm were protective camouflage. He'd had his reasons for tonight's violent behavior. For once, he'd even taken the trouble to explain them to her. In fact, she'd felt closer to him tonight than at any time since her return to Texas. Maybe if she waited up they could talk some more. Maybe...

But the hours passed, and Cal didn't come home. Laura tossed and turned, picturing Honey in his arms, the secretary crying out his name in a frenzy of passion. Her regret slowly turned into a hard lump of anger. She'd been right in the first place. Cal was ruthless, and cruel, and a womanizer to boot.

She finally drifted into a fitful sleep vowing that she'd never crawl for Cal or any man. She was through playing the role of the lovesick schoolgirl and being rejected at every turn. The next move was up to Cal Sinclair.

Chapter Five

The next day Melissa had the sniffles, and Juanita insisted that she stay in bed. The child was inconsolable until Laura thought of a compromise. "Listen, sweetheart, if you promise to be a good girl and stay home today, I'll take you into Houston for a shopping spree just as soon as you're better. I've been needing to buy some things for myself, anyway."

"Can we go tomorrow?" Melissa asked excitedly.

"Why sure, if you're all better tomorrow. So you snuggle down under those covers, and do your very best to get well."

Melissa nodded, and Laura planted a kiss on the little girl's feverish forehead.

Packing a lunch, she rode out to the glade alone and spent a peaceful, enjoyable afternoon working on the background of the portrait. By four o'clock, she was reluctantly getting ready to head back to the ranch when the sound of approaching hoofbeats diverted her attention. Looking up with a thrill of anticipation, she wondered if the rider would be Cal.

Mounted on a big bay gelding, Steve Randall broke through the surrounding ring of trees and Laura suppressed a sigh of disappointment. She had to admit that he cut quite an intriguing figure in tan jodhpurs and a charcoal-grey jacket over a white shirt and dark tie. A smile tugged at Laura's lips despite her annoyance. "The country squire rides again," she murmured.

"Laura! I'm glad you're still here. I couldn't get away any earlier." Steve's high black riding boots gleamed as he swung free of the English saddle and jumped lightly to the ground.

"Do you really think this is wise?" Laura asked, her smile fading.

Steve came toward her, a lopsided grin on his cleanshaven face. "I thought we made a date last night."

"Well, you thought wrong," she told him, making her displeasure obvious.

"Okay. So I guess you're still mad at me," he said with what was meant to be charming candor.

Laura laughed, but her voice was grim. "Come on, Steve! You proposition me and all the while you're engaged to Delphine with the wedding a week away. I think I have a right to resent that."

"One thing has nothing to do with the other," Steve said in a tone of an adult trying to reason with a petulant child.

"Are you serious?" Laura asked, a little shocked that even Steve could be so cold.

He shrugged nonchalantly. "Don't be so naive, Laura. I'm marrying because it will help my career. I need someone to be my hostess, to serve as my partner at company social events. Delphine had a few rough edges, but with my coaching she's turned into an attractive and sophisticated lady. You seem to bring out an unbecoming streak of jealousy in her—"

"Through no fault of yours," Laura inserted, amazed as always by the way this man could manage to justify anything.

"Through no fault of mine. But other than that, she's perfect. She's already familiar with business practices. She's got a good head on her shoulders, but absolutely no ambitions of her own. And Delphine has money, old Texas money. Her family has so much money they don't even act rich, they just go about their business as if they were ordinary people." He gestured toward the pond. "They don't even have a swimming pool. They have a water hole. My God, it's like something out of Norman Rockwell."

Laura had to keep from smiling. This time he wasn't going to charm her into agreement. "Steve, you don't have to marry anyone for their money. You'll have your own money eventually. In a few years—"

"A few years isn't now, Laura. Besides, marrying this girl will give me something money can't buy: social position. You know how far the Sinclair name will get me in this state? Maybe as far as the State Legislature. Maybe even farther."

Laura frowned. "Henry used to say that a person's name and family were only an accident of birth. His children had to earn his respect. They had to earn the right to trade on the name he'd made for himself."

Steve's face reddened with anger as though she had insulted him. His voice rose, and he spoke in a pronounced New York accent that made a lie of his usual cultured tone. "That's all well and good when you're sitting on your butt counting your millions, but in my world I had to use every advantage I had just to survive."

Laura tried not to gape in open astonishment. So there was something to Steve beyond his polished veneer of cool control. She'd suspected as much, but there had been little evidence of it before now.

With visible effort, Steve collected himself. The moment passed as if it had never happened. "Come on, Laura," he said calmly, "ideals are one thing, but we're talking reality."

Laura stalked to her horse and stowed her art supplies. "Don't talk to me like I'm a child just because I don't happen to share your moral values—or should I say your lack of values. You should have told me about your engagement to Delphine when you made that pass at me in New York. Even if it didn't matter to you, I had a right to know what I was getting into."

Steve's blue eyes twinkled. "Laura, you've been turning me down for years. If I'd seriously thought that there was any danger of your taking me up on my offer, maybe I would have told you."

Laura groaned in exasperation. "The key word in that statement is *maybe*."

"What can I say? I am what I am. I intend to give Delphine as much as I can in return for what I take from her, but no one's ever going to own me."

Laura faced him squarely. "And if I were to tell her about this conversation?"

Steve's mouth settled into a hard line. "Then I'd be forced to deny it ever took place. Besides, it wouldn't do any good for you to go to Delphine. She'd only assume you were lying in order to break us up." His voice softened in response to Laura's grim expression. "Hey, now.

Stop worrying for no reason. Delphine loves me. She wants to marry me. She'll be happy, you'll see."

He looked so much like an earnest little boy that Laura couldn't help smiling. "You're really hopeless. Don't you want to be in love with the woman you marry?"

A shuttered look came over Steve's face and his voice sounded curiously hollow. "Love? I've seen some ugly things happen in the name of love, Laura. I've seen lives ruined, people destroyed because they couldn't control their emotions."

Laura searched his face, wondering just what scars were hidden behind that impassive exterior. "I've seen that, too, Steve. But it doesn't have to be that way."

"It does for me," Steve said with bleak finality.

All at once, Laura didn't see a cold, ruthless man. She saw a lonely, hungry child. She reached out to touch his arm reassuringly.

That was the scene that met Cal's eyes as he rode his horse into the glade at a slow pace. It would have appeared innocent enough to any objective observer, but on a primitive level Cal sensed Randall's desire for Laura. He had first noticed it the moment Laura had come into the living room fresh from New York, and it had been there again during the confrontation in Laura's bedroom. He could read it in the other man's gestures, in the tone of his voice, even in the stance of his body. He knew Randall wanted Laura as surely as if the other man had told him so. Unfortunately Laura's feelings were harder to read, but the expression on her face as she looked at Randall stirred a feeling of irrational anger within him.

Cal had no proof that they were lovers, but he could tell that Randall was someone Laura respected and admired. That alone was enough to turn his stomach. Randall exemplified everything Cal despised. He was a phony, smooth-talking, money-worshiping hypocrite, a carbon copy of the man who had seduced Eve into running away to Europe with him and then left her to die alone in a rat-infested hovel. It was Randall and his world that had lured Laura away from the ranch in the first place. Cal had offered her love, honesty and faithfulness, and she had scorned them all to seek the empty rewards that Randall's way of life promised. Cal had been unable to prevent her from leaving then, and he had nothing new to offer her now. That realization washed away whatever remaining objectivity he possessed. He stopped short of admitting to himself that he wanted to claim Laura as his own. All he knew for certain was that he couldn't abide Randall having her.

Neither Steve nor Laura heard the rider approaching until Cal's voice rang out in the still air. "Get away from her."

Laura started in surprise, and Steve turned to confront the other man. "Now just a minute—" he began, but Cal cut him off.

"Mister, a blind man could see that you don't give a damn about Ellie, but she loves you so I'm willing to accept you into the family. If you want to keep things that way, you'd better get back to the house right now. My sister's been a snarling banshee since she came back from her walk and found you gone. She insisted that you were coming here to Laurie and damned if she wasn't right. I should have let her ride along like she wanted to. Maybe this tender little scene would have convinced her just how much you really care about her feelings."

Mounting his horse, Steve reined it around to face Cal. For an awful moment, Laura thought her boss was going to charge his accuser like some knight in an ancient tournament. Then she saw the anger fade from his eyes and a humbly sincere expression take its place. Sighing in relief, she knew he'd remembered just how much he had at stake. The one thing Steve didn't need was to make an open enemy of his future brother-in-law, the influential head of the Sinclair Company.

"I understand your concern for your sister," Randall said evenly. "And I can see how my meeting Laura here could be misinterpreted. I honestly just wanted to talk to her privately."

Cal's voice was laden with disgust. "Save it for my sister. I know your kind and just how far you can be trusted. A few years ago, I would've run you off my place on a rail—no matter what Ellie thought about it. But I've made my own mistakes since then, and I've learned from them. Now I have the sense to allow other people the same opportunity. Even so, mister, you're trying me to the end of my patience. Now get out of here before I change my mind."

The totally cold sound of Steve's voice as he responded raised the hairs on the back of Laura's neck. "Just watch how hard you push me, *mister*. I may start pushing back."

Then the businessman deliberately turned to Laura. "We'll finish our conversation soon," he promised.

With a parting look that dared Cal to contradict him, he rode away at a leisurely pace.

Cal watched until Randall passed out of sight. Then he turned his attention back to Laura. "All right, Laurie, I want the truth and I want it now. Did you come to the ranch because Daddy sent for you, or did you follow Randall here to bust up the wedding? Is that why you've been playing up to me, to make him jealous?"

Laura felt like literally pulling him down off his high horse. How could he believe she'd do something like that? Despite her best intentions, her temper flared, and she lashed out at her tormentor.

"I'm not 'playing up' to anyone, and it's certainly not any of your damned business who I see! I'm sure no one was checking up on you and Honey Lamb last night."

Cal's mouth smiled, but his eyes were devoid of humor. "Lambert. Her name is Lambert. She's a darned good secretary. In fact, she's darned good at everything she does."

Laura struggled against the unreasoning rage she felt. "I suppose you were sleeping with her even when my sister was alive!"

The lines in Cal's face deepened, and his voice turned cold. "Your sister, my loving wife, was wearing out half the male population of Texas. All a man...any man had to do was snap his fingers, and she was available. I guess that's another thing you two had in common."

Dragging on the reins, Cal wheeled his horse around and started to ride away. Laura stood in the glade, feet planted shoulder width apart, fists tightly balled. Her face was flushed with rage, and she spat out her words through clenched teeth.

"Well, maybe you just weren't man enough to hold either of us, Cal."

She regretted the lie the moment it escaped her lips. Her only thought had been to hurt him the way he'd hurt her, and she had instinctively gone for the groin. Now her words crackled in the still air like an invisible charge of static electricity, and she was powerless to take them back.

Cal pulled his horse up so hard that it whinnied and almost reared. His eyes locked with hers in cold fury, and a chill ran up her spine. For the first time in her life, she was truly afraid of the man before her. Without stopping to think, she put more distance between them, sprinting toward her horse as though the devil himself were pursuing her.

If she had stood her ground, Cal might have ridden away, leaving her with nothing more than that terrible look to remember. But when he saw her turn and run for her horse, some instinct more ancient than the memory of modern man galvanized him into action. He spurred his mount forward, his vision clouded by a dark red mist of anger.

Laura heard the thudding hoofbeats close behind her, but didn't dare take the time to look over her shoulder and judge Cal's progress. Her heart hammered from the adrenaline pumping into her system, she gulped in air, and her straining legs propelled her faster than she had ever run before. She was only a few steps from her horse and almost sure that she was going to reach safety, when she heard the whistling hum of the lasso.

The loop passed over her head and Cal pulled it tight, pinning her arms to her sides and jerking her off her feet. Her breath was knocked out of her, and she lay on the ground as dazed as any roped calf.

The figure of the tall cowboy was darkly silhouetted against the blue sky. He went down on one knee by her side and tilted his hat back slowly so that she could see his face. The expression in his eyes was still as hard and unyielding as granite, his jaw set. Laura shivered involuntarily in the warm sunlight.

"Girl," Cal said, his voice low and even, "you've been nipping at my heels ever since you came here, like you were daring me to turn and fight. Well, you are about to get what you've been asking for. You can have it nice, or you can have it rough. The choice is up to you."

Laura swallowed hard and tried to sort out her feelings. Her attraction to this man was strong. His touch excited her, and she knew that she wanted him, but she was also angry at him for the way he was treating her, and angry with herself for letting him get the upper hand.

Taking a ragged breath, she forced herself to smile at him. "Nice is always better," she whispered huskily.

Cal hesitated for a moment, as though weighing her sincerity. Then he loosened the rope and slipped it up over her head, freeing her arms. He was still down on one knee, which gave her the advantage she needed. He was caught off balance as well as off guard when her fist connected solidly with his jaw.

Laura had one foot in the stirrup before he caught up with her again. Grabbing her around her slender waist, he dragged her away from her horse. She reached backward, blindly clawing at his face. With an oath, he pushed her away from him.

They stood facing each other like two gunfighters on the street of an old western town. Laura was free for the moment, but Cal stood between her and the horses. She was trying to come up with some plan of escape when she realized that he was actually smiling at her.

"Damn, girl! You don't fight fair," he said with grudging admiration.

Laura stared back at him, beginning to see the humor of the situation. "I fight the way you taught me to, so you have no one but yourself to blame."

Cal rubbed his jaw ruefully. "I guess you're right about that . . . in more ways than one."

Brushing the dirt off her jeans, Laura avoided his searching glance, finding it easier to spar with him. "And what was all that garbage about 'you can have it nice or you can have it rough'?"

Cal had the grace to look embarrassed. He kicked at the nonexistent pebble in the grass. "Hell, you made me mad. I said what you made me feel."

"So now the big, bad man's going to rape me?" Laura taunted, enjoying his discomfort immensely.

Cal's gaze snapped back to meet hers, and his voice was a low, sexy drawl. "Didn't figure I'd have to."

"Why you—"

She swung at him again, but he dodged and grabbed her arm, using it to pull her firmly against his chest. She trembled as she stared into the eyes that she knew so well, the eyes that had haunted her dreams.

"What are you really doing back here, Laurie?" he asked her softly. "What is it you want from me?"

Laura met his questioning gaze openly and knew that she had to tell him the truth, no matter what the consequences. "Your father doesn't think he has long to live, and he feels he can't die and leave Melissa in a house without love. He's asked me to take her away with me."

Cal released her and stepped back, his face registering blank astonishment. "He's asked you to take her? He dotes on that child. He'd be lost without her. And what about me? I'm her father... at least in name." He paced a few steps and then turned back to her again. "Lord knows, I haven't been a good daddy to her, but that doesn't come easy to me. I can't help the way I feel. Every time I look at her, I see Eve."

"But surely you must have some good memories of Eve. You loved her for a long time, ever since we were children." She held her breath, telling herself that she didn't care what he had to say on that subject, but knowing that she did care terribly.

Cal took off his Stetson and stared into the distance. "I thought I did, God knows. But then for a while I thought that it was you I really loved."

Laura's heart thumped painfully in her chest, and she suddenly found it an effort to continue breathing.

Cal pushed ahead, every word precise, on target, a deadly weapon. "But when you left here, I realized that the thing between us had just been a mirage, something that had never really existed."

"Don't say that, Cal. It was real to me."

The hard, gray, cynical eyes bored into hers. "Was it?"

His callused thumb gently traced the full curve of her lower lip before his mouth touched hers. His kiss was slow and tender at first and then, all at once, it became fierce and demanding.

Laura's body responded. But a warning buzzer sounded in her head. He'd been with Honey last night and now he wanted her. He didn't really care. He was just using her for temporary satisfaction, or maybe to try and get back at her for what had happened so long ago. She couldn't take the pain of being close to him again.

She pushed away from him, gasping like a drowning swimmer. "No, Cal, I—"

He grabbed her arms and pulled her to him again, covering her mouth, his lips and tongue insistent. She sighed helplessly as he slipped a hand inside her shirt to caress one firm breast. Lowering his head, he traced a path of fire to the rosette tip, his hat falling to the ground unnoticed.

Desire blotted out all thought in Laura, and she became a being of pure feeling and emotion. Moaning low in her throat, she locked both hands in Cal's thick black hair and pressed his eager mouth closer against her body.

She felt an all-consuming flame engulf her as he pulled her down onto the soft, green grass.

The feel of his hard body on top of hers, the taste of his tongue in her mouth, the sound of his voice murmuring her name, had her shaking in his arms. She felt his heart pounding in rhythm with hers and watched him quiver beneath her caressing fingers, glorying in the knowledge that his need equaled her own.

They touched each other everywhere, hands racing, in a frantic search for flesh. Not taking the time to undress her, Cal pushed her shirt and bra aside and surrounded her breasts with shaking hands until only the hard pink tips remained uncovered.

"Damn, Laurie! It's been so long," he whispered huskily. "Too long."

Abruptly he sat up, tugged off her boots, and then stripped her from the waist down. His gaze was intense as he stood above her and began to unbuckle his belt.

All at once, his fingers paused in their task. Away from the burning touch of her flesh, he searched her eyes with his. Laura heard the doubt and mistrust creep into his mind as surely as if he'd voiced his thoughts aloud. She knew with sudden certainty that he was going to turn and walk away from her.

In a gesture as old as time, she held out her arms in supplication. She saw his chest rise and fall as if he were fighting for air.

"Cal," she whispered, making his name a benediction. "Please."

With a muttered oath, he tore open his jeans and covered her body with his, kissing her, caressing her. His swollen flesh pressed against hers demandingly. Locking her slim legs around his hips, she opened herself to him and sighed as he eased into her.

Lying quietly under her equally motionless lover, she savored the feel of his warmth filling her so completely. It was as if they were the only two people in the world. There was no Honey, no Steve, no Melissa, just Cal and Laura. She wanted to stay suspended in the joy of this moment for all eternity, with no future to worry about and no past to regret.

Cal framed her face between his hands and kissed her tenderly. A look that was a combination of agony and ecstasy crossed his features and he whispered a self-conscious apology. "Laurie, I don't think that I'll be able to... wait for you."

She looked up at him and traced the curve of his cheek with one slim finger, devouring him with her eyes. "It's all right. I feel the same way. I want you so much."

With a groan, he buried his face in her neck, and his thrusts shook every fiber of her body. Her breath began to come in short gasps, and her fingertips pressed into the straining muscles of his shoulders. Then he shuddered convulsively, and drove into her so hard that she could no longer tell where her body stopped and his began.

"No!" she cried in disappointed protest. But before she could complete that single syllable, his final strokes caught her and swept her over the edge, carrying her to the limits of feeling.

Rolling onto his side, he took her with him, their bodies still joined. He pillowed her head with one arm, the roundness of her cheek filling the hollow in the center of his chest. His hands remembered the curves of her back and rediscovered the silken softness of her hair.

Laura listened as the beat of Cal's racing heart slowed and steadied. She became part of the sound, part of the man she held in her arms. She closed her eyes, feeling secure, content and totally relaxed. She had Cal back now, and no other person, no misunderstanding, no harsh words would ever separate them again.

She was almost asleep when a feather-soft tickling called her back to consciousness. Looking down, she saw Cal's fingers rubbing against her flesh. His half-hard manhood began to move inside her with a slow, tantalizing rhythm, and he smiled down into her flushed face.

"You should have known I wouldn't forget you," he said lightly. But his eyes gave the words deeper meaning, and Laura's heart soared.

Continuing his sweet massage, Cal dipped his tongue inside her mouth, kissing her thoroughly until she trembled on the brink of paradise. Then his head moved down while Laura strained upward, arching her breasts toward his lips. But he was still too far away. Looking deep into his eyes, she cupped one breast and lifted it to his mouth.

"Laurie..."

He said her name with a vehemence that made it both a curse and a prayer, and she felt him grow fully hard inside her. His tongue had barely brushed her skin when great pulsating waves of feeling burst within her, and her cry shattered the afternoon quiet.

For a long time afterward they both lay still, unwilling to break the spell, to separate into two again. Then Cal leaned over her, blocking her view of the Texas sky.

"Promise me, Laurie," he whispered. "Promise me that you'll never let that damned fool touch you again."

"But, Cal—" she protested.

He looked at her sternly, refusing to debate the issue. Even he didn't understand the fierce possessiveness he felt, the sudden onslaught of pure emotion that defied rational thought. "Promise me."

Laura felt the same indignation that she had when he'd accused her unjustly before, but now it was tempered by a new and even stronger emotion—fear. She was afraid of that look in Cal's eyes, afraid that he would get up and walk away as if the last hour had never happened.

Swallowing her anger, she did what she'd vowed only last night she'd never do. For the sake of peace she said the two little words that he wanted to hear. "I promise."

She took a silent oath that someday, somehow, she would prove her innocence to his complete satisfaction. On that day he'd apologize for doubting her. Unaware of the truant thoughts beneath her calm exterior, Cal kissed her gently then rolled onto his back with a sigh.

Idly Laura's eyes focused on his lower body, and suddenly she swallowed hard, her face paling a little. "You didn't use anything."

Cal turned his head toward her, blinking in confusion. "What are you talking about?"

Then he saw the scared look on her face and understood. He sat up abruptly. "Hell's bells, Laurie!"

Laura wilted under his accusing stare. "Well, last time you took care of things!"

Cal frowned, perplexed by her words. "Laurie, that was seven years ago, not yesterday. Then, you spoke right up and said there was a problem. Today you never once mentioned it. Why not?"

"I—I—" A flush crept over Laura's face as she realized the truth of what he'd said. How could she explain to Cal that while he'd gone on to gain increased experience and sophistication, her sexual development had come to a dead halt? After Cal, the caresses of other men had left her cold. She'd dated occasionally, but there had been no one special enough to make her feel the way that Cal had.

She realized now to what extent she'd been dwelling in a fantasy world. Cal had really lived the past seven years. She had drifted through them, her career the only real thing in her life. She'd thought of this afternoon as a continuation of their original affair. The rules had been set before, so naturally Cal would know he was supposed to protect her.

How could she have been such a romantic fool? She'd been swept away by the absolute joy of being touched by him again, and nothing else had mattered except the love she'd felt. That was another thing she couldn't explain to Cal. Oh, he'd enjoyed her body, but she certainly hadn't heard him make any declarations of love. She'd been stupid to expect to pick up where they'd left off. Obviously she was nothing special to him, just the latest in a long line of women he'd satisfied and been satisfied by over the years.

In a few days, unless a miracle happened, she'd be leaving Sinclair Ranch for good. What if she were pregnant? The idea settled in her mind as if it had always belonged there. If she couldn't have Cal, maybe she'd be lucky enough to carry a part of him with her, a baby she could love and cherish. A child without any history of hurt and betrayal. She hadn't been ready to even consider something like that a few months ago, but now—

"Were you planning to take a little souvenir back to New York to remember me by?" Cal's tone was light and almost teasing, but the eyes probing hers were deadly serious.

"Are you crazy?" Laura exclaimed, startled into a vehement denial by his uncanny ability to pick up on her thoughts.

She hadn't planned what had happened. She'd never meant to take more from him than he was willing to give.

She had to convince him of that, or he'd never trust her again! So she told him what she thought he'd want to hear.

"Listen, my career is just starting to take off. I'm up for a big promotion. The worst possible thing that could happen in my life would be for me to get pregnant with your baby."

The wall that Cal had so carefully built around his emotions suddenly cracked wide open, and he hurt as he hadn't hurt in years. He'd learned from bitter experience never to trust a woman with anything he truly valued. Yet today he'd plunged right ahead with Laura like some blind, witless fool, not giving a thought to the consequences. Now he was paying the price.

His smile was mocking, his tone resentful and sarcastic, as he stood and zipped his jeans. "You sure weren't thinking about your almighty career down there in the grass a few minutes ago. But I suppose a slipup now and then doesn't matter much to you. If the test comes out positive, you'll just fix things and I'll never know the difference."

Without waiting for confirmation or denial, he turned away and began walking toward his horse.

Laura was stunned by his words, his sudden change of mood. She had tried to reassure him, but she'd sounded cold and uncaring. She couldn't let him leave like this.

"Cal, wait! That's not what I meant."

She ran after him and grabbed his arm. He jerked away from her as if she'd scalded him. "I don't want to hear any more lies. What happened here today was an accident, a mistake. It's over between us, Laurie. It's finished. That's the final word."

Laura stared after him, despair becoming anger, anger building slowly into rage. He'd roped her like an animal. He'd made love to her and maybe even gotten her pregnant. He'd accused her of having an affair with his sister's fiancé and had as good as called her a liar when she'd denied it. Then he'd had the gall to ask her to promise that the nonexistent affair would be ended. Now, even after she'd betrayed everything she believed to make that promise, he was walking away from her again.

Ever since she had arrived she'd tried her best to be considerate and understanding, and all he'd done was spit in her face. She'd felt guilty because she'd abandoned him to her sister's tender mercies, sorry because he'd been hurt. Well, what about her pain, her hurt?

She watched Cal put his foot in the stirrup and suddenly something inside her snapped. All the emotions she had kept so carefully under control for so many years came pouring out like water bursting through a broken dam. She heard the blatant agony of a woman's screeching voice and hardly recognized it as her own.

"I hate you, Cal Sinclair! I hate you! I hate you!"

Cal lowered his foot from the stirrup and turned to face a raging harpy, his eyes wide in disbelief, his mouth slightly open in astonishment.

Laura's hoarse, ragged vocalizations seemed to be coming from somewhere deep inside, a raw, ugly place that had never been opened to the light before. "All these years every time... every time I wanted a man to touch me... it was never... no one could..." Dimly she was aware of her own choking sobs and rambling words. "Now you're going away again... and I... I hate you... I..."

Drawn by a compulsion he couldn't control and an emotion he refused to acknowledge, Cal retraced his steps.

Laura felt strong hands on her arms. She tried to slap and scratch him, wanting to hurt him, wanting to make him suffer for the pain he'd inflicted on her. But he held her easily, drawing her so close that no space remained between them.

"Don't hate me, Laurie," he whispered, his voice barely audible over her sobs. "Don't hate me," he murmured, his breath warm in her ear.

Suddenly all the tension drained away and left her exhausted. She collapsed against him. He staggered, and they both fell to their knees on the ground, her body limp in his warm embrace. He pulled her unresisting form onto his lap and rocked her back and forth, crooning to her as if she were a baby, one big hand smoothing her wild, tousled hair. Gradually her sobs quieted, and she lay still against his chest.

It felt as though time was suspended for endless moments. Then Cal broke the silence, his voice sounding hesitant. "I'm sorry, Laurie. I didn't think you really cared what I said or did. I guess I was wrong."

"But you still don't trust me," Laura whispered dully. "You still don't believe in me."

The voice that answered belonged to a very old and bitter man. "I can't give you something that's not in me, Laurie. Belief, trust, love. I don't know what those words mean anymore."

Laura thought about what he'd said for a moment. Was it worth the cost in pride and pain to keep pursuing this man? He was as good as telling her that it was hopeless, but something inside her refused to give up. She loved him too much to quit now. Gathering all her tattered courage, she reached out to him one last time. "Belief, trust, love…maybe we can remember what those words mean—together."

There was a lengthy pause before Cal finally gave her a grudging one-word response. "Maybe."

To Laura it was the most wonderful word in the world. It meant that she still had reason to hope. She managed a weak smile. "Got a handkerchief, cowboy?"

Taking the white folded square that he thrust into her hand, she turned her face away, trying to repair some of the damage her crying had wrought.

"How do I look?" she asked, turning back to him.

Cal examined her face critically. "Like you lost your best friend."

She looked at him with red-rimmed eyes, seeing the change in him, catching a glimpse of the feelings he'd been so careful to keep hidden before. "Thought I had."

"You thought wrong."

Cal's eyes were radiant as he kissed her lightly. "I know just what you need," he said with the hint of a boyish grin.

"You already gave me that," Laura told him. "And you did it very nicely, too."

"Had your limit, have you?" he asked with lifted brows as he pulled off his boots and socks. Then he got up and slowly unfastened his jeans. Laura watched as they fell away, and he stood before her fully revealed, his perfect body dappled with patterns of shadow and sunlight. He pulled her to her feet, and soon the rest of her clothing joined his on the ground.

"Now what?" Laura asked, her lips tingling in anticipation of his kiss.

"Now this."

Before she could even protest, Cal had lifted her off her feet and carried her toward the crystal-clear pool.

"No!" she shrieked. "Don't you dare!"

Cal gave her a wicked smile. "Turned into a city girl, I see. Won't dip your manicured toes into anything that isn't chlorinated."

Laura struggled to break his hold as she felt the cool water begin to lap at her skin, but she might as well have saved the effort. When he reached a point where the water came up above his waist, he released her and let her slide slowly down the length of his body until her feet were securely on the bottom of the pond.

Wetting his fingers, he gently bathed her swollen face with the cool water until she was almost purring her contentment. "Feeling better?" he asked sweetly.

"Umm," Laura sighed.

"Good!" Cal's hand fanned the water, and what seemed like half the pond flew up and hit Laura in the face.

"You dirty, sneaking—" She sputtered, wiping her eyes.

They splashed and played in the sunlit pool, frolicking like children. Laura felt young, alive, and full of mischief. A glow of happiness flooded her. Laughing, she jumped toward Cal, flinging her arms around his neck and dragging them both underwater.

Cal's mouth found hers and his hands molded her body to his. They broke the surface, breathless, and Laura brought her legs up to surround his hips. He kissed her slowly, with excruciating expertise, leaving her aching for more. Pressing the burning softness of her cheek against his rougher skin, she moaned as she felt his body harden against hers. She was totally unprepared for the sharp, strident shriek that froze her passion as though a witch's spell had turned the pool to ice around her.

"You dirty slut! First you try to seduce my fiancé, and now I catch you with my brother!"

Startled, Laura turned her head to look at Delphine. The girl was standing on the bank of the pool livid with rage, shaking her fist at them like a crazy woman.

A blush spread over Laura's whole body, and she pressed even closer to Cal in a desperate attempt to hide her nakedness. She cringed under the obscenities that poured from the younger woman's mouth as Delphine reviled her. Gradually anger overcame embarrassment, and she opened her mouth to reply, but Cal spoke first.

"Shut up, Ellie. Shut up now. I don't give you orders about how to live your life, and I'd appreciate the same courtesy from you. Now get home before I climb out of this water and find a bar of soap to wash your mouth out. I said *move*!"

Delphine stepped backward, momentarily cowed. Then she glared at Laura, her voice cutting through the still air like a knife as she delivered her parting tirade. "I hope someone hurts you, Laura Wright! I hope someone hurts you like you've tried to hurt me!"

Laura stared at Delphine, almost hypnotized by the intensity of the gray eyes that were so much like Cal's. Before she could find words to deny the charge, the other woman had disappeared into the ring of trees that surrounded the glade, leaving a cloud of foreboding lingering in the sultry air like the scent of cheap perfume.

Chapter Six

In the clear, fresh light of the following morning, the previous afternoon's scene in the glade seemed unimportant. Laura felt content, rejuvenated and glad to be alive. She resolved that no one was going to take that feeling away from her through jealousy, suspicion or petty resentment.

As she got out of bed, her eye was drawn to a beige rectangle of paper that was lying on the hot-pink rug near the door. As excited as a teenager, she knelt down on the carpet and reached out with trembling fingers to open the note. She recognized Cal's bold, sprawling handwriting immediately.

Laurie,
I was looking forward to having breakfast with you today, but I have to leave for work, and you're still sleeping. (Too much exercise yesterday??) Why

don't you come to the big city and stop by my office? I'll take you somewhere special for lunch.

Cal

Laura smiled at the reference to their lovemaking and pressed the letter to her heart. Then she noticed the travel alarm on her bedside table. It was already past eleven! Leaping to her feet, she raced to the closet and hastily pulled out the blouse and slacks she'd worn on her trip from New York. She'd have to run down to iron them.

Zipping up her jeans and pulling on a shirt, she threw open the door and rushed headlong into Steve's arms.

"You scared me to death!" she exclaimed. "What are you doing out there?"

Grabbing her elbow, Steve pulled her out into the hallway. "You and I are going to have a talk," he informed her in no uncertain terms. "We're going to have a real conversation in full view of everyone who cares to look."

Propelling her down the stairs, he indicated the living-room couch. "Sit," he commanded.

"Now listen here," Laura flared, "I'm in a hurry!"

Steve was notably unimpressed. "If you want to keep your job, I suggest you spare me a moment of your time."

Laura thought it over then reluctantly sank down onto the soft leather, still clutching her clothes.

Steve settled into an armchair across from her. "I heard about your little frolic in the pond yesterday. It served to draw some of Delphine's suspicion away from me, but I think you've lost your mind."

Laura shot to her feet, her face burning. "I don't have to listen to this!"

Steve held up a hand to forestall her leaving. "I'm sorry. I apologize, Laura. I don't happen to care for your choice of lovers, but you're right, of course. It is none of my concern. Please listen to what I have to say."

Steve breathed a sigh of relief as Laura sat back down. "What I really wanted to tell you is that I've made plane reservations for the day after tomorrow. I'm going to see the new International Inns in San Antonio, Austin and Dallas."

"And you want me to go with you," Laura said, anticipating the direction the conversation would take.

"If you're still interested in becoming district manager."

Laura contemplated Cal's probable reaction to such a trip. She and Steve would definitely be gone overnight, and that little piece of news wouldn't be well received. Everything was so wonderful with Cal right now, but it was also incredibly fragile. She had the feeling that if she made one wrong move, the whole tentative relationship would collapse like a house of cards.

"Why do I have to go with you this time, Steve?" she asked a trifle desperately. "Maybe in a couple of weeks—"

Steve interrupted her impatiently. "You're supposed to go back to New York next week, Laura, or were you thinking of riding off into the sunset with your cowboy instead?"

Laura looked up quickly and met Steve's mocking eyes.

"I wouldn't count on it happening, Laura. Don't give up everything you've earned over the years for the sake of an illusion. He hasn't promised you anything in return, has he?"

Laura slowly shook her head.

"Then don't be a fool. You're my choice for district manager, you're already in Texas. From a purely business standpoint, it's absurd for you not to go."

Laura knew that what Steve said was true. She also knew how Cal was likely to see it. Suddenly she thought of another complication. "Does Delphine approve of my going on this trip with you, Steve?"

"No, Delphine does not approve. But if she thinks that will alter my plans, she's sadly mistaken. Like I told you yesterday, no one owns me, Laura." Steve leaned forward, his voice intent. "Ever since you arrived here, Delphine has subjected me to crying fits and farfetched accusations. After yesterday's fiasco, I decided I'd had enough of her jealous hysteria. I told her last night that if she wants to marry me, she'll have to learn to understand and respect my business obligations. I won't spend the rest of my life catering to the whims of a paranoid shrew—not even for all the—"

"Money in the world?" Laura finished for him.

He gave her a mischievous grin. "You said that, I didn't."

Laura sighed. Steve might be willing to discount Delphine's feelings, but for her the situation was different. She was in love with Cal. It was true that he hadn't made her any promises, yet she couldn't bring herself to say yes to Steve knowing how Cal would react. If only she had time to wait until their relationship was on more solid ground before putting it to the test. Well, the longer she put off the decision, the better chance she had.

Laura stood up, effectively terminating the conversation. "I'll let you know as soon as I can."

"That's the best you can do?" Steve asked in disbelief.

"That's the best I can do."

Steve sighed and ran a hand through his hair. "I won't try to coerce you into going if you really feel you can't, Laura, but do me one favor. At least stop by and see the International Inn in Houston."

Laura nodded, relieved by his concession. "Of course I will, Steve. I doubt that I'll have time today, but I'll do it before I... leave Texas."

The uncertainty of the future weighing heavily on her mind, she walked into the kitchen. "Nita, do you have time to run an iron over these clothes?"

She stopped suddenly when she saw Melissa sitting at the kitchen table. The little girl had on a full-skirted, ruffled blue dress and white patent leather shoes. She held a small matching purse in her lap, and her pale golden hair was done up with blue silk ribbons. Her face lighted up as Laura entered the room.

Wiping her hands on a dish towel, Juanita walked forward to take the clothes from Laura, distracting her attention. "I suppose that you heard that Mr. Randall and Delphine had a terrible argument last night after they came back from their rides. For a while, I thought that they would call off the wedding, but this morning they are lovebirds once again."

Laura smiled in reluctant admiration of Steve's persuasive powers. "She must really love him."

"Yes. And she thinks he is—what is the word?—sophisticated. She met him while she was visiting a friend in New York. He must have seemed different and exciting to her. She thinks he is from one of the best families, with not so much money now, but with famous ancestors. Henry has not told her the truth. He thinks she would only be angry with him for hiring a detective and he is probably right."

"Are we going soon, Laura?" Melissa asked, tugging at her arm.

Juanita clucked at the child. "Let her have a cup of coffee, little one." She turned to Laura with an apologetic air. "The little *señorita* is so excited. She has been sitting here since ten o'clock waiting for you to wake up."

Laura's heart sank as she remembered her casual promise of the day before. It had been easily made, and then easily forgotten in the heat of her reborn passion for Cal. She wanted so badly to be alone with him today, to talk about the past—and the future. Lord knew what his reaction would be if she showed up with Melissa. It was on the tip of her tongue to make some excuse, to say the words that would free her for the day. But when she looked into the child's happy, expectant face, she suddenly felt ashamed of her selfish thoughts.

Smiling, she took Melissa's hand. "You look so pretty today! We're going to have a real good time. You'll see." Cal would never learn to accept Melissa if he were allowed to keep avoiding her. This was a perfect opportunity for father and daughter to get to know each other better.

An hour and a half later, Laura and Melissa stepped out of Laura's car in front of the Sinclair building in downtown Houston. Laura gazed at the towering structure, admiring the skillful melding of glass, concrete and steel. It radiated strength, grace and power. Just like Cal, she thought proudly.

Laura smiled at Melissa and caught her staring up at the cloud-shrouded building openmouthed. "Haven't you ever been to your daddy's office before?"

The little girl shook her head so solemnly that Laura's heart contracted. She remembered the hours young Cal had spent in this building, sitting on Henry's knee while the elder Sinclair made multimillion-dollar manufacturing deals. She had played tag with Cal and Eve around Henry's huge oak desk, laughing and screaming until Henry had thrown up his hands in defeat, roaring to his secretary, "Get my calls, Lucy! No sense trying to work in this madhouse. We young 'uns are goin' out for ice cream."

Laura and Melissa rode one of the quietly humming elevators up to the top floor and stepped out onto the lush, rust-colored pile carpeting of the ultramodern executive offices. A circular Lucite-and-chrome receptionist's station had been added in the years since Laura's last visit. She blinked at the transformation. Gone were the oak paneling, the leather furniture, the smell of cigar smoke. Everything was bright, plastic and sterile.

A pretty, well-dressed young woman looked up at Laura through the transparent shielding of the receptionist's area. "May I help you?"

"I'm Laura Wright. I'm here to see Cal Sinclair."

"Do you have an appointment?" the receptionist asked, looking at her doubtfully.

"Yes. For lunch."

The woman raised one eyebrow. Punching buttons on the telephone, she spoke quietly into the receiver.

"Please go right in. It's the door at the end of the hall."

Laura walked on by, Melissa's hand clutching hers tightly. She found Honey sitting at Lucy's old desk looking unnervingly beautiful in a royal-blue suit that clung to her ample curves.

The secretary smiled at Laura in greeting. "Well, how nice to see you again. And how are you, Melissa?"

Before either of the visitors had a chance to reply, the door to Cal's office opened. His eyes met Laura's in a long, open stare that communicated his desire for her more clearly than words.

Laura felt a soft glow spread over her face, and she looked away, pleased, but suddenly shy. She noticed with some satisfaction that Honey's mouth had dropped open in astonishment.

"Come into my office for a minute, Laurie," Cal said easily. "I have something that I want you to see." Then he noticed Melissa standing by his secretary's desk, and he looked at Laura questioningly, his eyes putting up their guard again. "I didn't know you were bringing the child," he said coolly.

Laura swallowed hard, ashamed of her newfound fear of displeasing this man. "I promised her yesterday that I'd take her into town," she explained.

Cal nodded shortly. "You wait out here, Melissa, and we'll be right back. Honey, you see that my daughter has something to keep her busy, will you?"

Ignoring his secretary's openly inquisitive stare, Cal ushered Laura into his office and closed the door. She was surprised and pleased to see that the room was almost exactly the same as when Henry had ruled the company from the old leather chair. But she had time for only a cursory glance before Cal swept her into his arms.

His kisses left her light-headed, and she melted into his embrace as though she had never been absent from it. She felt his cool hands on her warm flesh as he unbuttoned her blouse and caressed her bare skin.

"Cal, we can't. Not here!" She shivered as he nuzzled her ear.

"Why not?" he demanded in a husky whisper. "It's my office, isn't it?"

Pressing her back against the door, he leaned the lower half of his body into hers, and Laura felt the delicious sensations of the day before return in full force.

"Cal," she whispered as he rubbed the silky hair of his mustache across the throbbing peak of her breast. She couldn't restrain her moan of pleasure as she felt herself grow hard inside his mouth. Her love for him seemed to fill every part of her. She dropped her purse to the floor and encircled him with her arms.

Then the phone rang, and Cal pulled back with a resigned sigh. Giving her a final kiss, he walked over to his desk and picked up the receiver. As he talked, Laura began to rebutton her blouse. Cal watched her, looking woebegone as her skin gradually disappeared beneath a cover of cloth. When his conversation ended, he hung up the telephone and came back around the desk to claim her, a feral gleam in his eye.

Laura took a deep breath and held him away from her reluctantly. "You promised me lunch," she said lightly. "And Melissa's waiting."

The gleaming eyes narrowed briefly, and for a moment Laura thought that he'd wrestle her to the floor and take her then and there. But his expression softened, and he lifted her hand from his chest and kissed it as if he were a knight and she his fair lady.

"Where are we going, anyway?" Laura asked quickly, struggling to keep from drowning in the depths of those eyes.

"You'll find out," the Texan told her mysteriously. He winked and gave her a light slap on the fanny that made her yelp in surprise.

"Watch your hands, cowboy," Laura warned him, more amused than angry. "I'm a woman, not one of your prize fillies."

"Yes, ma'am," Cal said with mock contrition. "But still and all, I think I'll have you saddle broke by week's end. You betcha." He pinned her up against the door for a last, lingering kiss.

"Just leave your spurs at home," she whispered as she held him close against her.

"You're taking all the joy out of my life, Laurie," Cal told her. "You sure you don't want to—?"

"I'm sure!" Laura exclaimed, interrupting him before he could discover how weak her willpower was where he was concerned.

He brought her hand down to touch the hard outline below his belt. "Your loss," he said with a wicked grin.

Releasing her, he lifted a cream-colored Stetson off his desk and turned back toward her. "Well, you ready?"

Laura flexed her tingling hand, remembering the feel of his body and already beginning to regret her decision to defer their lovemaking. "You never said where we were going."

"You're right. I didn't." He smiled enigmatically and straightened his tie. "Well, how do I look?" he asked, tugging at the vest on his three-piece suit.

"You look like a handsome and prosperous man who heads one of the most prestigious companies in the country."

"Aw, shucks, ma'am," Cal told her, laying on the accent. "I'm just a good ol' boy at heart. Give me an open range, a good horse and a lovin' woman, and I got all I need in this here world."

"Tell me another one, Cal."

He gazed down at her thoughtfully. "You know, Laurie, kidding aside, it's not all that far from the truth. When I'm on the ranch, that's the only time I feel any peace inside. This place, this monster that Daddy built here, it takes and it takes until it drains a man. You can lose yourself in it.''

''I know. I've been possessed by my job for the last seven years.''

The reason for their mutual obsession remained unspoken between them.

Laura reached up to touch his face in understanding, and he kissed her open hand, his mustache tickling her palm. He smiled at her, and the haze of weariness that had shrouded him seemed to suddenly evaporate.

''Come on, woman,'' Cal said, taking her arm. ''Let's go kick up some dust.''

''This is so perfect, Cal! I don't believe this place is still here.''

Laura beamed at him across the brightly colored floral centerpiece on their restaurant table, sipping her margarita from a salt-rimmed glass.

Leaning back in his Mediterranean-style chair, Cal smiled in satisfaction. ''I thought about taking you to a fancy French restaurant, or to one of the places I go for business lunches, but then I remembered how you used to love Mexican food.''

Their waiter approached with a basket full of fresh, hot sopipillas—pillowlike rectangles of soft dough. Laura tore one open, poured honey into the steaming center, and placed the delicacy in front of Melissa with a smile.

A stray dribble of sweet, sticky fluid lingered on the tip of her index finger, and she automatically raised it to her lips. Then her smile froze as she noticed Cal's eyes following her every move with rapt attention. Blood rushed to her face, and her whole body began to throb in response to the wanton implication of that look. Cal smiled at her, knowing just what buttons he had pushed and enjoying her reaction immensely.

Then Melissa giggled, amused by the unusually intense expressions on the adults' faces. The waiter cleared his throat discreetly. Cal reluctantly returned to studying the menu. "Let me see if I can guess what Laurie's going to order," he mused thoughtfully. "Chicken enchiladas, a soft beef burrito and a big bowl of homemade chili."

"Lord, don't forget that chili!" Laura admonished the waiter. She smiled at Melissa as she tucked a napkin beneath the child's chin. "One bowl for me, one bowl for Daddy and one for Miss Giggles here." Predictably Melissa giggled again.

"Your granddaddy used to take Laurie and me here to eat chili when we were just little ones," Cal told his daughter.

"And when we weren't so little," Laura reminded him. She sighed. "Those were the good times."

Cal nodded. "You bet. Sometimes I sure wish Daddy were here running the company, and I was back knocking around with no responsibilities. It seemed to come so easy to him. He enjoyed it. I know he did."

"To Henry," Laura said, raising her margarita in a toast.

"And to the good times ahead," Cal murmured softly.

They clinked glasses lightly and sipped their drinks, and the strolling mariachis drifted over to their table to play just for them. To Laura, it was a dream come true.

After lunch, they drove to the Galleria, Houston's largest shopping mall. Laura and Cal strolled around hand in hand while Melissa gaped at all the displays in the store windows.

"She's a good little thing," Cal told Laura with a touch of surprise. "She hasn't been a minute's trouble all day."

She squeezed his hand. "You wouldn't be so amazed at that if you'd get to know her better."

They drifted around lazily, stopping for a moment to watch the ice skaters gliding on the big rink in the center of the mall. Then they moved on, making their way through the throngs of shoppers, not pausing again until Laura admired a silk print dress in the window of an exclusive women's clothing store.

"You know," Cal said, standing at her shoulder, "in a couple of days, we're having a big barbecue so that all our unsuspecting friends and neighbors can come and meet Randall. And the day after that's the wedding. You ought to get something to wear."

"I was just thinking that myself," Laura admitted.

"Well, let's go in and get it taken care of."

"This place doesn't have the style of clothing I usually buy," Laura said with a decisive shake of her head. "That dress just isn't what female hotel managers are wearing this year."

Cal took her arm firmly. "But this would be for a party. Let's go in, and you can at least try some things on and get an idea of what you're looking for."

"I don't think..." she began, but Cal was already dragging her into the shop.

For the next hour, she modeled sequined dresses, jeans and fancy Western shirts for Cal and Melissa. As she had suspected, there wasn't a tailored suit in the store. The two Sinclairs were a very animated audience, cheering or booing each selection. For the barbecue, Cal approved a pair of tight white jeans and a matching fringed shirt trimmed with silver thread.

"It's perfect," he told the saleslady. "You got a hat and boots to go with it?"

"I believe we have the lady's size, sir," the woman told him eagerly.

"Cal, this is ridiculous! I'm not going to buy anything here," Laura reminded him in an urgent whisper.

"I want to see the total effect," he insisted.

With a resigned sigh, she obediently put on the hand-tooled white boots and settled the matching hat firmly on her head, pulling the brim down over her eyes.

Cal grinned at her and shook his head in admiration. "Girl, you look like you never left Texas! Now shimmy out of those duds, and let's see something really dressy."

Laura sank onto a chair, exhausted. She leaned back against the wall, and the hat's brim tilted down to cover her eyes completely. "I'm all tuckered out! This high fashion is a hard business. I've tried on so many dresses already."

"What about that little blue dress in the window? I saw you looking at it before."

Laura glanced over his shoulder at the dress. It was pale blue silk material overlaid with a barely visible leaf print in a slightly lighter hue. It had a scoop neckline and a low-cut back with short, fluttery sleeves that were mere wisps of material. The fitted bodice and waist gave way to a slim, layered skirt consisting of three consecutive ruffles.

Laura frowned, searching for the right words. "It's so..." She wanted to say, "feminine," but then wasn't a party dress supposed to be feminine?

She'd spent so many years of her life downplaying her femininity, wanting men to treat her as an equal, to take her seriously in the business world. It was as if that dress represented everything she had tried to leave behind when she'd left Cal: her youth, her vulnerability, her sensuality. Eve's pink dress had been a blatantly sexual parody, a Halloween costume that had evoked no feelings in her other than a sense of the absurd. The dress in the window reminded her far too much of the feelings of incompleteness she'd been experiencing lately. It reminded her that she, like everyone else, needed to be loved.

"It's so... frilly," she said lamely, finally completing her sentence.

Cal lifted off her hat and kissed her firmly on the mouth. "You're right. That's just why I like it. Not that you need to wear clothes at all. You're pretty enough to go around in the altogether if you want."

"Not likely!" Laura exclaimed, pleased, but flustered by the intimate nature of his remark. She glanced around anxiously to see if Melissa had overheard, but the little girl was occupied by a costume jewelry display near the door. Relieved, Laura got up from the chair. "Let's go, Cal. We've wasted enough of this lady's time."

But Cal was already talking to the saleslady. "We'll take what she's wearing and the blue dress in the window. And if you have a pair of shoes to match, we'll take those, too."

"Now just one darned minute," Laura flared.

Cal looked at her, all innocence. "Do you have clothes to wear to the barbecue or the wedding?"

"No," Laura began, "but—"

"Are these appropriate?"

"Well, I guess so, but they're not what I usually wear."

"How many weddings and barbecues have you gone to in the past seven years?"

"Well... none," Laura admitted.

"Well, there you are," Cal commented as if that explained everything.

Laura shook her head, hoping to clear it. "Cut it out! I know what I . . ."

Suddenly she saw the credit card in his hand. With a shriek, she leaped toward him and grabbed it just as the startled saleslady was reaching for it. She waved it under his nose as if it were damning evidence, and he stood accused of a heinous crime.

"Don't you dare! I earn perfectly good money, and I can pay for my own clothes, thank you very much. I don't need handouts anymore."

Cal held up his hands in defeat, eyes downcast, uncharacteristically humble. "Yes, ma'am."

Laura slipped his credit card into his jacket pocket, and triumphantly handed her own American Express Gold Card to the waiting saleslady. It wasn't until Cal raised his eyes, and Laura read the mischief in them, that she realized she'd been had.

"Dammit, Cal, I told you I didn't want those clothes!"

Cal looked down at her, not at all repentant, and turned on his considerable charm. "Aw, come on, Laurie, loosen up. I was just having a little fun. We can go to another store if you want, but those things sure do look pretty on you."

Laura hadn't worn frivolous clothes in years, but then she hadn't had anyone to wear them for. It was a sobering thought to realize that she had enough tailored suits in her closet at home to last the rest of her solitary life. She searched his face for a glimpse of her future, while he frowned in puzzlement at her change of expression. Finally she decided he was right. It was high time she loosened up.

"I think I'm going to enjoy wearing those clothes," she told him with a smile.

He opened his mouth to speak, but she laid a finger across his lips. "Say one more word," she warned him, "and I may change my mind."

She pulled her finger away hurriedly when he attempted to nip it. "Behave," she said as she saw the saleslady approaching with the charge form.

After making arrangements to have the clothes delivered to the ranch, she retreated to the dressing room and quickly threw on her clothes, flashes of heat pulsating through her body as she thought about Cal. As she looked at her partially clothed body in the mirror she could almost feel his hands on her, and the memory of his lovemaking made her tremble.

When she finally returned to the sales area, he was waiting for her with a small package under his arm.

"What's that?" Laura asked curiously.

"Oh, I just bought a little something to make up for all the inconvenience we put this lovely lady through." He tipped his hat at the gray-haired saleslady, and the woman giggled like a schoolgirl.

"I see you haven't lost your touch with women," Laura said archly.

"You'd better hope I never do," Cal told her, giving her a brief hug.

With Melissa in tow, they walked on through the crowded mall until Cal paused in front of a jewelry store window. "You remember that game Daddy used to play with us, Laurie?"

"You mean the 'what if' game?"

"That's the one. Well, what if you could have anything in this store. What would you pick?"

Laura walked around from window to window, carefully studying the displays. Finally a heart-shaped arrangement of diamonds caught her eye. It dangled at the end of a delicate white gold chain, glittering seductively under the artificial light.

"That. I'd pick that," she said decisively.

Melissa stared at the shimmering pendant, pressing her hands against the glass as if to touch the bauble. "It's the most beautiful thing in the whole, wide world!" she exclaimed in awestruck tones.

"And probably one of the cheapest items in that store, sweetheart," Cal told her.

Almost involuntarily, he reached out to stroke the child's gleaming blond hair. When the little girl started in surprise, Cal immediately withdrew his hand.

Laura opened her mouth to try to explain to Cal that the child just needed a chance to get used to this new side of him. In the end, she held her peace, instinctively knowing that the words would only make Cal feel more uncomfortable.

"Well, I don't care if it is *the* cheapest thing in the store, Caleb Sinclair," she said lightly, as though nothing had happened. "It's pretty, and I like it."

Cal lowered his head in mock defeat. "I guess you should know what's pretty, you being a high-toned, big-city woman."

"I know what I like and there's one thing I crave more than anything in the world right now." She snuggled up to him and peered into his eyes meaningfully.

"What's that?" he asked, trying to sound indifferent.

"Ice cream!" Laura cried, pulling away from him. "I must have ice cream."

Cal groaned. "You always were a tease."

"You love it!" she declared in tones that dared him to refute her statement.

"You're right," he admitted. "I love it so much that I want to spend the rest of the afternoon with you."

Laura stared at him in surprise. "You mean, you're going to take the whole afternoon off? Just like that?"

Cal smiled at her expression. "That's the advantage of owning your own company. You can take off as much time as you want. Actually this two-week period is supposed to be my yearly vacation. I'm not supposed to be working at all. But sometimes they just can't seem to do without me."

His eyes met hers openly. "In the beginning, being at work gave me a good reason to stay away from an unhappy home. Now it sort of fills the gaps in my life. I always thought I'd have a family of my own." He glanced at Melissa and sighed. "I mean, the kind of family I'd always imagined having—a wife who loved me, children I could be close to. But things just didn't work out that way."

Laura felt a pain deep in her chest. She wanted so badly to ask him if they could start over again and have that family together, but she was afraid of his answer. Don't push, she thought. It's too soon.

"You can be close to Melissa, Cal. You're spending the day with her today. That's a start." She hesitated, then plunged ahead. "After we finish shopping, why don't we take her over to Astroworld? I know she'd love that."

Cal put an arm around her waist. "Do you come along as part of the bargain?"

Laura couldn't help smiling. "Just try to stop me!" she said, returning his hug. "Come on, Melissa," she called. "Your daddy's going to take us for ice cream, and later we're going to Astroworld!"

But the little girl didn't hear her. She was still standing with her hands pressed against the jewelry store window, gazing at the shimmering heart.

* * *

After finishing their ice cream, the trio continued their circuit of the mall. Along the way, Melissa acquired a pint-size cowgirl hat, a bottle of brightly colored nail polish and some barrettes with her name on them. Laura bought three suits in the style she was accustomed to wearing, as well as some other much-needed clothing. She'd need the suits if she went on the business trip with Steve, a fact she carefully refrained from mentioning to Cal. Of course, she'd have to bring the subject up for discussion soon, but she couldn't quite bring herself to ruin their day. She refused to think for even one minute about the future, afraid that her newfound happiness would dissolve like a child's sand castle at high tide. Instead she clung to the present with all the tenacity of a drowning woman clutching a life preserver.

"Isn't that your company, Laurie?"

Following Cal's gaze, Laura noticed that she was standing near an entranceway which led from the mall into the main lobby of an adjoining hotel. A sign proclaimed that an International Inn would be opening there soon.

Laura peered through the huge chrome-and-glass double doors and saw several men at work in the lobby. Her practiced eye identified them as carpenters and electricians. She also observed a harried man in a dark blue suit in deep discussion with a short, balding man. The short man threw his arms wide in a gesture of exasperation that made Laura smile in recognition.

"Would you mind if we took a few minutes to check this place out?" Laura asked eagerly. Business had been so low on her list of priorities today that she hadn't even bothered to ask Steve where the Houston Inn was located. But now that she was actually on-site, she couldn't wait to inspect the new hotel.

Cal shrugged. "I don't think there's any way I could stop you."

Ignoring the No Admittance sign, she opened one of the big double doors. With Melissa and Cal following behind her, she made her way around stacks of ceramic tile, rolls of carpeting and other assorted obstacles.

The attractive young man in the blue suit broke off his conversation and looked up with a frown when he saw them approaching. "I'm sorry, but no one's allowed in here. As you can see, we're not open for business yet."

"Laura Wright!"

She was suddenly swept up in an exuberant embrace. The short man planted a kiss on each cheek before releasing her. "Darling," he raved, "you look ravishing!"

Laura smiled with genuine affection. "Paul, it's good to see you." She turned to Cal who was eyeing the beaming man suspiciously. "Cal Sinclair, I'd like you to meet Paul Pierre. He's the decorator for all our International Inns. And this is Cal's daughter, Melissa."

Paul shook hands with Cal and, bowing, kissed Melissa's hand. The little girl smiled shyly and hid her face.

"What a little angel!" the decorator exclaimed.

The man in the blue suit offered Laura his hand. "I'm Jim Reyes, the manager here. I'm sorry about that reception. I didn't know who you were."

At Laura's blank look he continued. "When I talked to Mr. Randall this morning, he said that the new district manager would be visiting, but I wasn't expecting you today."

Laura blinked in surprise. She hadn't anticipated this. She quickly glanced at Cal to gauge his reaction, but his face told her nothing of his thoughts.

Apprehensively she turned her attention back to Reyes. "Actually my promotion isn't official yet, but I really would appreciate a tour."

"Of course," Reyes agreed, giving her a megawatt smile. "Right this way."

Leaving Pierre mumbling dispiritedly about plaid fabrics, Reyes took his visitors to see the restaurant and kitchen, the laundry and the gift shop and, finally, several of the finished hotel rooms.

"The theme, as you can see, will be Great Britain," he told Laura between comments about the cost of towels and sheets.

"The theme of the inn I manage in New York City is France."

"New York City," Reyes echoed thoughtfully. "Will your promotion be leaving a vacancy?"

"*If* my promotion becomes official, I expect that my assistant manager would take over the hotel for me," Laura told him as they all returned to the lobby. "Why?"

Reyes hesitated, as if debating the wisdom of what he was about to ask. He was quite obviously a man in torment. "Well," he began almost reluctantly, "I'm thrilled with my position here at this new hotel, but the truth of it is, my wife has just been offered a wonderful job in New York City. I was hoping that it might be possible to transfer there."

"I can speak to Mr. Randall about it," Laura said doubtfully, "but I think I already know what his answer will be."

"Please understand," Reyes added hastily, "I'm perfectly willing to work anywhere the company needs me, and I know what I'm asking. It's just that this means so much to my wife. I gave her my word that I'd try."

"I totally understand your position," she assured him. "And I sincerely envy your wife, Mr. Reyes. Thank you for the tour."

Leaving the manager speechless with surprise, Laura waved goodbye to Pierre and followed Cal back out into the mall.

"There's a man who loves his wife," Laura commented to no one in particular.

"There's a man who's not going any higher in the company if he keeps putting her career ahead of his."

Laura stopped walking and turned to look at Cal. "Maybe that's not as important to him as his wife's happiness."

Cal smiled at her and shook his head. "You're not roping me into this conversation. He's your employee, not mine. Tell me, are you going to give him his transfer, seeing as how you envy his wife so much and all?"

Laura frowned at him in annoyance as she resumed walking. "I know what Steve will say. This is a new hotel and it needs an experienced manager. My hotel is well-established, and my assistant could probably take it over and do a credible job, but he wouldn't be trusted to transfer here and handle a brand-new hotel. Which means, in order for Reyes to transfer, another experienced manager would have to be found to replace him. Steve just went to a lot of trouble to move Reyes here. He wouldn't agree to move him again unless the circumstances were very special."

"So why didn't you deny the transfer right then and there?" Cal asked curiously.

"Because a transfer from one region to another comes under the jurisdiction of the regional manager, who in this case is Steve Randall," Laura answered. "I'm not even the district manager, yet. I'm just the manager of a hotel in New York.''

"But the district manager's job is yours if you want it?'' Cal persisted.

Laura nodded, and they continued walking for several minutes, the tension palpable in the air between them. Laura felt a tightening in her stomach that warned her trouble was coming. She hadn't wanted to face this yet. Why couldn't I just have had today? she thought miserably.

"And if you take this job,'' Cal continued, "where will you live?''

Laura drew a deep breath. "Dallas. The district offices will be there. Of course, I'll be traveling a lot from Dallas to Austin, Houston and San Antonio, and to the regional headquarters in Miami and the main headquarters in New York. I'll be pretty busy. Dawn till after dark. You know how it is.''

Cal nodded, staring at the ground. "Yeah, I know how it is all right.''

Laura wanted to take him by the lapels of his expensive suit and shake him until his teeth rattled. What does that mean, Cal? she thought. Does that mean you know what it's like to work so hard that there's no time for anything else, or does it mean you think I'll take this job and have no time left for you? Do you care, Cal? I haven't heard you say that you love me. You haven't asked me to give up my job to stay with you. And, oh, lord, what would I say if you did?

And because she was afraid that the answers to those questions would end the only real happiness she'd known in seven years, she didn't say anything at all.

"Look over there, Daddy! There's the Astrodome! That's where we went to the big rodeo last February." Melissa stared out through the bars of the sky ride in the air high above the one-hundred-and-sixteen-acre Astroworld complex.

Laura only had eyes for Cal. She felt like a child again as they disembarked near the Kiddieland section of the park. She held his hand and sipped a soft drink as Melissa boarded a giant, multiseated yellow caterpillar. Laura watched the contraption go around and around on its track while Melissa laughed, waving at them each time she passed by.

"It's so easy to be happy when you're that young," Cal commented pensively. He appeared to be watching his daughter, but his thoughts seemed light-years away.

Laura squeezed his hand. "I think people create their own misery or their own happiness to a great extent. It all depends on what your expectations are and what you're willing to settle for."

Dropping her hand, Cal leaned against the fence surrounding the ride, still staring straight ahead. "And you, Laurie? What are your expectations?"

"I expect to spend the rest of this beautiful day with you," she responded evasively, dreading the results of a confrontation.

He turned to face her, his eyes searching, probing. "Is that all there is, Laurie? Just this one minute, this one afternoon, this one week?"

Teetering on the verge of declaring her love, Laura decided at the last second to keep her feelings to herself. Even in their most intimate moments of the day before, Cal hadn't confessed to love her or expressed any desire for commitment. She remembered the pain he'd cost her in the past, and she felt as if she were standing in quicksand waiting to be sucked into the depths of the same old misery again.

"How do you feel about it, Cal?" she finally countered, answering his question with one of her own.

His eyes bored into hers for a long moment, but they revealed nothing of Cal's true feelings. His mouth became a thin, hard line. "I'm not sure yet," he finally told her.

When Melissa's ride was over they escorted her from the caterpillar to the motorboats, then from the boats to the kiddie airplanes, without exchanging another word. Laura stayed close to Cal, near enough to touch him, yet she held back, feeling as if they had just played a high-stakes game of chess that had ended in an uncomfortable stalemate. Traces of tension lingered in the air, forming an invisible barrier that separated them more effectively than a thick concrete wall.

Cal and Laura were alone at the huge, rectangular table. He sat at the head, she sat at the foot. Steve and Delphine had gone out on the town together, and Juanita was eating dinner with Henry in his room. Exhausted by the excitement of the day, Melissa had fallen asleep before eight o'clock.

They kept up a polite conversation throughout the meal. Cal spoke about his plans to further modernize the ranch, and Laura told him what it was like to live in New York. As if by mutual agreement, nothing that would remotely touch upon the future of their relationship was discussed.

She looked up from her plate several times and caught him staring at her, a contemplative expression on his face. But when their eyes met, he'd suddenly become ab-

sorbed in the positioning of his napkin or the need to re-
fill his half-empty water glass.

The lump in Laura's throat grew until she couldn't
even pretend to eat any longer. She stood. "It's been a
long day. I think I'll go up to bed now."

Cal finally looked directly at her. "I'll be up in a minute," he said softly. "Okay?"

Laura nodded and fled the room. She felt farther away
from Cal than when she'd first arrived. She could deal
with his anger better than with this polite noncommuni-
cation.

Still pondering the problem, Laura entered her room.
Her eyes fell on a conspicuous patch of white in the middle of the pink bedspread. It was a shopping bag from the
Galleria dress store that she had visited earlier. Inside she
found a sheer black nightie. The accompanying note
read: "Here's one more little thing I'd like you to model
for me."

Laura smiled as she held the exotic outfit in her lap.
She vowed that tonight she would show him how much
she loved him. If she couldn't bring herself to risk the
words, then her body would speak for her. She'd make
him understand.

In a moment, she was pulling on a pair of tiny black
nylon panties. Then she drew the rest of the outfit over
her head. Gazing at her reflection in the mirror, she felt
her face go hot. The garment left almost nothing to the
imagination. Every detail of her body was visible through
the transparent material. Laura had stood naked in front
of Cal and felt no self-consciousness at all, but something about the blatantly provocative wisps of flimsy
cloth made her feel awkward and ill at ease.

She jumped as she heard the soft knocking at the door
that connected her room to Cal's. With a trembling hand
and a pounding heart, she turned the knob. Cal stood in

the doorway clad only in a pair of blue pajama bottoms, his muscular chest was bare.

She felt his eyes rove over her all-but-naked body, and the tips of her breasts rose and pushed against the sheet material as if he'd touched them with his fingers. Slowly he walked forward and took her in his arms, teasing her tongue with his own. Then his lips moved lower, and he drew nylon and nipple into his mouth together.

Laura quivered with desire as she felt his hands slip under the insubstantial panties and cup her bottom. She wiggled as he trailed his fingers over the soft skin covering those sensitive curves.

"Cal, that tickles," she giggled, squirming against him even more, the uncomfortable tension that had existed between them only moments before suddenly forgotten.

"What you're doing tickles me, too." Starting at the shadows where her buttocks joined her thighs, he slowly drew his fingernails up over her skin with a pressure that was firm enough to stimulate, but light enough to leave no marks.

Laura gasped and arched against him. "Stop it, Cal! You're driving me crazy!"

"Oh, no," he said with a grin, his voice playful. "I know your secret now."

Shifting his arms, he lifted her and carried her to the bed. She kicked her legs and squealed in a halfhearted protest as he rolled her onto her stomach, but he held her easily with one arm across her back. Using the same hand to draw the nylon panties up until they became a thin line resting in the valley between her buttocks, he continued to stimulate her, licking and sucking her skin, rubbing his mustache across it and nipping her gently. His other hand massaged the wet crevice between her thighs until she writhed under him.

"Cal," she pleaded breathlessly. "Let me up. I want to touch you, too."

"What will you give me?" he asked.

"Everything I have," Laura said, and meant it.

The pressure on her back lifted, and she turned over and lay still, trying to catch her breath. Her eyes met Cal's and her heart overflowed with her love for him. She felt the words of love poised on the tip of her tongue, but fear held them back. Instead she told him with her eyes. Raising her hand, she stroked the silky softness of his newly shaven cheek, and he bent down to brush her lips with a kiss as light as a falling feather. He whispered her name, and she dared to believe that she saw love in his eyes, too.

"Let me touch you, Cal," she breathed. "Be still and let me show you . . ."

Leaving the sentence unfinished she pressed her hand against his shoulder and moved with him as he rolled onto his back. Taking his hands, she folded them around the brass rods of the headboard.

"You're not allowed to move," she told him with a mischievous smile. "You're at my mercy now."

He looked up at her, not at all intimidated by his position. "I always have been," he told her softly. "You just never realized it."

"Cal . . ." Laura leaned forward to kiss him, and love soon transmuted into passion as she nibbled his lips, tracing them with her tongue.

His breath coming faster, he sought her breasts with his mouth, but Laura moved out of his reach, sitting upright astride his pajama-clad hips. Twining her fingers in the lush dark hair under his arms, she tugged on it gently as she moved slowly against the hard male flesh lightly imprisoned between her thighs.

"Enjoying yourself?" he asked.

"Umm." Laura leaned forward to explore the hollow in his throat with her tongue. "You're sweating," she murmured, tasting salt.

"Your fault," Cal told her, his eyes following her progress with interest as she lowered her head to the small brown nipples almost buried beneath dark chest hair.

Out of the corner of one eye, she saw Cal's hand move. Sitting up, she pushed it back to its original position. "I'm not finished yet," she told him with mock sternness.

He looked up at her through half-closed lids, his eyes dark with passion. "That's what I'm afraid of."

Her lips followed the swirling line of hair to his navel as her nails stroked down his sides from his underarms to his hips. He shifted under her as she explored the depression in his abdomen with her tongue, and his eyes followed her again as she moved even lower.

With her tongue, her mouth and her hands, Laura began to express all the love that she'd refused to put into words. She soon found that willingness, enthusiasm and a few helpful suggestions from Cal could adequately compensate for her lack of experience.

Laura's latent sensuality burst into full bloom as she listened to Cal's moans and his whispered endearments. She watched as his hands tightened on the bars of the headboard and the muscles in his arms flexed until she thought that he would surely bend the metal.

Unable to contain her rising excitement any longer, she sat up and reached over to get one of the little foil packets she'd found in the bag along with her new nightgown.

Cal watched her fumbling, a wry smile twisting his sweat-dewed features. "Can I move my hands now, ma'am?" he asked.

Laura returned his smile. "I think you'd better."

Together, his hands guiding hers, they accomplished their objective. ✓

"You'll know how next time," he told her, his eyes watching for the reaction in hers.

Joy flooded her like warm sunlight. Next time. At the moment, those seemed like the two most beautiful words in the English language.

She leaned forward to kiss him, and the repressed passion of their day together burst into new flame as she felt his body slowly merge with hers. She sat up, and he unfastened her nightgown, baring her breasts to his eager eyes. Wetting his fingertips in her mouth, he tantalized one and then the other until Laura felt her excitement spiraling out of control.

She bent to kiss his cheeks, his eyelids and finally, his full expressive lips, knowing that she had never loved him more than she did at this instant. Her body seemed to melt into his as he captured her breasts and his mouth sought out the hard, sweet tips.

Pushing herself up, she grabbed the headboard of the bed with both hands, moving her hips faster and faster, looking down into her lover's eyes through a mist of overwhelming ardor. She felt his fingers move down over her abdomen, tickling and probing, seeking out the most sensitive part of her body.

Wave after wave of rapture washed over her until she thought that she would faint from sheer pleasure. At the same time, she felt Cal thrusting under her as he reached the climax of passion. Each stroke lifted her higher and higher until a second crest swept her away.

When he at last grew still beneath her, she fell forward and lay, spent, against his heaving chest. She clung to him fiercely, drained and glowing with fulfillment. In that moment, she knew beyond a shadow of a doubt that she could never leave him again.

Chapter Seven

The next morning, Laura came downstairs to find Juanita scurrying around the kitchen like a crazy woman. "What's going on?" she asked as she poured herself a cup of fresh, hot coffee. "More preparations for the barbecue?"

Juanita laughed and shook her head. "Everyone has been preparing for that accursed barbecue for weeks and weeks. No, what I do now is different. I am making a birthday cake for the little one."

Laura looked at her in surprise. "You mean today is Melissa's birthday?"

"I thought that I had told you! Ay! I am getting to be a silly and forgetful old woman."

"You've been saying that for at least twenty years, Nita."

"*Si,* my darling. But now it is finally true!"

Laura gave the housekeeper an affectionate hug and began to help her with the birthday preparations. "Where's Cal this morning?" she asked after a moment, trying to sound casual.

Juanita looked at her with eyes that missed nothing. "He went to the airport an hour ago. He is flying to Dallas for an important meeting, and he will not be home until after dinner."

"But what about Melissa's birthday celebration?" Laura asked with a frown. "He's not going to be here for that?" Yesterday, she'd been sure that Cal was drawing closer to his daughter.

Juanita shrugged. "It is the same every year. He is particularly not going to be here because of that. When I reminded him this morning, he growled at me and said he would have his secretary go out and buy Melissa a gift."

Laura felt a deep pang of hurt and disappointment— on her own account as well as Melissa's. She had awakened this morning alone in her bed with only the nightgown to remind her of the intimacy of the night before. Cal hadn't even left her a note.

The housekeeper put an arm around Laura's shoulders. "He said to tell you 'good morning' for him."

Laura looked at the other woman sharply. "You're telling stories, Nita."

The old housekeeper raised her voice in uncharacteristic annoyance. "Well, he would have said so, if he had the sense of a goat!"

Laura giggled in spite of herself and pushed the sharp little feelings of betrayal and doubt aside. She'd have it out with Cal tonight. The invisible barrier stretching between them had to come down. When he finally got home, she'd tell him about the business trip with Steve.

She took a long, shuddering breath as she anticipated his reaction to that news. But first...first she'd tell him how she felt about him, how she'd loved him all these years, how she hadn't been able to forget him.

But what if he asked her not to go on the trip, to give up her promotion? Laura knew that she wanted to keep working in the business world though she didn't want it to be her entire existence. She wanted to have time for her art, for a home life and to have a family with Cal.

But if he didn't ask her to give up her job, could she still take the promotion knowing that she'd hardly ever get to see him? Or could she keep her job in New York instead and see him even less?

Similar thoughts continued to plague Laura at odd moments throughout the day, even though she tried her best to stay busy. Leaving Juanita to finish decorating the cake, she accompanied Melissa to the child's room to select an outfit for that evening's party. Somehow, Laura was appointed to help dress Melissa's multitude of dolls for the event, as well.

It was after lunch before she was able to slip away and begin putting the finishing touches on her portrait of Melissa. She'd decided to rush it through and give it to the little girl as a birthday present.

Behind the closed door of her bedroom, she worked steadily through the afternoon. She'd lost all track of time until she heard Juanita calling her from the hallway. Wiping a streak of paint from her arm, she moved to open the door. Juanita stood outside, almost hidden behind an armload of boxes.

"What on earth—" Laura exclaimed.

The housekeeper entered and set the packages down on the bed, chattering excitedly about how the parcels had just been delivered. Some of the boxes bore the label of

the women's clothing store in the Galleria that Cal and
Laura had been in the day before. The rest contained the
three suits and assorted items she had purchased in another shop.

Juanita clapped a hand to her forehead. "I almost
forgot the most important thing!" Pulling a large square
black velvet box from her apron pocket, she handed it
over to Laura.

Laura stared at the box for a moment before she
opened it. Inside was the diamond pendant that she had
admired, winking up at her from a bed of black satin.

"¡Que lindo!" Juanita exclaimed. "How lovely!"

Laura took a deep breath, certain that despite everything that had happened in the past Cal truly loved her.
"It's the most wonderful present anyone ever gave me,"
she whispered fervently.

All at once, she was looking forward to the night ahead
instead of dreading it.

The whole family was present for dinner that evening
with one conspicuous exception: Cal. Even Henry was
there, presiding over the table from his wheelchair, a
blanket covering his knees.

Laura let her fingers glide over the rough surface of the
pendant as it rested in the hip pocket of her old Levi's.
She wanted Cal to be the one to fasten the golden chain
around her neck. She wanted to hear him declare his love
openly once and for all. And if it wasn't love that he felt
for her, well, then she wanted to know that, too. Watching the clock nervously, she waited for him to arrive.

"Aren't you listening to me, Laura?"

She started in her chair. "I'm sorry, Henry. I'm afraid
I wasn't paying attention."

The old man looked at her reproachfully. "I was saying that I'm glad you don't get all gussied up just to come down to the dinner table. It was a damned fool practice that sister of yours started. I never saw a woman with more clothes than that one. Even Ellie doesn't have that many."

"Oh, Daddy," the girl exclaimed, her drawl creeping back, "when are you gonna stop pickin' on me?"

"When you learn some sense!" the old man told her.

Choosing that moment to dim the lights, Juanita carried in the double chocolate cake with its six bright candles.

"Make a wish, sweetie," Delphine urged after everyone sang "Happy Birthday."

Melissa squeezed her lids shut, and her lips moved silently. Then, opening her eyes, she blew out all the candles to great applause.

Delphine gave the child a large, beautifully wrapped package that contained a lacquered music box. Opening the cover, Melissa revealed a miniature cowgirl twirling to the accompaniment of winking lights and the strains of "The Yellow Rose of Texas." She laughed, clapping her hands in delight.

Juanita planted a huge kiss on Melissa's cheek, then handed her an embroidered, ruffled dress that she'd made for the upcoming barbecue.

"Thank you, Juanita," Melissa said very formally. Then she broke down and gave the housekeeper a hug.

Next it was Laura's turn, and she nervously unveiled the portrait for all to see. There were gasps of admiration as all eyes turned to the vision of the beautiful child dressed in white sitting in the grass holding a lapful of daisies. The sunlight sparkled in her hair, turning it to spun gold, and her eyes were as blue and deep as the waters of the pool behind her.

"Frank!" Henry called with new vigor in his voice.

The old cowboy was at the other man's side almost immediately. "What is it, Henry?"

"Get one of those useless lugs who call themselves cowboys to dig that old frame out of the storeroom, the one that used to hang over the mantel."

Frank hesitated. "What about the picture that's already in it?"

Slapping his hand down on the arm of his wheelchair, Henry growled at his old friend. "I want the frame, just the frame! We're all steppin' outside for a little while, and I want this fine portrait of my granddaughter hanging up over yonder when I get back. Understand?"

Muttering to himself discontentedly, Frank stalked out of the room.

Melissa was standing in front of her portrait, entranced. "Do I really look like that?" she whispered to Laura.

"That's only a painting, Melissa," Laura told her. "You're much, much prettier than that piece of canvas could ever be. And you're nice, and smart, too. Those things don't show in the portrait, but they're more important than being pretty."

There was a pounding on the table that reverberated throughout the room, and everyone turned to face Henry. "We're all going outside now," he declared, gesturing for Juanita to take charge of his wheelchair. "I want to give Melissa my present."

The patriarch led the way out onto the back porch with the others trailing in his wake. In the yard below them stood a young wrangler holding the bridle of a black Shetland pony.

Melissa screamed in glee and ran for the steps. "Hold on, young lady!" Henry exclaimed, grabbing her arm as she flew past. "I want a kiss."

Flinging her arms around her grandfather's neck, Melissa hugged him with all her might. "Oh, thank you, Granddaddy!"

Then she was off down the steps. The wrangler tipped his hat with a grin and helped the little girl up into the red, custom-made saddle.

"Lead her around for a while, boy!" Henry ordered.

They were still on the porch when Cal's car drove up. Swinging into the driveway, he climbed out of the beige Mercedes dressed in a gray business suit that matched the color of his eyes. He carried a briefcase stuffed with papers, wearing a pensive, strangely melancholy expression on his handsome face.

Scrambling down from her pony, Melissa ran to her father expectantly, her reserve forgotten in the excitement of the evening. "Daddy! Daddy!" she called. "What did you get me for my birthday?"

Cal stood stock-still and stared at the little girl in surprise. Melissa came to a halt a few feet in front of her father, gazing up at him in innocent anticipation.

With a sinking heart, Laura realized that Cal had totally forgotten about Melissa's birthday present. She hurried down the steps trying to think of something, anything, that would soften the blow and preserve the fragile bond that had been developing between this man and his child. Suddenly she felt the hardness of the diamond pendant at her hip, and she remembered the gaze of adoration Melissa had directed at the jewelry store window.

Without stopping to think of the consequences, she pulled the trinket from her pocket. "Your daddy gave me this gift to give to you because he didn't think he'd be home in time for your party.''

With a wrench of her heart, she placed the delicate chain around the child's neck and fastened it securely.

Melissa gasped in delight. "Oh, Daddy, it's just what I wished for when I blew out the candles!''

But Cal wasn't looking at his daughter. He was staring at Laura, the expression in his eyes as raw as an open wound. He remembered how seven years before, he'd offered her another piece of jewelry—his mother's ring. She'd refused that ring and with it his love. And now he saw that same scene being reenacted; Laura was giving his diamond heart away as if it meant nothing to her, as if he meant nothing to her. Cal had been half expecting something like this, but that didn't lessen the familiar, bitter sting of betrayal he felt. Without even realizing it, he'd begun to trust her, to believe that she wanted more from him than just a good time in bed. Now his anger and his pain was so strong, so deep, that the intensity of his own emotions frightened him. He had only one thought: to reach the shelter of his room before he lost all control.

Laura felt her heart shrivel as the man she loved passed by her and went up the back steps two at a time. She hurried after him, past the frowning Henry and the smirking Delphine, only to bump squarely into his back as he came to a sudden halt in the living room. When Laura recovered her balance, she saw that he was staring at the newly hung portrait of Melissa. Then his eyes traveled to the other older painting that stood propped up against the couch. It was Laura's portrait of Eve.

Numbly she looked from one canvas to the other. Feature for feature, the two faces were identical, even to the tilt of the chin and the expression in the eyes.

Cal dropped his briefcase and strode over to Eve's portrait. With an oath, he flung it into the fireplace. Then he stood watching the flames consume the lovely face until nothing was left but black ash.

Laura approached him hesitantly. "Cal, I didn't realize . . . not until just now when I saw the two of them together."

He turned to look at her, his expression so filled with hatred that Laura quickly took a step backward. "It's as if she had never died!" Cal grated out the words. "Every time I look at the child's face, I can't help but see the evil witch who was her mother."

"That's not Melissa's fault, Cal! She's just a sweet, innocent child."

Cal's mouth curved in an ugly sneer. "Just like you, Laurie? All sweetness and love and innocence. Like what you did to me tonight, for example?"

Swallowing hard, Laura spoke quickly, trying to explain, wanting desperately for things to be right between them again. "I know it was wrong to give your gift away, Cal, but I didn't stop to think about that. It meant so much to Melissa—not because of what it is, but because she thinks her daddy picked it out for her."

Cal's voice was cold. "Don't even bother with some made-up explanation, Laurie. I've known enough lying, deceitful women to last me a lifetime. The truth is you thought I was trying to fence you in again, to interfere with your precious career, and giving away the necklace was your way of telling me to back off."

"I wasn't even thinking about my career—"

"Maybe that explains why you didn't bother to tell me about the little 'business trip' you're going on with Randall tomorrow. My sister was kind enough to enlighten me on that score this morning. I guess that saves you the trouble of leaving me a note—if you were even going to do that!''

Laura's face paled. ''Do you really believe that I'm going away in order to sleep with Steve? Do you really believe that I gave that necklace to Melissa to show you that I don't care about you?''

Cal took a deep breath and exhaled it slowly. When he finally answered her, all the anger had faded from his voice. He sounded unbearably weary. ''I don't know what to believe, Laurie. I only know that I can't cope with this situation. I don't want to cope with it. I lived in a self-made purgatory for too many years. I barely survived the climb out of it, and I'm not going to go back for anyone. Not even you.''

''Cal—'' Laura began, but he went right on talking as if he hadn't heard her.

''I tried to tell you the other day that I don't know anything about trust or love anymore. I tried to warn you, but you wouldn't listen. Now you can deal with the consequences.''

He turned away from her and headed toward the stairs. When he'd tried to leave her in the glade, she'd been enraged because he hadn't given her a chance to try to make him love her again. Now she'd had her chance, and she'd failed. She'd failed because he simply wasn't ready to love anyone.

She wanted to shake him, to make him realize how much he was hurting her and how much he was hurting himself in the process. Instead of doing it physically, she tried to do it with words.

''So you're finally going to let Eve win. You're going to let what she did to you destroy our relationship the way you've let her destroy the relationship you could have had with Melissa.''

Cal turned back toward her. His voice was quiet, but his words sliced to the center of her heart. "Our relationship? You mean what we had in bed together? That's the only place we ever had a relationship, Laurie."

A searing tide of anger swept through Laura. She struck out and felt the solid impact of her blow travel from her fingertips to her shoulder as the palm of her hand cracked against Cal's cheek.

"You're not the man I loved!" she cried accusingly. "You're cruel and vicious—so filled with hate that there's no room in you for love anymore. You killed the man I used to love, then you buried him under self-pity and fear and bitterness!"

The red imprint left by Laura's fingers provided the only trace of color in Cal's face as he stared at her without a hint of emotion. "You're wrong, Laurie. I may have buried him, but you killed him. On a cold winter morning seven years ago."

Shaken to the bone, Laura watched as Cal bounded up the stairs to his room. Hot tears rose to her eyes and cascaded down her contorted cheeks. It wasn't fair! she told herself. Everything had been so good, so right. Just when she'd thought there was a chance for them... But if what he'd just said was true, then really there had been no chance at all.

Laura stood motionless for what seemed like an eternity, replaying Cal's awful words in her head. Then she realized that she wasn't alone. Turning, she met the unreadable eyes of Steve Randall.

All at once, she was certain that he'd been a witness to the whole hideous confrontation. Shame burned her like a red-hot iron. She hated Cal for exposing her like this, for turning her strength to weakness, her confidence to doubt, for making a man who had respected her see her as an object of pity.

"Are you going with me tomorrow?" he asked softly.

"Yes," she heard herself respond, as if the rest of her life still had meaning. "Yes, of course I'm going."

Steve nodded once and then walked back outside.

Suddenly Melissa came out of nowhere and threw all the weight of her small body against Laura's, wrapping both arms tightly around the woman's slender waist.

"Don't cry, Laura! Come back to my birthday party. I'll let you ride my pony."

Gazing down into the little girl's dancing eyes, Laura found balm for her ravaged heart. She brushed the remaining tears from her cheeks and tried to put all thoughts of the moody, vengeful Mr. Cal Sinclair aside. Cupping Melissa's upturned face in both her hands, she planted a kiss on the child's golden hair.

"Now how could anyone refuse an invitation like that?"

Chapter Eight

We do have a plane to catch, you know.''

Hunched over her morning coffee and a steaming bowl of oatmeal that Juanita had foisted on her, Laura looked up at Steve with red-rimmed eyes. Her head throbbed dully from an almost sleepless night, and she was in no mood to be hurried by anyone.

''I'll be ready in twenty minutes, Steve. I just have to put my suit on and do my makeup. Now please let me drink my coffee.''

Self-consciously, she wrapped the terry cloth robe Juanita had lent her tightly about her. She felt old, unattractive, and emotionally bankrupt. She had no idea how she was going to get through breakfast, let alone the trip with Steve.

Then Delphine came into the kitchen and made her misery complete. ''What? Not ready for your 'business trip'?''

Laura sighed. Delphine had told Cal about the trip and exacted her pound of flesh, but apparently she still wasn't satisfied. By rights Laura should have been furious with her, but she didn't feel anything at all. Nothing seemed to matter.

"If I had a choice," Laura said, her voice barely above a whisper, "I wouldn't be going. But it happens to be part of my job. As far as I'm concerned, you're welcome to come along with us as a chaperon."

"That won't be necessary," Steve interjected. He took Delphine by the shoulders and turned her to face him. "Now I thought we'd settled all this. So far I think that I've been very patient with these childish tantrums of yours, but you have to get used to the idea that I'm a businessman. I have to travel extensively, sometimes with Laura. If you can't accept that, then maybe we should call off the wedding."

Steve's velvet-smooth voice only made the threat hidden behind his soft words more potent. The angry color left Delphine's cheeks. Her gray eyes widened, and her lips began to tremble. Suddenly Laura didn't see the sophisticated, well-dressed woman who stood before her. Instead she saw the chubby, lonely, ugly duckling that Delphine had been as a child.

Don't let him do this to you! Laura wanted to yell. She knew that above all else Steve respected strength. The way that he was using Delphine made her feel ill. But then hadn't she been just as weak as Delphine? She'd let Cal violate her self-respect repeatedly, and all she'd gotten out of it was temporary physical satisfaction. He'd made her miserable everywhere but in bed. Maybe he'd been right when he'd said that their only real relationship was a physical one.

Laura left her coffee on the table and slipped quietly from the kitchen. On her way upstairs, she glanced at the closed door of Cal's room. Her lip curled in contempt. He was sitting in there, waiting for her to leave. The Cal Sinclair she'd known seven years ago had had his share of faults, but cowardice wasn't one of them. Now he didn't even have the backbone to face her.

Simmering with resentment, she burst into her own room, interrupting Juanita in the process of making the bed.

The housekeeper examined Laura's face questioningly. "What new calamity has occurred, my precious one? Is it Mr. Cal?"

Laura began to pace back and forth, her expression intense. "I'm sure you overheard what happened last night—I'm sure everyone did. He called it quits between us, and now he's holed up in his room, waiting for me to go away."

"You were getting too close to him, and that frightened him very much," Juanita began. "He is so afraid to love again."

"I don't care what his reasons are anymore, Nita! I'm sick of going half crazy playing 'he loves me, he loves me not.' I'm sick of pushing one step forward only to get shoved two steps back. The bottom line is I can't love him unless he wants to be loved. And after last night, I'm not sure what I feel for him."

"It is so difficult for him. He has lost so much in the name of love that he does not believe he can ever win again."

"And I can't make him believe it. That's something he's got to do for himself." She paused, savagely twisting the tie on her robe. "I should have left when he first told me to go."

Juanita held out her hands beseechingly. "Laurita—"

"No! It's over, Nita. It was his decision, not mine, but I've got to learn to live with it. Help me do that, please." She ran a hand through her hair distractedly. "I have to hurry now. Steve's waiting for me."

The housekeeper sighed and pulled the satin quilt up to cover the pillows. "I hope that you are not going to do anything that you will regret later."

Laura's impatience reached an apex. "If you don't mind," she said coolly, "I think that I'm old enough to make my own decisions."

Her face stiffening, the old woman moved toward the door. "You are right, of course."

A wave of remorse washed over Laura, and she reached out to touch Juanita's arm. "I'm sorry," she said sincerely. "I'm so upset right now. I want to get away for a while. I have to!"

The housekeeper nodded, patting Laura's hand with a smile. "I will get you a garment bag for your pretty new clothes."

A few minutes later, Laura was packing her underwear and accessories. Deciding to wear a charcoal-gray suit and a pale, peach-colored blouse, she zipped the other two suits she'd bought into the garment bag. She was on her way back to the world she belonged in. Before she was finished, she'd make the Sinclair fortune look like small change. She'd show that damned cowboy that there was life after Cal Sinclair!

She dressed and rushed through her makeup, applying concealer to mask the dark smudges under her eyes and using the curling iron to shape her hair into long, smooth curves that formed a flattering frame for her face. Staring into the mirror, she decided that she liked what she saw. The single-breasted jacket and the long, straight skirt she wore emphasized her slim figure without frills or fuss. This was the Laura Wright she knew—successful, assertive, with self-respect to spare.

She didn't falter until she descended the stairs. In her mind, she pictured Cal standing in his usual position by the fireplace. She imagined how he'd turn and look up at her. His eyes would glow with pride as they swept over her from head to toe and back again.

"You look great, Laurie!" he'd say. "Have fun on your trip, and be sure to call me tonight. I'll be counting the minutes until you come home."

In reality, the living room was empty. The man secluded in his bedroom was a stranger to her, a stranger who'd be relieved if she never came back again.

"I'll have fun all right," Laura said aloud, biting off each word. "With someone who'll be glad to have the pleasure of my company."

She ran to the front door, wanting only to get out of the house as fast as possible. But as she reached for the knob, it swung toward her and Steve stepped inside.

"I'm glad to see you're ready, Laura. The car's out front. I have to get my suitcase from my room. If you want to leave those things, I'll take them out when I come back down."

Laura forced a smile, grateful for his consideration and for his tact in avoiding any mention of her obvious lack of composure. "Thank you for offering, Steve. I can manage."

Laura went outside, closing the front door firmly behind her. She stowed her bags in the open trunk of Steve's rented car and walked around to sit in the passenger seat.

As she waited, she remembered a similar day seven years before. She was leaving Cal again, this time for good. Oh, she'd be coming back to the ranch, but not to

Cal. It was time to move on, time to pick up the pieces and look to the future.

She massaged her temples, praying that her headache would go away. What on earth was taking Steve so long? She glanced at her watch. They were going to miss their plane. All at once, she had a horrible thought. What if Cal had come downstairs to confront Steve? It seemed unlikely after the things he'd said, but . . .

Just as she was about to go back into the house to find out what was happening, the door opened and Steve came hurrying to the car. After placing his suitcase in the trunk, he got in beside her and started the engine.

"Is everything all right?" Laura asked anxiously.

Steve gave her a questioning look. "What do you mean?"

"Nothing," Laura muttered. She leaned back in her seat feeling foolish and more than a little disappointed.

As they left the driveway, she looked up at the window of Cal's room. For a moment she thought she saw a flicker of movement behind the curtain, as if someone were watching her from above. Then she ascribed it to more wishful thinking and a chance gust of wind.

"This, as you've probably guessed, is called Alamo Plaza," Laura told Steve with a smile.

Her mood had greatly improved. She'd managed to sleep on the plane and, by the time she's awakened in San Antonio, her headache had completely disappeared. They'd rented a car at the airport and driven directly to the new hotel. They'd ordered lunch in and had a long, productive meeting with the manager. Laura had been impressed with the man and the way he ran his establishment. Even though it was in the same construction chaos as the International Inn she'd visited in Houston, she could clearly see its potential. When Steve had introduced her as the new district manager, she hadn't bothered to protest.

Now Steve had slowed to a stop at a red light in front of the Alamo Plaza. The small stone chapel with its distinctive arched top was visible nearby, its double wooden doors positioned between four inset columns. The red-white-and-blue Lone Star flag of Texas flew above the Alamo, its material rippling in the breeze.

Laura's thoughts drifted back to the time when Henry had brought her, Eve and Cal to this spot. He'd told them all about the Texans' battle for independence and about the Mexican side, too. He'd really made Bowie and Crockett, Travis and Santa Anna, come alive for them.

Determinedly blocking out the memories of Cal that threatened to overwhelm her, Laura settled back, casually noting the white, high-rise hotel looming directly ahead of them on Alamo Street. She frowned when Steve pulled up at the entrance.

"What are we doing here?" she asked, puzzled.

"This is where we're spending the night," Steve told her matter-of-factly. "Our flights to Austin and Dallas aren't until tomorrow, and our own hotel certainly isn't ready for guests yet."

Laura opened her mouth to object and then shut it again. What was there to say? She'd expected to stay overnight somewhere. The company was picking up the tab, so why not choose the best?

Waiting quietly in the sumptuous lobby while Steve checked in, Laura began to feel ill at ease. She'd traveled with Steve before, but somehow this time it was different. They usually stayed at International Inns, where their conduct came under the scrutiny of dozens of fellow company employees. Here she felt vulnerable.

At last Steve approached, followed closely by a suit-case-toting bellman. Laura's feelings of apprehension increased in direct proportion to the number of floors traveled as the elevator carried them to their destination.

"May I have the pleasure of the new district manager's company for dinner?" Steve asked as they followed the bellman down the hallway that led to their adjoining rooms.

Laura shook her head. "I'm kind of tired, Steve. I think I'll beg off tonight."

"You're still mad at me because I didn't tell you I was getting married—"

"Steve!" The last thing Laura wanted was to open that subject again, especially within earshot of a third party.

"I apologize, Laura. I'll even get down on my knees if you insist. Now come on, let's be friends again."

Laura hesitated, trying to hold on to her resentment, but it was rapidly disintegrating in the face of Steve's charm.

"Truce?" he asked hopefully as the bellman unlocked the door to his room.

"Truce," Laura agreed with a resigned sigh.

"Great! I made dinner reservations for eight o'clock. Let's meet in my room at seven-thirty."

As she undressed, Laura began to wonder just what she had let herself in for. Then she decided that spending the evening listening to Steve talk about his relationship with Delphine was preferable to sitting in a lonely hotel room brooding over Cal.

She showered and then pulled on a white blouse and one of the suits she'd bought at the Galleria. The jacket was double-breasted and multihued, with subdued tones of jade, royal-blue and black. The skirt was slim and jet-black and fell well below her knees.

When she was ready Laura knocked hesitantly on the adjoining door. It swung open to reveal Steve, who was wearing a perfectly tailored blue suit with a matching silk tie. He gave her a low whistle of appreciation. "You are magnificent."

Laura laughed self-consciously, more pleased than she'd ever admit. For once Steve's flattery was just what she needed.

"You're not so bad yourself," she told him, quickly maneuvering him out the door before things could get more personal.

With a glint of amusement in his eye, Steve allowed himself to be led.

They had dinner five hundred and fifty feet above street level in the Tower of the Americas Restaurant. Steve ordered the wine, and they drank, ate and talked about the new hotels, pausing often to watch the lights of the Alamo City slide past as the restaurant slowly revolved. Laura felt completely at ease in his company, and she enjoyed herself thoroughly.

When they were done, they walked back to the hotel at a leisurely pace. Steve pointed out constellations in the clear, dark sky.

"Why, Steve," Laura said teasingly. "I didn't think you'd spare the time for a glance up, let alone take the trouble to actually watch what goes on there."

He gave her an uncharacteristically self-conscious smile. "When I was a kid, I spent a lot of time looking up at the night sky. I always wanted to fly up there and get away..."

His voice trailed off without explanation, but Laura sensed that he was thinking of the poverty and misery of his childhood. For some reason, his remark made her feel closer to him than she ever had before.

"Steve," she began impulsively, "can I ask you a provocative question?"

"They're my favorite kind."

"You've been trying to get me into bed for years, but you've never once mentioned marriage. Aren't I wife material?"

"You'd make the worst possible wife!"

Laura stared at him reproachfully, perplexed and a little hurt.

"Oh, come on, don't look like that," he said as they crossed the hotel lobby and entered the waiting elevator. "It's nothing personal. It's just that you have your own career, your own responsibilities. Where would you find the time to play a supporting role for me when you're center stage yourself twelve hours a day?" He shook his head decisively. "I want you as one of my executives. And ... the position of mistress is still open."

Laura was intrigued despite herself. "But once you're married, why would you need the liability of a mistress? And, why me?"

His gaze met hers as they left the elevator and walked toward their rooms. "I find you attractive in a physical sense, but, more than that, I think you're the first woman—the first person—I've ever been able to be totally honest with. You know exactly who and what I am, but instead of being repelled, you're ... dare I say, fascinated?"

Laura smiled in grudging acknowledgement. "Well, to tell you the truth, sometimes it's a close call."

They had reached the door of Laura's room, and she began to fumble in her purse for the key. Steve put his hand on her arm, and she raised her eyes to his automatically.

"Stay with me tonight, Laura."

At that instant Laura knew, despite everything, she still loved Cal. With all the good reasons she had for saying no to Steve, Cal was the first she thought of.

Steve read her answer and the reason for it in her eyes. He took her by the shoulders and shook her gently, as if she were a misguided but beloved child. "You and Sinclair are wrong for each other, Laura. You may love him, and he may love you, but you spend all your time pulling in different directions because neither of you is willing to give an inch. You'd never be happy together. You and I, we're going in the same direction. Your career goals fit right in with my plans."

"A career's not enough for me anymore, Steve," Laura said, determined that he understand her reasoning. "I'm changing. It started before I came back to Texas, before I even saw Cal again. I've proved that I can make it in business and be a success, but I don't want it or need it the way I used to. The trouble is, I don't seem to be very good at getting what I do want. You said that Cal loved me. I only wish that were true."

"You love him very much, don't you?" Steve asked, stroking her hair gently.

It was the first time he'd touched her as a friend instead of as part of a seduction ploy. She looked down to hide her surprise. "You know I do."

Steve pulled his hand away and stared at the plush carpet. "I wasn't going to tell you this, but... remember this morning when it took so long for me to get back to the car with my suitcase? Well, Sinclair was the reason. He came out of his room especially to talk to me. He threatened to remove certain parts of my anatomy if I, and I quote, 'took advantage' of you.''

Laura almost forgot to breathe. "Cal said that to you? This morning?"

"Yes. Can you believe it? I told him that as far as I was concerned, he was the one who had taken advantage of you."

"What did he say to that?" Laura asked softly.

"What could he say? He just glared at me in that charming way of his. Then he changed tactics and offered me a very lucrative investment deal—"

"That you turned down?"

Steve straightened his tie with a negligent shrug. "I do have my pride. Besides, if I had taken him up on the deal, I'd have been admitting that my intentions toward you were less than honorable. And let's face it, I am marrying the man's sister on Sunday."

"Of course," Laura commented. "You do have to keep up appearances."

If Cal had cared enough to say what he had to Steve, then she was sure she could eventually convince him to take another chance on their relationship.

As if from somewhere far away, she heard Steve talking again. "I'm going to get some sleep. We have an early plane to catch and a long day ahead of us tomorrow. We'll be flying to Austin, then Dallas, and back to Houston."

"Steve, wait," Laura cried, coming out of her trance as he moved to unlock his door. "Thank you for telling me about Cal, and I'm sorry if I . . . disappointed you tonight."

Steve smiled. "You have done many things to me, Laura Wright, but you have never once disappointed me.

Good night. And good luck with Sinclair. Something tells me you're going to need it.''

Laura let herself into her own room and sank down on the bed, a little stunned by the genuine affection she'd felt radiating from her boss. Imagine Steve, of all people, trying to convince her that Cal loved her! It seemed that everyone kept telling her that—everyone except Cal himself.

But she hadn't said ''I love you'' to him, either. Would that have made any difference? Suddenly she couldn't wait to tell Cal how she felt. Earning back his trust might take months or even years, but she intended to make that investment. He was the only man she wanted, now and forever. When she got back to the ranch, she'd tell him that in no uncertain terms. Eventually, no matter how long it took, Cal Sinclair was going to love her again.

Chapter Nine

It looks like we're in for a real downpour," Steve said, squinting at the black clouds massed in the sky.

Laura took the garment bag and overnight case that he handed to her. "You're right about that. You'd better put the car in the garage. I'll see you inside."

Turning, she ran into the house, hoping that Cal was home. But as she entered the living room, she knew from the tense, anxious look on Juanita's face that something was desperately wrong. "Tell me what happened," Laura demanded apprehensively. "Tell me everything."

"There is little to tell, Laurita. Mr. Cal was in a black mood after you left yesterday. He rumbled around the house like an angry tiger until late afternoon. Then he had me pack some food for him. He took a bottle of tequila from the bar and went outside. Frank saw him ride out on Dancer with a canteen and a bedroll, but he does not know to what destination."

Laura breathed a sigh of relief. "If he took a bedroll, it means he was planning to camp out for the night. I'm sure he's all right, though that bottle of tequila does have me worried."

"But his secretary called early this morning. Mr. Cal missed an important meeting today, and that is not like him. The men have been combing every inch of the ranch for hours without finding any trace of the *señor*. And the weather! The men say that there will be a bad, bad storm."

"I'll bet there's one place they didn't look," Laura said.

"Tell me where, and I will send someone immediately."

"No," Laura told the other woman, "I'll go. There's something I have to get straight with Cal. Now's as good a time as any."

Out in the stable, she saddled Taffy, the gentle buckskin she'd been riding since her arrival. Setting her feet in the stirrups, she guided the horse toward a rocky outcrop visible in the far distance.

It was nearly nightfall when she reached her destination, and the gathering storm seemed ready to break at any moment. Gazing up at the rough face of the low cliff, Laura remembered long-gone days.

As children, she and Cal had explored all the caves here, searching for buried treasure, acting out stories of ancient Indians and pirate raids. The cliff had also been a refuge, a hiding place to flee to when pressures built up at home or school. She had even sworn a blood oath with Cal that neither would ever relate their adventures to any outsider. To Laura's knowledge, she and Cal were still the only two people who knew the caves existed.

Dismounting she sought the beginning of the steep path that led to the first cave. She climbed slowly and carefully in the gusting wind, fully aware that one misstep could mean a broken leg or worse.

At last she reached the hidden entrance to the dark, rocky chamber. Breathing heavily, she turned to look out over the valley below. Towering storm clouds cloaked the setting sun. Lightning sliced across the dusky sky, and rolling thunder seemed to vibrate the very rock beneath her feet. As she watched from the shelter of the cave's mouth, the outside world disappeared behind a solid curtain of rain.

The sound of a striking match caused her to whirl around, and she saw a light flickering in the darkness behind her.

Cal had thought he'd made the right decision when he'd let Laura leave. He'd thought that all his pain and confusion would depart with her. Instead his jealousy, anger and frustration had built to a fever pitch. Like a wounded animal, he'd retreated to the cave to hide himself from the rest of the world. But he hadn't been able to find refuge from the relentless torment of his own thoughts.

For hours he'd sat in the pitch-dark cave and imagined Laura lying in Randall's arms. He could almost hear her mocking laughter, and his own rage threatened to choke him. Now, just when he'd convinced himself that he'd never see Laura again, she was standing before him like a vision from a dream. He smiled ruefully. Even though she'd come back this time, in a day, a week, a month, she'd disappear again; she was just as insubstantial as any dream. Why did she have to keep torturing him like this? Why couldn't she just leave him for good and get it over with?

He lowered the glass chimney on the kerosene lantern and carefully blew out the match. "I came here to be alone, Laurie," he said, his voice sounding strained as he fought to hold his overtaxed emotions in check. "Why can't you respect that?"

Laura walked forward into the cave, squinting at Cal in the dim light. He was sitting cross-legged on the floor, his handsome face covered by black stubble, the dark half circles under his eyes only emphasizing their grayness. Then Laura noticed the half-empty bottle of tequila standing on the floor of the cave by his side. "You shouldn't be drinking all by yourself up here, Cal. It's dangerous."

Lifting the bottle to his lips, Cal took a long, deliberate swig. "Just what makes my actions any of your damned business?"

Here was the opening Laura had been looking for, but Cal's hostile glare seemed to freeze her declaration of love before it could reach her lips. "I . . . care about what happens to you," she said awkwardly. The hesitant words failed to convince even her.

The sound of Cal's dry chuckle bounced off the cave walls. "Sure you do, Laurie. In your own way. But a man can't trust your brand of caring. At the first sign of trouble you take the easy way out, tuck tail and run."

Laura tried to hold on to her patience. "I didn't 'run' anywhere, Cal. Not this time—not even after you said all those horrible things to me. I just went on an overnight business trip."

"Oh, yeah. The innocent little business trip," Cal said sarcastically. "If everything was so innocent, why didn't you tell me about the trip to begin with?"

"I was going to," Laura asserted. "But Delphine beat me to it."

"Don't make me laugh! As sure as I'm breathing, Randall left my house intending to take you to bed. What went wrong, Laurie? Weren't you good enough to make that two-faced bastard give up my sister's money?"

Laura flinched, hurt and angered by the ugliness of his insinuation. "I went to a lot of trouble to get up here, Cal, because I wanted to talk to you. But you're a worse listener drunk than you are sober." Turning away abruptly, she walked back toward the cave entrance.

The condescending tone of Laura's voice only stoked Cal's temper. She'd given away his necklace, slapped his face and then gone gallivanting across half of Texas with his sister's fiancé in tow. Now *she* felt insulted because he dared to question her motives. He was flayed and bleeding, and there she stood—cold, remote, untouched by the pain he felt. Suddenly he needed to wipe that holier-than-thou look off her face, to make her hurt the way he was hurting, want the way he was wanting.

Getting to his feet, he started after her, his face almost sinister in the lantern light. "What's the matter, Laurie? Does the truth hurt? Or maybe I have it backward. Maybe Randall wasn't enough of a man to satisfy you, and you need me to finish the job."

Laura whirled around with a sharp cry of outrage. "You disgusting, conceited—"

Cal dragged her into his arms, firmly wedging his hard body against hers. "That's what you want from me, Laurie. That's all you've ever wanted. Why don't you save us both a lot of trouble and just admit it?"

"Let me go!" Laura demanded, her voice shaking with helpless rage.

"Not yet," Cal told her huskily, his breath warm against her cheek. "Not until I make you forget that Steve Randall was ever born." His lips traced the pulsing curve of her throat down into the cleavage showing above her blouse, and despite her resolve Laura's breathing quickened.

"Please don't," she pleaded, fully realizing for the first time that her feelings for Cal put her completely at his mercy. She didn't want it to be like this. She wanted him to take her in love, not in anger. But her body was a wanton traitor that refused to obey her will.

Ignoring her feeble protest, Cal swung her off her feet and carried her to his soft, down-filled sleeping bag. The pearlized snaps of her blouse opened one after the other with loud pops. It took him only a second more to unhook the clasp that held the front of her bra together. Then her full breasts fell free, exposed to the cool air of the cave. Cal lowered his head to savor their sweetness.

Laura made an effort not to react to his caresses by trying to hold on to the anger she had felt at first, but it was no use. Her passion caught and flared like dry tinder, her response to this man as natural and inevitable as the rising of the sun. When he began to remove the rest of her clothing, she lifted her hips to help him.

"I see your attitude has changed a little bit," Cal commented, his hands doing things that made her tremble with longing. "Tell me this doesn't feel good, Laurie. Tell me you want me to stop."

He reached over to retrieve the tequila, and Laura's heart pounded with a savage excitement she had never known before as he tilted the bottle and the liquor spilled downward in a shining arc. The amber-colored liquid splashed across her breasts, and she turned her face away to avoid the splattering droplets. Then Cal's tongue was chasing the rivulets of fiery fluid over the silky surface of her quivering skin, his new beard just rough enough to deliciously stimulate every nerve ending.

Laura's eyes closed and her breath came in short gasps as the remainder of the tequila flowed along her stomach and down between her thighs. Cal's tongue swirled around her navel, probing, teasing, spiraling farther and farther downward.

Just as she was approaching the point of no return, he suddenly drew away. Laura bit her lip in frustration and tried to hold back a groan.

Cal's face hovered above hers as unreal as an image in a dream. "Don't stop," she heard herself whispering.

"What do you want, Laurie?" he persisted. "Tell me what you want."

"I want you to love me, Cal," she said softly, her heart in her eyes. "Just love me..."

He stared down at her, and for a moment she thought that he was going to take her into his arms and kiss her. Then his expression hardened,

"I'll love you," he said fiercely.

Pushing her legs apart, he knelt between them. She gasped as he entered her with a single hard thrust. Then his body was slamming into hers with a jarring force that drove her almost insane with passion while his hand moved upward to tease her nipples and then downward again to rub the hard button pulsating between her legs. Laura moaned as a thousand fireworks went off inside her head, and her body seemed to explode like a star gone nova.

"That was one for you, Laurie," Cal murmured, his hot breath tickling her ear. "Want me to stop now?'"

"I...I never want you to stop," she told him shamelessly, almost sobbing with need for him, with love that refused to be denied.

"I'm glad you feel that way, sweet, 'cause tonight I'm going to go for the world's record."

Chapter Ten

The sun shining through the entrance of the cave woke Laura, and she blinked in the early-morning brightness. She sat up stiffly, flinging aside the thick flap of the sleeping bag that had been drawn up to cover her nakedness, aching in a dozen different places as a result of a night spent on a hard rock floor. Glancing about, she discovered that she was alone.

Laura buried her face in her hands and let shame and despair have their way with her. She had been a fool last night, a weak fool; Cal had believed that she was an easy mark, and she certainly hadn't done anything to undermine that opinion. She blushed as she remembered the things he'd done to her, the way he'd used her.

Last night, Cal had employed every bit of erotic knowledge and all the sensual talent he possessed to arouse her, to repeatedly bring her to peak after peak of satisfaction. Through it all, he had remained totally separate from her, giving nothing of himself, even when their bodies were joined in the most intimate way possible. Over and over again, he had proved relentlessly, unmistakably, that he could manipulate her feelings at will, while she had no power to touch him at all. In the end, she had turned from him in despair, begging him to go away and leave her alone.

Now, in the cold light of morning, Laura felt a chill wave of hopelessness wash over her. And then the anger came. It grew until she shook with its force. Cal had done the one thing that she could never forgive—he had taken her dream, the memory of gentleness and love that she had held like a sacred flame within her heart throughout their years of separation, and he had trampled it in the dirt. Now all she had left was harsh, uncompromising reality. He had finally forced her to face the truth; she meant nothing to Cal Sinclair, absolutely nothing at all.

By sheer willpower, she stood and pulled on her clothes. Packing up Cal's bedroll, she extinguished the old lantern and began the long descent to the valley below. She found her horse near the base of the cliff, grazing contentedly on the rain-drenched grass. Taking a deep lungful of cool, sweet-smelling air, Laura wiped the fine leather saddle dry and then mounted.

Lost in thought, she let the little mare choose their course. She was startled when she looked up and saw the ranch buildings looming ahead. She knew she didn't belong there anymore, but she'd be damned if she'd give Cal the satisfaction of leaving now. He probably thought he'd succeeded in breaking her spirit, but she'd show him that she was capable of taking his worst and dealing it right back to him.

Cal was standing alone in the sunlit kitchen pouring himself a cup of coffee when Laura entered the house. He looked up as the door opened, a mixture of regret and resignation in his eyes. Even in the grip of the unthinking, desperate jealousy that had compelled him to confront Randall before the business trip, he'd shown some measure of self-control. He'd threatened the other man and tried to bribe him, but he'd stopped short of using brute strength to prevent Randall's departure with Laura. He had stepped aside and allowed the businessman to walk out of the house unscathed, for the same reason he'd let Laura leave seven years earlier. He'd known that he couldn't hold her by force, that if she stayed it had to be her choice or her presence was meaningless.

But in the cave last night, he'd been more than a little angry, frustrated and drunk. It had been easy to forget that simple truth. Selfishly, with calculated technique, he had sought to dominate Laura completely, to break down all her defenses and possess her totally. And in trying to do so, he had destroyed whatever tenderness and caring had existed between them. Finally she'd whimpered and turned away from his touch, but not before Cal had seen the dark side of his own soul reflected in her anguished eyes.

He would have given everything he owned to take back what had happened, to have the chance to live last night over. But that wasn't possible. He knew that there was nothing he could say to repair the damage he'd done, nothing that would heal the terrible pain he saw in her eyes. But he owed her the words. "I'm sorry if I hurt you, Laurie."

His words—an echo of those he'd spoken on a winter night many years before—and the caring look in his eyes, made Laura want to reach out to him just one more time, to tell him that despite all that had happened, there was a part of her that understood, and was still stubborn enough to love him. But that would have been the ultimate surrender, the ultimate degradation. She could well imagine his reaction to such an unsolicited declaration. First, there would be suspicious disbelief, then cold, bitter amusement and finally a gentle, but firm rejection shaded with overtones of contemptuous pity. That would cost her the last shred of pride she possessed. It would destroy her. So she held on to her anger with all her strength because it was the only defense she had left. She'd had enough. She didn't care about him anymore. She wouldn't let herself care.

"I'm sorry, too," she cried, her voice ragged with emotion. "I'm sorry I ever came back to this godforsaken place! And I'm damned sorry I ever met you!"

Suddenly she knew that she couldn't stay in the same room with him—not feeling as she did. She had to get away from him, away from this house, away from the ruin of her cherished memories. Hurriedly she turned to flee, not knowing or caring where she went.

Cal slammed his coffee mug down, sloshing half its contents onto the counter. He crossed the floor in two strides and reached for her arm. "Listen to me, Laurie...please. When we were together in the cave, I'd been drinking. I didn't know what I was doing. I didn't use—"

Seething, Laura jerked away from him, cutting him off in midsentence. "You think I didn't know that? Well, don't worry. Whatever happens, you won't have to tolerate the presence of another unwanted child in your house. Once I leave here, I won't be back like a bad penny. You'll never see me again!"

Without waiting for a response, she turned on her heel in disgust and walked out onto the porch. Making her way to the stable, she saddled a fresh mount, taking simple comfort from the animal's unquestioning acceptance of her voice and hands.

As she was finishing, Melissa rode up on her new pony, the diamond pendant gleaming at her throat. "Where are you going?" she asked eagerly. "Can I come, too?"

Laura shook her head. "No, I don't think so, baby. I was just going to the glade for a little while and—"

"Let me come," the little girl begged. "I can go swimming! I'll be good, I promise. And I have Midnight now, so I won't have to ride double with you anymore. I want to know what you saw in San Antonio, and Dallas, and . . ."

Laura sighed in resignation, interrupting the child's merciless flow of persuasive reasoning. "Okay. Go get your bathing suit, and ask Juanita for some food to take along."

With a whoop that would have been a credit to any of Laura's Indian ancestors, Melissa slid down from her pony and ran toward the house. Laura leaned her head against her horse's warm neck and tried unsuccessfully to recapture some of the equanimity that she had taken for granted only a week before.

A half an hour later, Laura and Melissa rode into the glade. The little girl quickly changed into her swimsuit and dived into the water. She broke the surface almost immediately, the diamond heart about her neck turned to shimmering fire by the sun.

Laura stripped to her underwear and swam for a while. She began to wish that she'd stayed at the ranch house where there would have been a tub full of hot water to ease her aches—all except the ache in her heart.

Climbing out of the pond, she lay down on the soft grass in the shade of the same tree that had sheltered her when she was Melissa's age. She remembered all the times that she and Eve and Cal had come here skinny-dipping after school—before they'd known that there was anything to be shy about. Now here she was a grown woman, Eve was dead and Cal . . . Cal was almost as out of reach as her poor sister.

Rousing herself from her gloomy thoughts, she called to Melissa. "You've been in that pond long enough now, honey. You're going to be as wrinkly as an old prune! Come on out of there before you get the sniffles again."

Obediently the child dried off and dressed. Laura unpacked a tablecloth and dug out the lunch Juanita had sent along. She watched as Melissa ate, but couldn't force herself to take a single bite.

After the remnants of the meal had been cleared away, Melissa stretched out on the checkered cloth with a yawn. "I'm tired, Laura. I'm gonna take a nap."

Laura ran her hand over the little girl's silky hair. "Sounds like a good idea, sweetheart."

Lying down next to the drowsy child, Laura fell into a exhausted sleep, her head filled with visions of Cal and their meeting in the cave. She relived that disturbing episode over and over again, waking with a start to find Melissa shaking her arm.

"I wanted you to wake up, Laura," the little girl explained. "You were having a bad dream. You were calling Daddy's name."

Laura sat up, still shivering from the impact of the last nightmarish scene that had flashed across her mind—the morning sun flooding the kitchen and illuminating the black despair in Cal's gray eyes.

Shuddering, she glanced at the darkening sky. "My lord, it can't be sunset already! Juanita's going to take a stick to me if we're late for the barbecue!"

Dressing quickly, she rounded up their mounts and they rode back to the ranch, arriving after dark. The whole yard was alight with hundreds of paper lanterns, and already crowds of people thronged around several tables laden with food. The smell of smoked beef rose tantalizingly from the barbecue pit, and the live music of a well-known country and western group drifted down from a newly constructed bandstand.

Juanita met them at the door of the house, wringing her hands. "I was so worried about you two. Where have you been? Come, little one, you have to get dressed for the party."

Bundling Melissa upstairs, the housekeeper left Laura to bring up the rear. She felt refreshed and renewed by the hours of sleep she'd had. Her mind was made up and she closed her bedroom door with new resolution. She'd managed to survive without Cal for seven long years. He wasn't the only man in the world; there were many others more interesting and much easier to get along with. She had a challenging job awaiting her and a new apartment to find. The last thing she needed was a stubborn, uncaring chauvinist to tie her down.

Laura was determined to enjoy herself tonight. She'd show Cal how little he meant to her and she'd show both the snotty Sinclair offspring just what she thought of them.

After showering, she dressed in the white outfit that Cal had picked out for her. It showed off her lithe, trim figure at its best and provided a pretty contrast to her olive skin and dark hair. Heads turned as she walked down the stairs. Her heart skipped a beat when she saw Cal look in her direction. But he turned away almost at once, the expression in his eyes dark and unreadable.

Laura swallowed hard and renewed her resolution to leave their relationship behind. Entering the yard, she was swept into the swirl of the crowd, exchanging greetings and compliments with people she hadn't seen for years.

She made the rounds, eating the delicious barbecue and drinking too much of the heavily spiked punch. She danced with a succession of young cowboys who smelled of tobacco, leather and after-shave. Flirting and laughing, she floated through the extravaganza of color and noise.

Somewhere in her travels, Laura latched on to Steve and dragged him out onto the dance floor. Pressing her body close to his, she reveled in the fire spitting from Delphine's gray eyes and the stormy looks Cal sent in her direction.

After the first tune, Steve introduced her to his cousin, Fred, who'd just arrived from Chicago.

"Fred is going to be my best man tomorrow, Laura. You remember, I'm getting married tomorrow," he said slowly, emphasizing every word. "I have to go dance with Delphine now, Laura. You dance with Fred."

But she clung to him steadfastly, her voice rising. "Oh, come on, Steve, just once more! I'll dance with Fred later."

Steve took her arm roughly and, guiding her through the crowd, directed her stumbling footsteps toward the house.

Laura frowned. "Where are you taking me?"

"I'm taking you in to Juanita," Steve said shortly, and she could hear the anger in his voice. "You need some black coffee."

"I don't want any coffee," Laura protested, trying to pull away from him. "I want to dance. I like to dance. I—"

Laura's conversation with Steve ended abruptly when she walked head-on into an object that had all the flexibility of a brick wall. She staggered backward with a surprised exclamation, and only Steve's hold on her arm prevented her from falling. She heard a deep chuckle that sounded eerily familiar.

"I'll be more than happy to oblige you, little lady. I like to dance, too."

Laura's eyes turned to focus on the large mass of a man that was blocking her path, and her giddy state of semi-drunkeness completely evaporated as a bolt of fear shot through her. Facing her was the giant from the night-club—the colossus that Cal had laid out on the floor!

"W-what are *you* doing here?" she gasped.

"Me and my friends was just drivin' around when we seen the lights and heard the music. We decided to come on over and join the party."

For the first time, Laura noticed the four burly strangers standing close behind the big man. The pervasive odor of unwashed flesh and the open leers on their faces did nothing to ease her mind.

While she was still trying to gather her muddled thoughts and decide on the best course of action, an arm with muscles like steel shot out and encircled her waist. She found herself being hauled up against the giant's hard, foul-smelling body. When he spoke, she grimaced at the smell of stale beer and sour breath.

"Come on, honey. Don't be shy. I been wantin' to dance with you ever since I seen you that night in the honky-tonk."

"Laura, do you know this person?"

All heads turned toward the source of the unexpected interruption. The intruders regarded Steve with a mix-

ture of contempt and astonishment. Laura's captor was
the first to recover.

"Who's this? Your daddy?"

Braying laughter erupted from the big man's support-
ers. They clapped each other on the back and stomped
their feet, apparently overwhelmed by their leader's uncharacteristic display of wit.

"Let her go—*now!*"

The words cut through the air like the crack of a whip,
and Laura whispered a prayer of thanks as she recognized Cal's voice.

Ripples of reaction seemed to spread outward from the
scene of the confrontation as the party guests began to
realize that something was wrong. People stopped dancing and gathered around, straining to see what was happening. Laura saw Frank push Henry's wheelchair to the
front row of spectators as an unnatural quiet descended
on the yard, punctuated only by expectant murmurs from
the crowd.

Laura felt tension flow through the huge body so close
to hers, and the giant abandoned all pretense of humor.
"Damned if it ain't that no-good ambusher from the
honky-tonk—same big mouth and all. This is a sorry
night for you, mister. I been dreamin' about meetin' up
with you again."

"I said, let her go," Cal repeated, his voice as cold and
cutting as tempered steel.

The big man actually grinned. "Just try and make me,
boy. I'll take you apart one piece at a time."

"You couldn't whip a newborn pup," Cal drawled.
"You're just a two-bit, yellow-bellied braggart. I put you
down once, and that was easier than drinkin' a cold beer
on a hot day. I'm gonna do the same thing tonight, and

then I'm gonna spit in your face—if I can figure out what end it's at."

With a roar the big man pushed Laura away and ran at his tormentor. Cal watched him come, then stepped aside at the last second like a matador nimbly outmaneuvering a charging bull. His opponent crashed into the crowd of spectators, taking a half dozen innocent bystanders down with him as he fell. Men yelled and women screamed as confusion and fear spread.

Cal turned to face the rising giant, leaving his back exposed to the big man's quartet of companions. They came at him as a group, but before Laura could call out a warning, she saw Steve moving to intercept them. He swung at one of the strangers, and the man went down. Henry tripped a second man with his cane and chortled as the intruder sprawled on the ground.

Then two of the Sinclair Ranch hands entered the fray. One took a blow that sent him reeling into the crowd. Trying to maintain his balance, he grabbed on to a young blond woman. Her dress tore, she shrieked, and he never saw the punch her husband threw. All at once the backyard erupted into a spontaneous brawl, a confusing blur of flying fists and rebel yells.

Laura quickly lost sight of Cal in the thrashing melee. Straining to catch a glimpse of him, she remembered the story he'd told her about how the giant had already crippled one man. Her apprehension grew with every passing second.

Suddenly a pair of combatants shifted, and she saw Cal near the bandstand. But her relief was short-lived. She watched in horror as a huge fist lashed out and connected with his face, knocking him against the bandstand with terrible force. Cal rebounded off the creaking wood and sprawled in the dirt as the giant reared up like a wounded bear. He got in two hard, vicious kicks to Cal's right side before the gray-eyed man grabbed the big metal-tipped boot and twisted his attacker to the ground.

Cal struggled to get up, but his injured side made him slower than his opponent. The other man caught him off balance and dragged him to his feet, locking him in a bear hug. He proceeded to squeeze with all his strength, grunting with the effort.

Cal's involuntary cry of pain galvanized Laura into action. She forgot her hurt feelings and her feigned indifference. No one was going to put her man in a wheelchair unless they went through her first!

Racing through the crowd, she grabbed an empty whiskey bottle off a refreshment table, and wielding it like a club, rushed into the fight. Swinging the weapon with all her might, she aimed a blow at the giant's temple. But the intruder saw the bottle coming. He dropped Cal with an oath and threw out his left arm to deflect the blow.

Laura was swept aside and propelled through the air like a leaf caught up in a hurricane. She hit the ground with bone-jarring force, executing a perfect belly flop in the dirt. As she struggled to breathe and cough the dust out of her lungs—all at the same time—she was dimly aware that her one venture into combat had resulted in inglorious defeat, and that somewhere along the way she had even lost the bottle.

Pushing herself up to a sitting position she desperately sought out Cal. A thrill of elation coursed through her as she saw him on his feet delivering punch after punch to the larger man's jaw and midsection. Following up his advantage, Cal grabbed the giant by the hair and rammed the hardest part of his own skull into the big man's forehead. Staggering, the man bellowed with pain.

Breathing heavily from exertion, Cal grabbed him again and slammed the man's head into the heavy beam that formed the corner of the bandstand. Once, twice, three times, and finally the giant fell down in the dirt and lay still.

With a groan, Cal sank to his knees on the ground beside Laura, blood oozing from a deep cut near his lower lip. His eyes took in her dirty face and dust-covered clothes, and he remembered how she'd rushed to help him. His heart swelled with pride and a depth of caring that shook him from the top of his head to the soles of his boots. He'd fought for her and he'd won. Now he wanted to reach out and claim his prize. But it wasn't that simple. This wasn't an ancient arena, it was the modern world. Laura wasn't a prize, she was an individual entitled to choose her own future. And that meant she'd be leaving him again. As strong as he was, he was helpless to prevent her going. And why should he even try? He knew better than most that love was just another word for pain. He'd had more than his fair share of that already.

As Laura looked at Cal, a primal feeling of exultation coursed through her. She forgot her anger and all she felt was love. He'd fought to defend her, and he'd emerged victorious. She wanted to tend his wounds and make him whole. She wanted to take her place by his side and never leave him again. Then she looked into his eyes, and the wary bitterness she saw there jolted her back to reality. She remembered that her dream was dead and that she didn't belong to this man or this place anymore.

Overcome by the hopelessness of her situation, she scrambled to her feet and hurried toward the house, barely noticing that the fighting had finally stopped. The ranch hands were making the rounds, righting overturned tables, trying to bring order out of confusion; but all that was nothing compared to the chaos raging inside her heart.

She made it as far as the living room before she encountered Juanita. The Mexican woman gasped and put both hands to her mouth. "In the name of all the saints," she exclaimed. "What happened to you? I heard some noise outside, but—"

"I'll explain later," Laura told her wearily. "Right now I just want to get upstairs and take a hot shower."

Juanita gasped again, and Laura turned to see Cal walking toward them. The front of his shirt was stained with blood from the cut on his face, and he moved slowly, favoring his right side.

He spoke carefully, as if fighting to keep the pain out of his voice. "Some of the boys are watching those guys until the police get here. I guess the party's over."

Laura wanted to run to Cal and hold him. She wanted to draw the pain out of his body and into her own. Instead she forced herself to remain still. He'd made it abundantly clear last night that he didn't want or need her attention.

"Oh, my goodness!" Juanita exclaimed, clucking over Cal's condition. "Tonight is truly a night for calamities! I was just coming outside to tell you that Melissa has disappeared. I cannot find her anywhere. I have searched and searched."

Cal took the housekeeper by the shoulders, his pain forgotten. "What do you mean, 'disappeared'?" he demanded.

"The little one and I spent an hour at the party, and then I got her ready for bed. Just as I was turning off her light, she sat up and began crying, 'I lost it! I lost it!' I tried to talk to her, but she would not tell me what she meant. Nothing I said could comfort her. Finally I went downstairs to make her some hot chocolate. When I came back with it a few minutes later, she was gone. No one I have talked to has seen her since.''

Despite his injuries Cal set off at a headlong run, Laura following him. They reached the stable together, soft, welcoming whinnies greeting their approach.

"Damn!" Cal exclaimed. "Her pony's gone—saddle and all.'' His face creased with worry. "Where the hell would she go this time of night? And why?''

"Oh, no!'' Laura gasped as a sudden insight hit her with frightening force. "The pendant, the diamond pendant! She was wearing it this morning when I took her swimming in the glade. Suppose she lost it then and went back to look for it tonight?''

Juanita's terrified voice came from behind them. "Dear God, protect her! I put her bathing suit over her shower door to dry. A few minutes ago, I noticed that it was missing. But I had no reason to think she would go to the glade!''

"That pool is twelve feet deep in places,'' he muttered. His eyes met Laura's, and, for the first time in her life, she saw naked fear there. Suddenly he was saddling his horse at breakneck speed, seemingly oblivious of his injured side.

Laura dragged out Taffy's gear. "I'm going with you.''

Cal glanced at her and nodded, not having the breath to argue. "Keep up as best you can,'' he said, swinging into the saddle. Then he was gone, riding over the rough ground at top speed, trusting luck and the grace of God that his horse wouldn't stumble in the dark and break both their necks.

Pulling the cinch on the saddle tight, Laura climbed up on her own mount and urged the reluctant buckskin into a gallop.

She and Cal arrived at the still, moonlit glade almost simultaneously, and Cal lowered himself from the saddle with a grunt of pain. His face pale and beaded with sweat, he walked toward the water calling Melissa's name. A large black shadow detached itself from the surrounding darkness and Midnight came forward to nuzzle his hand.

"Oh, God, no!" Laura exclaimed as her eyes fell on the motionless, white form floating face down on the glassy surface of the pool. Icy terror gripped her heart, and she stood riveted to the ground.

Throwing himself into the water, Cal swam out to his daughter's side. Carrying her from the pool, he laid her limp form gently on the soft grass.

Laura dropped down beside the child. "She's not breathing, Cal," she whispered as though afraid to speak the terrible words out loud. "She's not breathing at all!"

Cal pressed his fingertips to the side of Melissa's throat. "Her heart's still beating!" he exclaimed, in an eerie mixture of hope and despair.

Bending over the little girl's motionless figure, he forced the blond head back, covering the child's lips and nose with his own open mouth.

"Not too much air, Cal. Her lungs are a lot smaller than yours," Laura cautioned. She felt as if she were listening to a stranger speaking to her from a great distance, reciting long-forgotten details from some college first-aid lecture.

Cal breathed air into his daughter's lungs for what seemed like an eternity. "It's not going to work, Laurie," he said between breaths, his voice breaking. "My little girl's dead, and I never once told her that I loved her.''

Laura felt tears gathering in her eyes. He'd been hurt in the fight, he was tired, he was upset. She wanted to step in and relieve him, but she knew that she couldn't. He had to be the one to give Melissa back her life.

By sheer effort she stopped her tears. ''Don't start feeling sorry for yourself, Cal,'' she said firmly. ''Melissa needs you more than she's ever needed you before. Don't give up on her now!''

Suddenly, miraculously, the child began to cough and stir. Cal bent over the small body, not daring to believe that she actually lived. The little girl's eyelids fluttered open, and she focused blurrily on her father's face.

''I didn't lose it, Daddy. See? I didn't lose your present. It was in the mud at the bottom of the pool. I had to dive and dive. But I got it.''

She tried to lift her arm, and, for the first time, Laura noticed the white gold chain clutched in the delicate fingers of the child's right hand.

Cal swept Melissa into his arms and buried his face in her neck, his shoulders shaking convulsively. Then Laura was crying, too, releasing all the pent-up emotions of the last few hours.

After a long moment, Laura drew a deep, shuddering breath and watched as Cal got to his feet, still holding Melissa. He reluctantly surrendered the child to Laura while he pulled himself up into the saddle. In the moonlight, Laura could see that his face was contorted with pain. She wanted so badly to reach out and comfort him. Instead she silently returned his daughter to the shelter of his arms.

''I'm riding back to the ranch to get the car,'' Cal told her. ''Then I'm taking Melissa to the emergency room.''

"What about my pony?" Melissa asked drowsily.

"Don't worry, princess. Laurie will see to it that Midnight gets home."

Unable to restrain herself any longer, Laura reached up and hesitantly touched his hand. "Cal, I want to say thank-you for helping me tonight. I'm grateful for that and for all the times you've been there for me when I needed you. And I wanted to tell you that I accept the apology you made this morning. You did hurt me, but...I've hurt you, too."

Cal shook his head. "I don't know that I deserve your forgiveness, Laurie." But he solemnly held out his right hand, and Laura grasped it firmly with her own. He smiled down at her. "Thank you. And thanks for your help in the fight. If I live to be a hundred, I'll never forget the sight of you making your charge with that whiskey bottle."

Laura laughed in embarrassment. "I guess it was kind of ridiculous."

"It was the most beautiful sight I've ever seen." He paused then looked down at Melissa. "Most of all, thank you for giving me back my daughter. No one's ever going to take her away from me again. She's a Sinclair to me, no matter what her bloodline might be."

Cal made clicking noises to his horse, riding out of the glade at an easy walk. Laura heard his voice drifting back to her on the still night air.

"Princess, did I ever tell you about the time Granddaddy had to take me to the hospital? I was a little tadpole, no bigger than you."

"Were you scared, Daddy?"

"You betcha."

Laura watched them go until they were swallowed up by the darkness. A feeling of great joy filled her because

Cal had finally acknowledged his love for his daughter. But she felt great sadness because she wouldn't be around to see that love grow. What she'd been summoned back to the ranch to do had been accomplished.

With a supreme effort, she dragged herself up into Taffy's saddle. Rounding up Melissa's skittish pony, she started down the dark, lonely road that led back to a place she no longer had the right to call home.

Chapter Eleven

Juanita woke Laura at noon with the welcome news that both Cal and Melissa were home from the hospital and doing fine. In addition, the airline had delivered her missing suitcase. Juanita had brought it upstairs while she slept. Laura smiled at the irony of the situation; on the day she was leaving, her suitcase had finally arrived.

She lay in bed quietly assessing all that had happened to her since she had arrived at the ranch. She felt strangely serene and at peace with herself now that she had finally made up her mind to go. The sight of her leather bag and the errant suitcase standing packed and ready by the bed was somehow comforting. Her life had been on an even keel for years before she'd come back to this place. She hadn't really been happy, but she hadn't been unhappy, either. Steve was right. There was nothing wonderful about being dragged through life at the mercy of violent emotions. The unspeakable ecstasy and the abject misery that Cal had aroused in her had proved exhausting and had led nowhere.

After last night, she was Cal's friend again. From now on, he'd accept her as part of the family, and that was more important than any transitory love affair. Visits would be painful for her, but at least they'd be possible.

What if she went to Cal today with a declaration of undying love? He'd probably be embarrassed and uncomfortable at having to reject her—she'd be humiliated—and they'd both remember it every time they saw each other again. Once she'd been willing to risk that, but after last night she had too much to lose.

The same could be said of her job. It was comfortable, secure, profitable. It would become even more profitable with her promotion. She was wasting her time with art. She was wasting her time wanting more. From now on, she was grabbing for rewards that were within her reach. It was time to stop chasing rainbows.

Laura threw back the bed covers, pushing aside all negative thoughts. Ten minutes later, she was pulling on the blue silk dress that Cal had conned her into buying.

She looked in the mirror, and her heart ached dully as she saw the young, pretty woman who looked back at her. The dress seemed to shout, "notice me, need me, love me." It was an appropriate symbol of what might have been. Ignoring the feeling of melancholy that was attempting to take her over, she wound her hair into a sleek coil and pinned it securely. Soon, she had finished her makeup and was on her way down the stairs.

Wonderful smells were once again emanating from Juanita's kitchen. As Laura entered the room, she saw the Mexican woman directing a white-clad catering staff as they prepared mounds of hors d'oeuvres.

"Nita," Laura exclaimed, "everything looks wonderful!"

The older woman beamed. "Thanks to the good Lord and to all these helpers. The cake has just arrived and also the rest of the flowers. Frank is outside directing the men in putting up a big tent to serve as a dressing room for the women in the wedding party. And already most of the guests have arrived. Ay! There is too much for one poor old woman to remember!"

Laura impulsively embraced Juanita, sad to be leaving this one happy remnant of her childhood.

The housekeeper looked at her quizzically. "Ah, Laurita, how can you be unhappy on a day like this? It has been so long since there was a wedding in this house. Soon, maybe you and Mr. Cal . . ."

Juanita stopped in midsentence as Laura began shaking her head. "I'm leaving, Nita," she blurted out. "Today, after the wedding. Cal doesn't love me. He never really did . . . at least not enough to matter."

"You are wrong, my sweet, very wrong."

Laura was about to reply when the kitchen door flew open, and Honey swept in. "Juanita, please speak to the caterer. The champagne isn't the vintage Cal ordered. I suppose there's nothing that can be done about it now, but he'll certainly want the bill adjusted. And let me take out a tray of these cheese puffs. They're Cal's favorite, you know."

With a quick nod to Laura, the secretary whirled around and made her exit.

Juanita said something in Spanish that Laura didn't understand, but she was sure it wasn't at all complimentary. "The grand lady of the manor!" the housekeeper snapped sarcastically. "You would think that she was mistress in this house."

Laura was still staring at the door when the Mexican woman grabbed her by the shoulders and shook her. "Are you going to leave Mr. Cal to a woman like that, the way you left him to Eve?"

Laura hadn't seen Juanita's anger directed at her for many years. She blinked in surprise. "But what can I do?" she asked helplessly.

"The one thing you have been afraid to do: tell him exactly how you feel, tell him that you are willing to make a permanent commitment. You have not said these words to him because you are as frightened of him as he is of you. You are afraid that he will hurt you even more than you are hurting now. So go! Run away again. Go become a frightened, lonely, proud old woman. Be a coward like you accused him of being. No one can stop you. No one except Laura Wright."

Laura's face contorted as she realized the truth of Juanita's words. In spite of her physical intimacy with Cal, she had been withholding a vital part of herself because she was afraid of being rejected. And the thought of risking a permanent commitment to Cal scared her for another reason. They were both so stubborn, both so temperamental. As Steve had pointed out, it would never work. It would only mean more misery, more pain. And that just might destroy her. But what if it *did* work? Did Cal even love her enough to give it another try?

"All right!" she blurted out. "All right. I'll do it! I want Cal . . . forever."

"Then tell him so. Tell him today. But first, I think there is someone else you must talk to—for Delphine's sake, as well as your own."

Laura nodded in reluctant acceptance of Juanita's words. It was time to do what she felt was right no matter how painful that might be. She'd finally learned that

she could never run fast enough to escape her own con-
science. In the past, she'd paid bitterly for taking the easy
way out. Today that was going to change.

With a hammering heart, she forced herself to climb
back upstairs and to tap lightly on Steve's door. For a
moment, she thought that no one would answer, and a
feeling of panic flooded her. Had she come too late?
Then the door opened, and the groom-to-be stood
framed in the doorway.

He was dressed in white pants trimmed with black velvet and a long-sleeved white shirt with a ruffled front. A
purplish bruise covered almost half his face, and Laura
winced when she saw it.

"Oh, you're hurt! I didn't know. So much was going
on last night—"

Steve dismissed her concern with a wave of his hand.
"Delphine tried to hide this with makeup, but I don't
think it helped much. Anyway, it will fade soon enough."
He ran one hand through his hair, a sure sign that he was
feeling harried. "Look, Laura, I don't want to be rude,
but—"

Before he could shut her out, Laura pushed past him
into the room. "I need to talk to you, Steve."

He quickly looked up and down the hallway before
shutting the door and turning to face her. "I'd appreciate it if you spoke to me at the reception. I'm trying to
finish dressing for the wedding, and, as you know, my
wife-to-be is a jealous woman."

"Steve, it's your marriage I want to talk to you about.
It's the biggest mistake you're ever going to make."

Steve frowned as he threaded a stud through the slits
in one cuff. "I'm sorry you feel that way, but I'm not
changing my mind."

Laura slapped her palm on the shining dresser top, shaking the mirror and rattling a multicolored assortment of men's toiletries. "Listen to me, Steve. Delphine loves you. It's not going to take her that long to figure out that you don't love her. When that happens, she's going to feel cheated and miserable, and she's going to make *you* miserable."

Steve fixed the stud in place and met her eyes with a shake of his head. "You'll forgive me if I disagree with you. I think that Delphine and I can have a very civilized and mutually satisfying marriage."

Laura took a step toward him, both fists clenched. "If she were more like you, maybe. But she's not. She has emotional needs, Steve. She's a romantic, jealous, impulsive nineteen-year-old, and empty words aren't going to satisfy her for long. She's going to want more from you.'"

Involved in fastening his black cummerbund, Steve shrugged. "So we'll have children."

Suddenly all Laura could see was Eve. Selfish, headstrong, destructive Eve going headlong to hell, sure of her own invulnerability until she'd been caught in the web she'd spun herself.

"Dammit!" she yelled. "Stop what you're doing and listen to me. Now!"

Steve paused and gave her his full attention, too startled by the strength of her emotional display to be annoyed.

Laura continued, her tone one of quiet desperation. She had the horrible feeling that a seven-year-old mistake was about to be reenacted before her eyes. This time, she had to stop it.

"You've been in this house for almost two weeks now. You heard Cal talk about Eve the night of the birthday party. You've seen what his relationship was with Melissa. That's the result of a marriage like the one you're planning—a marriage based on a lie, a promise of love that never existed. Is that the legacy you want to give to your children, Steve?''

Steve slowly sat down on the bed and, leaning his elbows on his knees, rested his chin in his hands. "You're saying that I should call off the wedding?" he asked in a soft voice, staring at the floor.

It was the first time in six years that Laura had ever heard her boss sound unsure about anything. He looked so . . . human! With a shock she realized that she had succeeded in penetrating his phony facade and had at last made contact with the real Steve Randall.

Sinking down beside him, she laid a hand on his arm. "No, I'm not saying you should call off the wedding. Just, for once, lay your cards on the table. Tell her the truth. Tell her that you're not in love with her. If she wants to marry you under those circumstances, then at least you've warned her. Give her that choice, Steve—not just for her, but for yourself, too."

The stranger in front of her nodded his head. "I'll think about it," he told her. "I'll think about it."

Laura closed her eyes and slumped forward, relief rushing over her. Steve's statement was more than she'd dared hope for when she'd first entered this room.

Getting to her feet, she was halfway to the door before it occurred to her that she'd never asked Steve about Jim Reyes's transfer to New York. But now just wasn't a good time. Steve was trying to decide his own future, and she had some choices to make, too. Then an idea came to her with such illuminating swiftness that she couldn't help smiling to herself. She didn't know yet what was going to happen with Cal, but all at once, that was irrelevant. She knew what she wanted to do. She knew what was right for her.

Using as few words as possible, she told Steve what she had decided and the reasons behind it. When she'd finished, he simply nodded once.

"I'll arrange it, Laura."

She had expected a protest, or at least further discussion, but when he continued to sit as if lost in thought, she left the room, closing the door softly behind her.

She wondered what he'd decide to do about Delphine. She could usually predict Steve Randall's every move, but she had no idea who this new person really was. But, whatever happened, this time she hadn't run away. Maybe this time she'd made a difference.

As she stood in the hallway in front of Steve's room with her hand still on the knob, the door to Cal's room opened. He stepped out, and his eyes met hers. He was dressed in the same style of tuxedo Steve had been wearing, but his shirt was a pale shade of yellow. Only a small bruise on his lower lip testified to the beating he'd taken the night before, and Laura thought she'd never seen a handsomer man. She noticed that his eyes were roaming over her as if he were thinking similar thoughts. Then he saw her hand on the doorknob of Steve's room and his look chilled her to the bone.

She tensed as he walked toward her, but he ignored her, moving past without a word of recognition. Why had she ever thought that they could be friends? For them it had to be everything or nothing.

Her voice seemed unnaturally loud in the confines of the hallway. "We have to talk, Cal."

He gave no indication of having heard her until he reached the top of the stairs. "After the wedding," he told her curtly, not bothering to look up.

"No, now."

Cal paused in his descent and met her eyes directly. His were filled with anger, and Laura felt her heart sink past her knees.

"Give me one good reason why I should start taking orders from you," he demanded.

"Because I love you, Cal," Laura said, her voice trembling. "Maybe you don't want to hear that now, but I need to say it. Someday—in a month, in a year, in five years—you'll be ready to love again. When that day comes, I'll be waiting. I'm not going to give up on you, Cal—not today, not ever."

She closed her eyes and waited for his response. All she heard was an eloquent silence that spoke louder than any words.

Choking on tears, she turned and stumbled back down the hall to her room. She was halfway inside before Cal caught up with her. "Laurie..." he began.

Then he saw the packed overnight bag and suitcase standing ready by the bed. He closed the door and leaned back against it, shaking his head. His hoarse, derisive chuckle filled the room. It had a pained sound to it that set Laura's teeth on edge.

"You're running out on me again."

It was a flat statement of fact that left no room for argument. Laura heard resignation in his voice, but also a hint of something that was almost satisfaction, as if she had finally done exactly what he'd expected her to do from the moment she'd first set foot on the ranch.

All at once, her temper snapped. Bringing herself up to her full height, she shook her finger under his nose. "How dare you accuse me of running out on you? Ever since I arrived you've been telling me to leave. You even offered to pay me to leave. Now you have the gall to blame me because I'm finally going?''

Cal's eyes were filled with an old and bitter hurt. "It's the same thing you did seven years ago. You haven't changed.''

Laura's pain rose to match Cal's, but she fought the urge to answer him in kind. She couldn't drive him away again. She had to reach him, to make him understand.

She spoke softly, every word coming from her heart. "I want to apologize for what happened seven years ago.''

"'Apologize'?'' Cal echoed in surprise.

"Not for what I said about wanting to finish school and have a career. I was right about those things, absolutely right.''

"This is some apology, woman.''

"Just hush now, and listen! You were—and still are— very obstinate, very proud, and very sure of yourself and of what you believe to be right. In spite of these qualities, or maybe because of them, you're very easily hurt. You just hide it so deep no one can find it under all the anger. I didn't realize how deep until last night. Anyway, I was a fool to react the way I did to that ultimatum you gave me so long ago. If I had only taken more time— stayed an extra day—maybe we could have reached a compromise. But I was young, and I had a temper—''

"Had?" Cal interrupted, one eyebrow raised.

Laura glared at him. "Don't throw stones, mister. You never even tried to get in touch with me after I left. And then you went right ahead and married Eve.''

Cal looked at the floor, all the fight gone out of him. "You don't know how many times I picked up the phone to call you, how many letters I wrote and then tore up. Hell, I even made plane reservations. It was my damned-fool, stubborn pride that kept me from flying to New York. I was waiting for you to make the first move so I could save face. Then the night before my birthday, Eve talked me into going out with her. She was sweet, and sympathetic, and very, very loving. She also got me very, very drunk. When I woke up in a Mexican motel the next morning and found out that I was a married man, I couldn't even remember the ceremony. I figured I'd committed myself at that point. Besides, you never contacted me. You never gave me any reason to try and get out of the marriage. I thought you didn't care.''

Somewhere deep inside Laura, an old knot of pain and bitterness began to slowly dissolve. She hastened to explain her side of the story. ''I had reservations to fly down on your birthday. I was so miserable without you, I think I would have agreed to anything you'd demanded. But after Eve's call, I felt like a fool. I thought you'd only given me the ring in a moment of passion—that in the light of day you'd changed your mind. I thought that my body was the only part of me you'd wanted and that— after we'd slept together—your love had just fizzled out.''

Cal stepped close and traced her cheekbone lightly with his fingertips. ''I loved all of you, Laurie, seven years ago, seven hours ago. I was afraid that you didn't feel the same way about me. Oh, I knew you liked the things we did in bed together, and after your crying fit in the glade, I started to believe you cared for me. But I didn't think you cared enough to stay with me and work at building a real relationship. I tried to get you to tell me how you felt, what you wanted, but you shied away like you were hiding something. Then you gave the pendant away the same day I found out about your trip with Răndall—a trip you hadn't even told me about.

"Hell, for all I knew, you two were running off to-gether and never coming back. It was too much for me to deal with after what I'd been through before, Laurie. I just wanted to end it, to get away from all the pain, and the doubt, and the fear. When I let you go, I thought that I could make that decision and abide by it. But after you left, the feelings I was trying to escape didn't stop. They just got stronger and stronger until I thought I'd go crazy with jealousy. That's why I started drinking and . . . and treated you the way I did in the cave."

Laura's heart had soared at Cal's declaration of love, and she was desperate to reassure him. "I've never been with Steve that way, Cal. I've never been with any man but you."

"Not in all these years?" Cal exclaimed in amaze-ment.

Laura looked away, suddenly feeling self-conscious. "Well, it wasn't as if I didn't try. I'd go out with an at-tractive man, he'd touch me, and I'd feel absolutely nothing. I wanted to make love, but it was only you I wanted to make love to."

Cal examined her face and finally saw the truth there. He sighed deeply. "So I was wrong again. Lord, there are so many things I'd do different if I had the chance. For starters, I would've listened to those things you tried to tell me about your sister."

He paced the room, his eyes shadowed by dark mem-ories. "Eve didn't stay sweet and loving for long after we were married. She told me that it was my fault, that I wasn't paying enough attention to her. Every time I didn't give in to one of her demands, she'd raise a ruckus that shook the whole house. Then I found out from the family doctor that she was planning to have an abor-tion. I came barreling home and raised some hell myself.

We must have yelled at each other for over an hour. She ended up telling me that I'd better let her have the abortion, or else I'd be stuck raising another man's child.''

"Eve was capable of saying anything to get her own way, Cal," Laura reminded him gently, hurting for him as he relived the pain.

"That's why I don't know if what she said about Melissa was the truth or a lie. Maybe Eve wasn't sure herself. Anyway, I told her that if she went ahead with the abortion, I'd file for a divorce."

Cal looked at Laura and smiled grimly. "We stayed together for nearly four years after Melissa was born. I never slept with Eve once during that time—not that I was the idealized image of the long-suffering husband. I found consolation with a lot of women. None of them really meant anything to me. They were just a way to make the pain go away for a few hours. When I wasn't out catting around, I was working my tail off at the office."

He paused, his gray eyes haunted by the ghosts of old regrets. "I guess I can't blame Eve for leaving, but I don't know how she could get herself mixed up with drugs. It was a waste, Laurie—her life, her death. It was all purely a waste."

"Don't say that, Cal," Laura pleaded, touching his arm gently. "Because of my sister Melissa was born. That child is everything Eve could have been, but wasn't. It's almost as if she's Eve's second chance."

Laura paused, searching his face. "And what about us, Cal?" she asked. "Do we get a second chance?"

Cal looked at her with doubt in his eyes. "After all the awful things that have come between us, after all the hurt we've caused each other, I just don't know if it could work. But . . ."

He hesitated, and Laura realized with a shiver of dread that the entire course of her future depended on his next words. What if he still rejected her? What if she were forced to leave today as she had planned to do in what seemed like another lifetime? She'd still have her career, but she knew now with aching certitude that she wanted more out of life—and she wanted Cal to share it with her. Trembling, she waited for him to say the words that would seal her fate.

Chapter Twelve

Suddenly there was a brief knock, and then the door opened to admit Juanita. Laura blinked in surprise. It was as if she and Cal had been sealed off in a world of their own, oblivious of outside sights and sounds, even to the passage of time.

"Come, children," Juanita called. "Hurry, hurry! The wedding!" In her excitement, she omitted the honorary title that she'd tacked on to Cal's name ever since he'd taken over the Sinclair Company and instead called him by his childhood nickname. "Calito, you were supposed to give the ring to the best man. He has been looking all over for you! You will have to hand it to him after you escort Delphine down the aisle. Hurry now!"

With a muttered oath, Cal strode to the door. "Well, I suppose I've got to go through with this ridiculous charade."

Laura tried to keep up with Cal's headlong rush down the stairs, but she arrived in the backyard several seconds after him. She stopped behind the last row of spectators, involuntarily halted by the overwhelming solemnity of the occasion.

As the first notes of organ music rang out, Laura spotted Steve standing under a latticework arbor that was covered by dozens of yellow roses. He looked dignified and composed despite his marred face. His cousin, Fred, fidgeted nervously beside him. Fifty guests sat on padded folding chairs, giving the ceremony their rapt attention.

The first person to emerge from the specially erected tent was Melissa. Laura felt an impulse to grab the child and carry her back to bed. Then she smiled at her own rush of overprotectiveness. Melissa looked healthy and beautiful. Dressed in yellow chiffon, the diamond heart gleaming at her throat, she walked sedately down the aisle scattering white and yellow rose petals as she went.

Following Melissa came the maid of honor and then four bridesmaids, each dressed in yellow, wearing crowns of white roses and carrying white rose bouquets. The ushers escorting them were dressed in outfits that matched Cal's.

There was a murmur of anticipation as the piping notes of the organ announced the imminent appearance of the bride. She finally emerged, the reincarnation of Scarlet O'Hara in a hoopskirted, white lace wedding gown. She wore no veil, but a garland of baby's breath rested on her auburn hair like an angel's halo.

Then Laura's attention shifted to Cal who was standing at Delphine's side. Her eyes met his, and she returned his smile, imagining her own wedding day with Cal waiting for her at the end of the aisle. In her mind, she went over the conversation they'd had only moments before. He'd said that he loved her, but did that mean they could learn to live together without tearing each other apart? Would it be different now that they had declared themselves? She wondered what she would do if he didn't ask her to stay, and suddenly the warm day seemed chill.

As the couple passed by her, Laura looked into Delphine's face, and what she saw stunned her. Delphine didn't have the happy, carefree face of a young bride, but rather the thoughtful, saddened face of a disillusioned woman. Laura knew then that Steve had taken her advice. Had she done the right thing, or had she been wrong to interfere?

"Who gives this woman to this man?" the minister asked.

"Her father and I," Cal answered with a nod to where Henry sat on the sideline in his wheelchair.

"Do you, Steven Randall, take Delphine Sinclair to be your lawfully wedded wife, to love and to cherish from this day forward, for as long as you both shall live?"

"I do," Steve said in a clear, strong voice that resonated over the crowd. He turned and smiled at Delphine.

"And do you, Delphine Sinclair, take Steven Randall to be your lawfully wedded husband, to love and to cherish from this day forward, for as long as you both shall live?"

Laura wondered if the silence seemed long to the other guests, or if her imagination had gotten the better of her. When Delphine finally answered, Laura wasn't sure she'd heard correctly. Even the minister asked the girl to repeat her statement. The second time it rang out loud and sure.

"No, I don't,"

The bride turned to her erstwhile groom. "Thanks for being honest with me, Steve. Even after you told me that you didn't love me, I thought that I could go through with the marriage because I...I care for you. But that just isn't enough. I deserve better."

A tear fell onto the white lace of her wedding dress as she turned away from Steve. Then, her head high, she walked back down the aisle alone.

The guests broke into full conversation, speculation abounding. But no one was more surprised than Laura when Delphine passed the last row of chairs and came to a stop directly in front of her.

"I'm sorry for the way I treated you, Laura. I knew that something was wrong between Steve and me, and I blamed it on you. Now I realize I was wrong."

"I understand," Laura said gently. "I know what it's like to be in love."

A small smile hovered on Delphine's lips as she handed Laura her bouquet. "Here, maybe this will bring you luck. I won't be needing it. I'm going back to college and make something of myself—the way that you did."

Impulsively, Laura gave her a quick hug. "Good luck, Delphine."

"It's Ellie," the other woman called over her shoulder as she walked away. "I never did like Delphine."

A moment later, Steve came back up the aisle looking as if he were out for a leisurely stroll. His embarrassed cousin and a covey of chattering bridesmaids trailed after him.

Laura touched his arm as he passed, and he paused beside her. "Are you sorry?" she asked softly.

"You were right. It wouldn't have worked out. Next time I'll be smart enough to pick someone who's in it for the same reason I am.'' His expression turned thoughtful, and he gazed over her shoulder at something only he could see. ''Right at the end there, I realized just how much I'd lost. Now I can almost understand the decision you made this morning.''

He bent closer to her, his eyes twinkling. ''You remember what I said about you making the worst possible wife?'' he whispered. ''Well, if I'd thought there was any danger of your taking me up on my offer, maybe I'd have asked you, anyway.''

He grinned at Laura's stunned expression, then turned and looked straight into Cal's stern gray eyes. ''Sinclair,'' he warned, ''you'd better take good care of her.''

Cal shrugged. ''As much as she'll allow.''

Steve nodded. ''I'm familiar with the problem.''

The two men exchanged a rare look of mutual understanding before Steve walked away and disappeared around the side of the house.

''I'm not sorry he's leaving,'' Cal said, ''but there was something about him, something...'' He stopped speaking, searching for the right word.

''Fascinating,'' Laura supplied without thinking.

Cal turned to look at her suspiciously, and Laura was relieved when the crowd surged forward, temporarily separating them.

Suddenly, Melissa came running toward her. The child buried her face in Laura's skirt. Her heart overflowing with love and concern, Laura knelt down in the grass and held Melissa in her arms.

''What's the matter, sweetheart?'' she asked, caressing the silken blond hair crowned with a wreath of daisies.

Melissa hesitated and then spoke in a half-choked, fear-filled whisper. "Why is everybody leaving? Is it because of something I did?"

The enormous blue eyes looked up at her pleadingly, and Laura's heart melted. She pulled the child to her in a long embrace. "Oh, darling, no! It's not your fault. You haven't done anything wrong."

The preacher's voice, filled with a forced cheerfulness, interrupted Laura's remarks. "Well, folks, it looks like there won't be a wedding today after all. But Mr. Henry Sinclair has invited you all to partake of the reception feast as planned. No sense letting all that good food go to waste now, is there?"

Standing up, Laura pulled Melissa aside to make way for the departing guests and noticed Juanita hovering nearby.

"It is such a shame," the housekeeper murmured. "Everyone dressed up, all this food, all these guests, and no one is getting married."

All at once, Laura had a notion that all but took her breath away. And the more she thought about it, the more appealing the idea became. Why should she stand around waiting for Cal to make the first move? He'd asked her to marry him once before, and she'd left him flat. Maybe it was her turn to take a chance. Maybe Cal needed to hear that she was ready to make a total commitment.

Catching his eye, she worked her way through the crowd until she reached his side. Summoning up every last bit of courage, she cleared her suddenly dry throat.

"I've got a bouquet and a new dress, and this wedding's already paid for. So I was thinking ... Why don't we get married?"

Despite her bold intentions, her voice came out as a rather squeaky whisper. Cal's eyes widened, and he bent toward her. "I don't think I heard you right. What did you say?"

Laura took a deep breath and tried again. "Will you marry me?"

This time her question came out so loudly that everyone in the general vicinity turned their heads and gaped. The backyard became so quiet that Laura could actually hear herself blush.

But for once she didn't care if she made a fool of herself in front of the whole, wide world. She was going to marry the man she loved before another day passed or know the reason why.

"I love you, Cal," she declared, her voice strong and sure, "and I've been miserable without you all these years. I don't ever want to lose you again. I don't know if we can go the distance, Cal, but I want to try. Please, give us a chance."

Laura and fifty interested spectators waited for him to reply. There was a tense moment of total silence. Cal raised his eyebrows and gave her a look she couldn't read. Finally he brushed past her without saying a word.

Laura felt as if he were treading on her heart with every step he took. She wanted to sink into the ground and disappear. Why had she pushed so hard? She should have been more patient. She should have waited until he was ready.

Whirling around, she was about to go after him when she saw him not a yard away. He was bent over, his hands on his knees, looking at Melissa at eye level.

"Would you like Laurie to be your new mama?"

Laura squeezed her eyes shut, the blood pounding in her ears. After all the long years spent hurting and hoping, she couldn't believe that this moment was actually happening.

Melissa laughed, a delighted little-girl giggle that elicited a response from the assembled guests. "You betcha!" she said firmly with a determined nod that was pure Cal.

Her father's face lighted up, and he gave the child a big hug. "I love you, Melissa," he declared for all the world to hear.

The little girl wrapped both arms around Cal's neck and sighed deeply. "I love you, too, Daddy."

Cal straightened and moved back to Laura. "In any kind of love, there's always a risk of being hurt. I've known that for a long time. But last night I found out that I can't escape the hurt by trying to deny the love. I never stopped loving you, Laurie, and I do want to marry you—" Laura started to throw her arms around his neck, but he grabbed her wrists and held her away from him "—under one condition."

Oh, lord, Laura thought, here it comes. She felt as if she had been transported seven years into the past. Now he'd make his demands, and she'd have to respond. She was willing to give up almost anything for him, but if he insisted, if he demanded it as a kind of tribute, she didn't know how she would react. Had they come this far only to go their separate ways again? Numb with apprehension, she listened as he began to speak.

"When we talk later, we may find that we don't agree on every issue. You have to promise me that we'll stay together until we work out a compromise—even if it takes the rest of our lives."

He searched her face for reassurance, looking so expectant, so hopeful, that Laura wondered how she could have doubted his feelings for so long. "Caleb Sinclair," she whispered fervently, "you couldn't run fast enough to get away from me! This morning I finally decided that whether or not you wanted me, I wanted to stay in Houston near you and Melissa. And I wanted to have more time for my personal life, for the people and the things that are important to me. So I turned down the promotion. I asked Steve to give Jim Reyes the transfer to New York and make me the new manager of the Houston International Inn."

"You're sure that's what you want?" Cal asked doubtfully.

Laura nodded. "I'm sure. Whatever it was I had to prove to myself—or to you or Henry—I've done it. I've finally come back to what I really want—you and Melissa and my art. Who knows? Maybe after the hotel gets on its feet, I'll resign and open an art gallery. I'll combine business and pleasure."

Cal smiled. "Speaking of combining business and pleasure, I have a proposition for you. Don't say no until you've heard me out. I almost asked you a couple of times before, but . . . I guess I had to be sure you wanted me just for myself and for no other reason."

Laura looked at him questioningly. "What on earth are you talking about?"

"What would you think about helping me run the Sinclair Company? You already have the business background. I can teach you everything else you need to know. You'd be better at it than I am before long. You're a natural, Laurie, just like Daddy."

She tried to answer him, but he continued, his voice growing more enthusiastic by the minute. "We could share the job. That way I'd have time off for the ranch, and you'd have time off to paint, and we'd both have more free time to spend with Melissa."

Laura didn't have to think twice about it. The idea was so right for them that she wondered why she hadn't come up with it herself—maybe because she'd believed that Cal would never consider such a thing.

"I'll start as soon as I have the hotel running smoothly. I feel obligated to stay until then." She shook her head in amazed disbelief. "You know, this is the best idea you've ever had. The Cal Sinclair I used to know wouldn't have thought of it."

"And the Laura Wright I used to know wouldn't have had the confidence or the savvy necessary to do the job. I guess we've both grown up a little. Kind of nice, isn't it?"

"It sure is."

Laura grinned at the man she hadn't been able to forget. He looked down at her, his teeth flashing in the first honest-to-goodness smile she'd seen on his face in seven long years. He offered her his arm, and they walked down the aisle together, Melissa trailing after. Behind them, the guests hurriedly filed back to their seats.

Gliding toward the preacher, Laura caught glimpses of familiar faces and overheard snatches of conversation from the crowd. She saw Honey gaping at her from the sideline, speechless for once. In her elated mood, Laura had a wild urge to flash the secretary a V-for-victory sign. She suppressed the uncharitable instinct with great difficulty.

As they drew closer to the rose-covered arbor, Laura saw Henry sitting in his wheelchair to one side of the preacher. The patriarch was chuckling and stomping his feet with more color in his face than she'd seen in some time. Juanita fussed over him worriedly, but he motioned her away with an imperious wave of his hand.

Laura watched as Henry winked at the housekeeper. "You see there," she distinctly heard him saying to Juanita. "I told you that if I wrote Laura and asked her to come back to the ranch, she and Cal would get together again. And I was right. My plan worked."

"*Your* plan?" Laura heard Juanita responding indignantly. "I thought that it was *my* plan! I am the one who really brought them together."

Before Laura could even begin to realize the full implications of that conversation, she and Cal had come to a halt before the minister.

The clergyman looked acutely uncomfortable. "Do you have a marriage license?" he whispered.

Laura groaned inwardly. She'd known that it was too good to be true. For some reason, this marriage just wasn't meant to be.

"You just marry us, Reverend," Cal said in a voice that brooked no argument. "You'll have the license before the day is out."

"B-but ... but it's Sunday!" the clergyman stammered in confusion.

"I know what day it is—it's my wedding day. And you'll have your license if I have to pull strings all the way to Austin and mortgage this ranch to pay for it!"

Laura felt tears of joy gathering in her eyes. For the first time she really believed that Cal loved her. If the minister wouldn't officiate, she'd say her own vows in front of God and whoever else cared to listen.

"Cal, this is the happiest day of my life! I promise to love you just as much as I do today for as long as you'll have me. And I promise that if we have a problem in the future we'll always talk it over together. And I swear I'll never leave you again—no matter how many times you ask me to go."

Cal looked down at her, his eyes alight with adoration. "And I promise that you'll always be as beautiful to me as you are today. No person, not even a bad memory, will ever come between us again. For the rest of our lives together, I promise to tell you what my feelings are so we don't have to second-guess each other. I lost you once because of my own foolish pride and stubbornness, but you're not getting away from me again. Ever."

They gazed into each other's eyes and found the love that they had been seeking for so very long.

The preacher cleared his throat as though he weren't quite sure they were finished speaking. "Is there a ring?" he asked resignedly, totally disconcerted by the afternoon's strange happenings. Apparently nothing was going to proceed according to the usual format today.

Cal dug into his pants pocket and the green fire of his mother's ring sparkled in the sunlight. "Delphine was supposed to wear this today," he whispered to Laura. "But I guess it was always meant to belong to you."

Then her husband slipped the exquisite band onto her finger. His lips found hers in a lingering kiss, and Laura knew that she'd finally come home to stay.

Chapter Thirteen

The last guest was ushered out the door at ten o'clock, and Juanita shooed Laura away when she tried to lend a hand with the cleanup.

"Now you are the mistress of the house. It would not be fitting." The housekeeper tilted her head in the direction of the staircase, her eyes dancing with barely contained amusement. "Besides, I think that someone is waiting for you to go to bed."

Laura turned to see Cal, still clad in his wedding tuxedo, lounging against the banister at the top of the stairs. "If you don't hurry up, woman," he growled impatiently, "I'm going to be too old to do much more than keep your feet warm."

A trail of pink spread over Laura's face, and she glanced self-consciously in Juanita's direction. But the housekeeper had discreetly disappeared.

"The blushing bride," Cal drawled, teasing her affectionately. He tugged at his black velvet bow tie until it came undone, the ends flowing loosely down the front of his shirt. Unbuttoning that garment slowly, he stared down at her with mock concern. "You're not turning shy on me at this late date, are you?"

"I'll show you who's shy!" Laura exclaimed as she ran up the stairs and into her husband's waiting arms.

His lips moved over hers in a softly pulsating, almost reverent caress, and his tongue gently explored the soft inner curves of her welcoming mouth. Laura's nerves vibrated with a longing that seemed to radiate from the depths of her soul as she circled his waist with her arms, pulling his tall body close. When she finally tore her mouth away from his, she pressed her burning cheek against his cool white lapel.

"I may just faint, sir," she whispered with an exaggerated Southern accent.

"You do that, and you're liable to miss the best part of my performance," Cal warned her, his lazy smile making even her toes tingle. He grasped her face in both his hands and turned it upward, covering her eyelids, nose and mouth with warm, gossamer-soft kisses.

"Oh, Cal," Laura sighed. "It's always been wonderful with you, but this is something else. All the mistrust and the anger are gone. All that's left is—"

"Love." Cal finished the sentence for her. "For the first time in all these years, I'm certain-sure that you really care for me. And I'm going to show you just how much knowing that for a fact means to me."

Without any further warning, Cal lifted her off her feet and carried her toward her bedroom.

"No, Cal," Laura protested. "Not in there. Take me to *your* room."

"My room?" Cal said in surprise. "It's not a very romantic setting."

"It is to me," Laura told him, her eyes filled with warm memories of their very first night together.

Cal smiled in understanding, and changed direction. As they crossed the threshold of his room, he kicked the door shut behind them, and they were alone at last.

Setting her down on the quilt-covered bed, he slowly began undressing in front of his bride, the gleam in his eyes telling her that he knew just what erotic longings the sight of his partially clothed body inspired.

Laura gasped when he removed his shirt and she saw the multicolored bruise covering his lower-right rib cage. "Oh, Cal, I forgot you were hurt! And I let you carry me—"

Her husband smiled down at her and touched her face to reassure her. "They're just bruised, not broken. And tonight, believe me, I'm feeling no pain."

He continued to disrobe, flaunting every new inch of exposed skin as Laura's passion continued to rise. When she reached for him, he retreated with a teasing smile.

Laura laughed and clapped her hands, growing more excited by the moment. Cal, who had always been so ruggedly masculine, had relaxed and forgotten himself to the extent of putting on a show just for her. The miracle of it touched her heart, and the feelings it aroused in her body took her to a new level of sensuality that she hadn't explored before.

At last he stood completely nude in front of her, the hard lines of his body illuminated by the soft light of the room. By the time he joined her on the mattress, she was yearning for him body and soul. With trembling fingers she savored the satin-smooth perfection of his back and the dark, matted hair of his chest. She paused there only briefly before straying downward to stroke the hard physical evidence of his desire.

Laura was full to bursting with years of unrequited love that she couldn't wait any longer to express, and she protested when Cal pushed her hands away.

"Shh, Laurie. Don't. Let me go slow. Let me make it good for you."

He undressed her with painstaking care, lingering over every button and hook until Laura threatened to tear off the clothes herself. His only answer to her threat was a maddeningly superior smile as he continued at his snail's pace.

Finally she lay completely exposed to his gaze. She trembled as she watched him devour her body with his eyes and begged him to take her. But he only smiled again and began an agonizingly thorough exploration of her body with his warm hands and mouth.

She quivered as his tongue caressed the bottom of her foot and cried out as he found every nerve ending in each toe. The backs of her knees were also explored before he worked his way higher and, with a wordless exclamation, buried his mouth in the warmth between her legs.

"Oh, yes! Oh, please," she pleaded, but he would only take her to the edge of fulfillment and no further.

Ignoring her protestations, his fingers and tongue moved on to tease her rosy nipples, which were already ridged with excitement. Tears ran down her cheeks as he pulled her hands from him once more and, holding them pinned above her head, discovered every hollow and valley of her neck and ears, sucking and nibbling on her lobes as she ground her hips against his elusive body, silently pleading for more intimate attentions.

When he finally released her arms, she seized his well-rounded bottom in both hands and, with a cry of primitive triumph, guided him into the burning center of her passion.

He drew in his breath sharply, his soft gray eyes gently reproachful. "I was only trying to make it good for you, Laurie. I can't last long this way... not tonight."

Laura surged against Cal, almost crazy from wanting him. "I've got news for you, cowboy—neither can I."

With a groan, he began to thrust into her, and she lost all sense of time and place. She knew only that she was being joined—finally and irrevocably—to the man she had always loved. She gasped as spasms of pure pleasure racked her body, and she felt her husband find ultimate fulfillment in her embrace. Then she was floating reluctantly, but inevitably, back to reality, still locked in the circle of Cal's arms.

He stroked her face gently, almost reverently, running the tips of his lightly callused fingers across her cheeks and along her jawline. Then he barely touched his lips to hers.

"My wife," he whispered against her ear. "I can't believe it. Oh, Laurie. It's so right, so good. We should have been married years ago. We should never have been apart. I love you so much."

"And I love you," she answered, holding him tightly, still half afraid that he would somehow slip away from her again.

Later, Cal sat pulling his brush through her dark, shining hair while they watched the news on the bedroom television. "You don't know how many years I've dreamed of doing this," he murmured as he leaned back against the headboard with a satisfied smile.

Neither of them had a stitch of clothing on, but that seemed natural and right to Laura. With her back to him, she took a sip of the hot coffee she'd brought up from the kitchen and reluctantly decided to venture into dangerous waters. She wasn't afraid to do that now because she was certain of his love.

"What about Honey?"

He looked at her with a raised brow. "What about Honey?"

"Isn't there some other executive in your...our... company who could use a good secretary?"

Cal pulled away from her, his eyes teasing. "I guess since no woman under ninety could possibly resist my charms, I'll have to find some very efficient, little gray-haired great-grandmother to be my secretary. Or maybe a man would be better." He chuckled wryly. "We haven't been married twenty-four hours yet, and I'm already roped, tied and branded."

Laura bridled at the undertone of sarcasm she detected in his lighthearted words. Her lithe form became an unyielding, ice-cold block of marble in his arms.

"You can do what you want, Cal Sinclair," she told him through gritted teeth, "and I guess I can't stop you. But I'll never willingly share you with another woman again—now, or twenty years from now."

"Whoa, little lady. Simmer down to a slow boil. All this jealousy is real flattering, but there won't be any other woman."

He smiled at her doubting expression and began his soothing ministrations with the brush again. "I guess I could give Honey back to Jack Lambert. She used to be his secretary a few years ago. Of course, after they got married, he said that he couldn't work with her. Seems she didn't know who was boss anymore, so he sent her over to work for me."

Laura turned and gaped at him incredulously. "She's married?"

"Uh-huh," Cal replied, grinning like a mischievous little boy.

"Then what did you mean by that comment about Honey being 'darned good' at everything she does?"

"Well, she's a good secretary, and she's a good wife. She's certainly a good mother."

"She has children?" Laura's voice rose dangerously. "If all this is true, why were you out on a date with her?"

"Jack—her husband—was out of town, and I'd promised him I'd escort her to the bull-riding tryouts. He doesn't like her to go to nightclubs alone."

"No, I imagine not."

"Anyway, her mama stayed with the kids. Then when I took Honey home, the three of us sat down and had fresh-baked oatmeal-raisin cookies and hot chocolate."

The look of studied innocence on Cal's face had Laura so angry that she was practically bouncing on the bed. "And I tossed and turned half the night thinking that you...that she... Just where were you the rest of the night?"

"You had me so keyed up that I just couldn't relax. I went to the office to do some work, hoping that it would calm me down. I fell asleep on the couch there."

Laura gave him a hard stare. "And you weren't even pretending that there was something going on with her to make me jealous?"

Cal looked down at the brush, turning it over in his hand. "I suppose I was. I enjoyed getting a rise out of you. I guess I got more than I bargained for."

"From her or from me?" Laura asked archly.

"Come on, Laurie. You know what I mean." Cal stroked her silky hair tenderly. "When you left, you took all the meaning out of my life. I thought I'd never care about anyone or anything again until the day I rode up and found you in the glade. You're all the woman I'll ever need. There's no one else in the world I want."

Secure in her husband's declaration of love, Laura felt her body slowly relax as she was snuggled in his arms. But there was one more thing she had to settle.

"Cal, remember in the glade when I said that getting pregnant with your baby was the worst possible thing that could happen to me? I only said that to convince you that I wasn't trying to have your baby without telling you, and . . . Oh, it all just came out wrong. Actually in a couple of years, I wouldn't mind having a baby...or two...or three."

Cal looked uncomfortable. "I don't know what to say, Laurie. I haven't even figured out how to deal with Melissa yet."

Laura traced the outline of his generous mouth with one smooth fingertip. "It seems we've each come full circle in our thinking. I guess we're on opposite sides of the fence again, my love."

Cal smiled down into her upturned face. "You go ahead and have as many babies as you want, Laurie. I'll give you my full cooperation. Lord knows, it's probably the only way I'm going to be able to keep you tied down."

"What? Barefoot and pregnant?"

"Don't look so abused, woman. What about me? With you and my sweet-tempered Melissa, I'm already outnumbered. If you were to give birth to an ornery little female spitfire like yourself, I'd really be in trouble."

Laughing, Laura swatted him playfully on the arm. "You're not exactly an angel yourself, mister."

"And aren't you glad?"

He kissed her soundly. Then, turning her firmly away from him, he set the brush down on the bedside table. "Behave yourself now. I've missed the news, but I fully intend to see the sports. If you do as you're told, I might even let you sleep in my bed for the rest of the night."

"You're too generous," Laura murmured wryly.

For the next five minutes, she sat quietly beside her husband, listening to the TV drone on. Then, as if of their own accord, her eyes strayed downward. She began to stroke one muscular thigh. Little by little, she let her fingers trail down into his lap until they touched the velvet-skinned softness nestled there.

She heard a deep chuckle. "Haven't you had enough for one night, woman?"

Laura released her hold and looked back at his face seriously. "It's not that. It's just that I've never really had a chance to touch you when you're like this."

Cal's chuckle became a full-fledged laugh. "Like what?" he demanded, a twinkle in his eye.

"Like..." Laura began, turning to focus on the object of their discussion.

But a change had taken place. Her expression wavered between exasperation and amusement.

"Oh, Cal! You did that on purpose!"

Cal very deliberately used the remote control to turn off the TV in the middle of the baseball scores. Pulling his wife over backward until she lay flat on the bed, he covered her body with his own.

"You never change, Laurie. You're the one who did it, and there you go trying to blame it on me."

Laura opened her mouth to argue and found that Cal's tongue had slipped deftly inside. She was breathing hard when he finally pulled back to look at her face.

"I . . . you . . ." she faltered, trying to pick up the elusive thread of her reasoning.

Cal gave her an especially infuriating smile as he slid his body inside of hers. "I think I've finally discovered a way to have the last word in an argument with you."

Laura moaned and wrapped her legs around him. Grabbing his hips, she settled him even deeper within her until he filled her completely.

"You hush now, Cal Sinclair," she commanded in a low, husky whisper, "and just love me."

For once in his life, Cal did exactly as she asked.

* * * * *

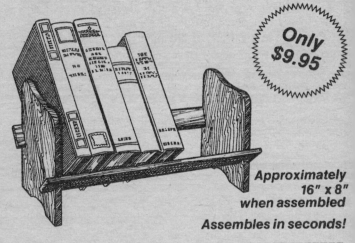

Silhouette Desire®

1989
IS THE YEAR
OF THE MAN!

What makes a romance? A special man, of course, and Silhouette Desire cele-brates that fact with *twelve* of them! From Mr. January to Mr. December, every month has a tribute to the Silhouette Desire hero—our **MAN OF THE MONTH!**

Sexy, macho, charming, irritating . . . irresistible! Nothing can stop these men from sweeping you away. Created by some of your favorite authors, each man is custom-made for pleasure—*reading* pleasure—so don't miss a single one.

Mr. January is Blake Donavan in RELUCTANT FATHER by Diana Palmer
Mr. February is Hank Branson in THE GENTLEMAN INSISTS by Joan Hohl
Mr. March is Carson Tanner in NIGHT OF THE HUNTER by Jennifer Greene
Mr. April is Slater McCall in A DANGEROUS KIND OF MAN by Naomi Horton
Mr. May is Luke Harmon in VENGEANCE IS MINE by Lucy Gordon
Mr. June is Quinn McNamara in IRRESISTIBLE by Annette Broadrick

And that's only the half of it—
so get out there and find your man!

Silhouette Desire's

MAN OF THE MONTH . . .

MOM-1

Silhouette Special Edition

COMING NEXT MONTH

#511 BEST LAID PLANS—Nora Roberts
Headstrong engineer Abra Wilson and cocky architect Cody Johnson
couldn't cooperate long enough to construct a hotel together—could
they possibly hope to build a lasting love?

#512 SKY HIGH—Tracy Sinclair
When client Jeremy Winchester insisted that pilot Meredith Collins
masquerade as his fiancée, she knew something was fishy—so why
did his pretense of passion feel so real?

#513 SMALL-TOWN SECRETS—Kate Meriwether
Their high-school reunion unveiled forbidden longings...but could
Reese finally beat the ultimate rival for Sadie's love without revealing
secrets that would tear the community—and Sadie's heart—apart?

#514 BUILD ME A DREAM—Pat Warren
Toy designer "Casey" Casswell created dreams for children...
and dreamed of having children. Pretty, practical Sabrina Ames
would be his ideal mate—if she weren't so terrified of marriage
and motherhood!

#515 DARK ANGEL—Pamela Toth
Julie Remington and Angel Maneros had crossed class boundaries to
fall in love, only to be thwarted by the bitterest misunderstanding.
Ten years later, they were facing temptation—and betrayal—
once again.

#516 A SUDDEN SUNLIGHT—Laurey Bright
When heiress Natalia awoke from a coma—pregnant—she didn't
remember the horrors she had survived. Nor did she remember Matt,
who claimed to be her lover, her fiancé....

AVAILABLE THIS MONTH: